P9-CAF-552

*For Elisabeth*
*Eleven Come Again*

# LIFE
# SAVINGS

## a novel by Linnea Due

spinsters book company
SAN FRANCISCO

Copyright © 1992 by Linnea Due
All rights reserved.

First edition.
10-9-8-7-6-5-4-3-2-1

Cover photo by Jill Posener

Spinsters Book Company
P.O. Box 410687
San Francisco, CA 94141

This is a work of fiction. Any similarity to persons living or dead
is a coincidence.

Printed in the U.S.A. on acid-free paper


The Spinsters Book Company desktop publishing system was
made possible by a grant from the Horizons Foundation/Bay
Area Career Women Fund and many individual donors.

*Library of Congress Cataloging-in-Publication Data*

Due, Linnea A.
    Life savings: a novel/by Linnea Due. — 1st ed.
        p. cm.
    ISBN 0-933216-89-0 : $10.95
    I. Title.
PS3554.U314L5      1992
813'.54—dc20                                      92-24439
                                                       CIP

# CHAPTER 1

"1179 Grayson Street." Dale Hayden lay down her clipboard and glanced over her reading glasses at the five women grouped around her. Needing those glasses had caused Dale a three-month-long crisis of confidence, Marcia Lanier recalled. What would happen when they all went into menopause?

"Grayson Street's in Berkeley," Carol Slezak reminded them, as if they hadn't known.

"And it's registered with the rent board," Reba Dresher added. Everyone but Marcia lived in Berkeley but they wouldn't dream of investing there.

Sarah Rabin said she'd heard at her last Architectural Heritage Association meeting that a two-flat Victorian junker right on San Pablo Avenue was for sale, but the owner wanted $265,000 firm because he thought someday the property would go commercial.

"Then he should fucking sit on it until it does," Carol snapped. She shoved bony fingers through her spikey gray hair, her weathered face grimacing, as if angry gestures could punish the greedy.

"Why don't we check the Open Houses?" Polly Taccone, ever the mediator, suggested quickly. Polly was Reba's lover and the acknowledged-by-everyone mother

1

of their child, in spite of the fact that fourteen-year-old Ruth was an exact duplicate of tall, gruff Reba, albeit feminized and young. Dale said Ruth proved virgin birth was still possible in the 20th century.

So Reba read aloud from the real estate section of Sunday's *San Francisco Chronicle*, which gave everyone an opportunity to snooze off, because if a house was listed, it was probably already taken. The buying mania in the Bay Area was at its peak in the summer of '89; in certain neighborhoods, people had begun walking block to block ringing doorbells asking if anyone knew of a house for sale.

Dale was looking quizzically at Marcia, one eyebrow raised. Something happened to you this weekend, she seemed to say, but what? Marcia shrugged. She had no intention of answering, at least not until she herself knew, which could take months at the rate she was going in the romance department.

Marcia had clear bright hazel eyes, a fresh open face that revealed more than she wanted or knew, and a quirky sideways smile that managed to be both shy and cocky. Dale, her best buddy for 23 years, was a few inches taller and rangy as a Texas longhorn, with that perpetually propped-up eyebrow and a grin on the move from sardonic to astonished. The two pals had been 86ed from a dozen dyke bars for fighting and out-and-out belligerence, but that was decades ago: Marcia was now 42, Dale 40, and they'd been sober 29 years between them.

"Oh, wait!" Dale interrupted Reba's sonorous reading and her own drawing of an antelope on her contractor's tablet. "I forgot. There's that place on 62nd Street."

"Below Telegraph or above?"

"Right above." They all considered. At least, Polly noted, it was in Oakland. But Sarah said she'd driven by and the house was just an ugly stucco box, not worth anyone's energy. Carol muttered that they weren't running a beauty contest and couldn't they just buy something please so they could stop having these meetings?

Marcia didn't mind the meetings that much—her rehab partners could be pretty funny—but tonight she had to admit she was completely distracted by what had happened Sunday afternoon, when she had run into a passing acquaintance at UC Berkeley's Botanical Garden. Lydia Fitzpatrick was conducting a field trip meant to interest freshmen in plant science, while Marcia was hiding out from all the Open Houses she should have been attending. When Marcia spotted Lydia, small and fiery, her dark hair cascading across her shoulders, Lydia was being trailed up a sun-drenched path by sixteen youths of various dimensions, all hanging on her words as, eyes flashing with passion, she described how plants use various enzymes to control the timing of their own flowering, fruiting, and ripening. Marcia tagged along behind, telling herself she was only interested professionally. In truth, she remembered dancing with Lydia at a friend's party a couple years earlier, but then losing track of her in the crowd. Now, when Lydia turned and spotted her hanging at the rear of the group, perplexed recognition flooded her light brown eyes, followed by something warm and wondering that drew Marcia in so quickly she nearly tripped over herself in surprise. Maybe it was because they'd startled each other that they were soon in such a fever to go to bed; making love was something they thought they would understand.

"You're a botanist?" Marcia had asked at a quickly arranged dinner, just before she'd started stroking Lydia's thighs under the table.

"Well, that's kind of complicated," Lydia had answered.

Marcia didn't see how it could be complicated, but it turned out that people who worked with plants could be biologists or molecular biologists or biochemists or geneticists, and according to Lydia, it didn't much matter what they called themselves. Marcia didn't delve into the subject further because once she'd reached under the table they were in a big hurry to get out of the restaurant. In fact, they didn't really cover anything in depth—like what they might do in bed—but since Lydia seemed to have a pretty good scenario in mind, Marcia just let her get on with it, supposing the friend who'd given the party had alerted Lydia to Marcia's sexual proclivities. They hadn't even discussed who might top and who might bottom, but when they both reached for the check and

Lydia caught Marcia's wrist instead and they got washed up in each other's eyes, neither emerged with a question. Marcia paid the bill, telling Lydia it was butch perogative on the first date. As she was signing the credit card slip, the imprint of Lydia's thumb on her wrist made her cunt throb deep inside, insistent as the pulse of a humming-bird's throat.

"What's the big grin for, doofus?" Dale asked, poking Marcia in the ribs.

"Oh, nothing," Marcia said, her face coloring as she found herself back in Polly and Reba's living room. Dale was watching her with a quizzical half-smile, but Marcia had already segued to a more pressing topic: why hadn't Lydia called since their entanglement on Lydia's bedroom floor? Wasn't it the way of lesbian love to commit instantly or never see each other again? It was true that as they were bolting their dinner, Marcia had given Lydia her lecture about how she wasn't interested in a relationship, she just wanted recreational sex, all the while caressing Lydia's ankles with her toes. This speech had proven unpopular in the past with prospective sex partners. Lydia, however, seemed completely unfazed, shrugging her shoulders and murmuring, "Fine. Agreed." Could Ly-dia have misunderstood, believing Marcia meant to limit recreational sex to a one-night stand? No. Impossible, not after they'd sunk into each other. How often does that happen? But maybe they'd gotten along so well they'd frightened each other off.

Dale poked her again. Marcia considered turning to her and saying, "Dale, I met this woman on Sunday, she's 45, a professor at Cal, I know I can talk to her even though we've hardly said a word to each other, we get along great in bed, and I think I really like her." Of course she would never say that, because first, saying it fucks it up and second, she didn't want a relationship. She really didn't. I'm not frightened, she swore to Dale in her mind.

Dale pointed at her watch. Yes, Marcia signaled with eyes thrown to the ceiling, the meeting was going on forever. What else is new? Dale began to add another antelope to the herd already galloping across her yellow tablet.

Marcia decided she really did have to think about something other than Lydia Fitzpatrick or she'd start remembering the actual sex and that would be fatal. She fixed on her other longtime friend Sarah, who, now that she was bothering to notice, seemed to be getting her marvelous tangled cloud of baby's breath hair styled—or something. Marcia had never been good with hair terms, since she just strolled into her barber's and let him have at it every six weeks or so, cropping it up around her ears while allowing the rest to fall to the side across her forehead. Dale went to a hairdresser to achieve a more feathered effect, but, as Marcia pointed out, Dale, taller and more raw-boned, needed a little extra to keep the straight censors at bay.

For years Sarah had seemed to Marcia like a comfortable old flannel blanket crumpled at the foot of the bed, and now suddenly she was dressing in fancy cowboy shirts and cords. Nevertheless she looked terrible, her eyes sunken and her cheeks sucked-in. Marcia was puzzling over this paradox when she realized that Reba was glaring at her. "What?" she asked. No point pretending she'd been paying attention.

Reba took her time repeating herself as Carol gazed at the ceiling, Sarah poked at her nails with an emery board (another oddity—Marcia was adding them up now), and Dale turned a page on her pad and began sketching a blocky shape that soon resembled a buffalo. All of them would, Reba said, once again and for the absolute final time, commit themselves to the figure they were willing to invest. Reba needn't mention (though she did) that the higher the combined figure, the more likely they would come out with a handsome profit. She did not explain why this was so, and no one asked. She reminded them that the primary intention was to pay wages for remodeling the house, thus allowing them to work for themselves, but their secondary goal was to sell it for enough profit to pay a decent return on their investment.

In truth, they'd come nowhere close to any of this, mainly because they couldn't find a house. In the shark-filled waters that characterized Bay Area real estate, houses sold within hours of listing, and often at prices ten to twenty thousand above asking. It had taken their group weeks to realize they had to make an offer the same day they saw a house, and another few weeks to realize they had to offer above the asking price. But they were still in such shock over the prices that they'd been unable to bear paying a quarter-million for a war-built stucco bungalow in Albany.

"We've got to get in the market!" Reba thundered, as if sheer volume would help

She was marching back and forth in front of them, expounding. It would have been more effective if she'd been mounted on a charger, but Polly gazed at her adoringly nonetheless. Marcia found the idea that after ten long years Polly still worshipped Reba to be like eating too much chocolate—sweet and a little sickening. Knowing who to fault was difficult: Polly, ever the cheerleader, or Reba, too tall to be Napoleon but otherwise a near-perfect match?

What a nutty crew, and all patched together by power-mad Reba: Polly and Sarah, Reba's current and ex; Dale, business associate and pal; painter Carol, armored in antagonism, who must have been in rare form when she met Reba to have even advanced her name; and Marcia herself, Dale's best buddy and the gardener. Marcia had no illusions that she and Carol had been added to the core foursome, who had worked on jobs together for years, as anything other than cash cows—Reba had made it clear that she believed gardening and painting to be common-laborer tasks which should be accomplished with as little outlay of time and money as possible. "Great," Marcia had said, stung but determined not to argue; with her job at the catering company she had very limited hours anyway.

Besides, she knew she was in this only out of greed, envious at watching speculators in her neighborhood sell for triple what they'd paid only a few years before. Early this spring, she'd been burning to invest her measly savings, hoping to roll it over on house after house, maybe even to quit her job and do landscaping full-time. By now, the middle of August, finding a fixer-upper at a steal seemed as likely as tripping over a diamond on the street, and Marcia had mentally consigned her money to a safe but steady climb in a CD. She came to these meetings as if she were going to the movies—let's take a trip to fantasy-land. Part of the ritual was every couple months they'd swear to tithe a cash amount to the god of make-believe: Dale had just now pledged to contribute $5,000 to the till.

"Ten," Reba said.

"Ten," Carol seconded.

Polly paused with her pencil above a 3 x 6 reporter's pad and took a deep breath. "Twelve." She had, at earlier meetings, made certain that everyone knew the money she was investing was hers alone, separate from joint funds with Reba. "Defining limits via high finance," Dale had remarked to Marcia with her customary hoisted eyebrow.

Sarah allowed that she had fifteen. Marcia wondered how Sarah had managed to amass fifteen thousand bucks doing construction work with Reba and Dale, but on the other hand, how had she herself saved so much from her catering job? "Fifteen," she said. Over the last couple months, she'd thought of dropping her contribution to ten, but from the start she'd decided to go for broke, and loyalty to the group now held her fast. Besides, she reassured herself, they couldn't find a house to spend it on anyway.

Polly had totaled it up. "Sixty-seven thousand dollars," she announced. She sounded breathless. "That's a lot of money."

They all agreed it was a lot of money. They all hoped it would be enough. Privately none of them believed it was. Marcia said she would go see the property on 62nd Street with Reba and Dale. As the gardener for the project, she wanted to examine the yard.

Dale stretched, loosening the critches in her back, and half-limped out to the front porch, Marcia strolling by her side. They stood shivering in the chill fog of a Bay Area August night, staring out at the dimly lit street. Dale said she wanted a cigarette.

"God, wouldn't that be great," Marcia said. They could bend close to catch the acrid flare of sulphur, then lean companionably over the porch rail to knock ash onto

7

Reba's unwatered lawn as smoke rose around their heads in the glow of the unshielded yellow lightbulb. "Maybe nicotine would make my fibroids shrink. What is it, six years?"

"Seven years, sixty-three days and counting," Dale told her. They had stopped together, entertaining each other for months with how murderous they felt.

"Jesus," Marcia said. "After ten it oughta settle down to a dull roar."

"Have you noticed that our lives are measured by how long it's been since we participated in the really blatant forms of our self-destruction?"

Sarah stepped out the door behind them, bringing a rush of light and laughter to the porch. She kissed them quickly and then hurried off down the walk.

"Sarah's seeing a younger woman," Dale confided.

"Ah," Marcia murmured. That explained the dressing up and the hair and even the sunken eyes. "How much younger?"

"Twenty-two."

"Twenty-two?"

Dale nodded.

I've been seeing someone too, Marcia imagined herself saying. No, you haven't, she scolded herself. You just slept with someone once.

"She's a Marine," Dale continued.

"A Marine? Peacenik Sarah is dating a twenty-two-year-old Marine?"

Dale nodded again, up—down. Marcia stared at her. It was incomprehensible. "What's going on here?"

Dale lifted her thumb and then her shoulder in an eloquent gesture of who-the-hell-knows, and Marcia felt a surge of affection for her. She opened her arms, and they hugged each other hard. "Thursday, four o'clock, 62nd Street," Dale called as Marcia clattered down the steps.

"Right," Marcia shouted back. She slid onto the sprung seat of her '66 Ranchero and sat for a moment before she started the engine. Finally, she thought, it was safe to remember.

She was down on her knees, her neck bent as if she meant to kiss the floor, but the focus of her attention was the woman standing over her, small and slender, with sweet downy cheeks Marcia could recall as clearly as if she were looking at a photograph, though she hadn't lifted her eyes to Lydia's face for several minutes now. Lydia was speaking with a voice even softer than her cheeks, in order to make Marcia strain to hear and therefore listen all the harder. She'd changed her professorial wear to Levis, Reeboks, and a black leather vest which revealed the curve of her breasts through the oversized arm holes—curves that set Marcia to thinking about running her tongue across the skin and into the fold underneath, so the hillock would butt up against her nose, and she could nibble across an acre of silk before she bumped into—

She hadn't heard the whoosh of the hand but her head rebounded and her cheek flashed red and she got wetter than before, maybe she would drown in her own juice before this was over. The other side too—turn the other cheek, Marcia. She couldn't recall from one second to the next if Lydia had actually said this or her mind had just hooked it and dragged it into her consciousness, a struggling fish pulled from the slow-moving stream that meandered through her brain. Sometimes that stream dammed up and threatened to engulf her with an overflow of thoughts, but not now, now her mind was miraculously clean and she wanted to keep it that way, keep it free for the sensations that inflamed her cunt and made her nipples tingle, standing erect in this cool room.

Lydia dropped to her own knees but still Marcia didn't look at her, didn't dare to, until Lydia took Marcia's chin in her firm fingers and tugged. Then Marcia did look and they didn't stop staring until Lydia caught her breath and said, "You like this, don't you?"

Marcia was still too dumbstruck by the warmth in Lydia's light brown eyes to answer. The consequent slap was without force, because Lydia was at an awkward angle, but Marcia didn't mind—it was the thought that counts. Another fish yanked gasping from that hellish stream. Perhaps she should write Hallmark cards.

Her nipples ached because Lydia was pinching them carefully. A radio went on in the flat next door. They both paused, then threw the distraction aside. Marcia wondered about Lydia's seventeen-year-old son. Well, even if he did come home he wouldn't storm into his mother's bedroom. Lydia dropped one hand to Marcia's cunt, and Marcia sagged, moaning. The hand moved away. Marcia cried out again, this time in anguish. She was allowed to put her own hands on the floor behind her. She was told to spread her legs as far as they would go. She was panting, her chest heaving. She couldn't hear the radio anymore, but she didn't think about it. The stream was going fast now, too fast to catch anything, thank god. Going so fast it faded to a dull roar, and her limbs were light, bones filled with air, and she was nothing but her cunt and her quiet and her openness. She could float to heaven on the stream between her legs, so much more elemental than the one in her head.

But that wasn't all, Marcia thought now, passing the car detailing lot at the corner of 50th and continuing along Market until she turned off towards the bay, gunning the Ranchero past a block-long warehouse until she reached a dimly lit residential street. She hovered in front of her house, leaning her head on the steering wheel of the old half-car, half-truck. There was, she thought, another kind of life-stream flowing under what we call "real." Good sex can dump you right into it. Had she even known that before?

It suddenly occurred to her that Lydia could have left a message on her phone machine. She docked the Ranchero in her next-door neighbor Robert's sacrosanct space, which would piss him off, but lately with Robert it was contention or nothing, and Marcia usually preferred something. She took her porch stairs two at a time, almost falling over herself in her eagerness to get inside.

The light on the phone machine glowed a steady maddening green. If she doesn't call by Thursday, I'll drop my Mr. Cool routine and call her myself, Marcia decided. Maybe I won't be able to wait—I might have to dump Mr. Cool tomorrow. Heaving a sigh, she crossed through her tiny living room to the far larger kitchen, with its big rear windows overlooking her back yard.

When Marcia had moved into her rental house in 1972, the yard had been a solid sea of knee-high weeds. Seventeen years later, it was a mini-wonderland of tall ferns, climbing vines, and specimen trees, made private by a solid line of birches at the back which let in sun but kept out noise and neighbors. Paths led to a barrel of water overflowing with parrots' feather and a grove of lavender and species geranium clustered around chalky pink boulders orange with lichen. Several commitment ceremonies had been held in Marcia's garden, but, Marcia couldn't help noticing, none of them had been hers.

Get off this topic, Marcia commanded herself. It's boring, stupid, and furthermore not even what you want. She put water on to boil for tea and stood by the stove, tapping her fingers on the bright polished chrome. It was possible that Lydia Fitzpatrick hadn't liked her, though if so, she'd certainly put on a good act. It was possible that Lydia Fitzpatrick had been abducted by tiny space people and was even now praying Marcia would rescue her. Marcia poured boiling water over her Earl Gray teabag and stared at her inner wrist, picturing Lydia's thumb print there, as if the pale skin had been indelibly stamped with an invisible brand. You wish, she thought, and then, no, you don't.

A bass beat started pounding from her bedroom, joined seconds later by a hypnotic chant: "Hey bitch, saw you last night with my man Leroy, he ain't nothin', ain't nothin' but a toy, gimme your honey, bitch, gimme that honey, you know Leroy he ain't got no money."

Marcia strode across the blue ceramic tiles of her kitchen, across the oak flooring of her bedroom, and stuck her head out the open window: "Bil—l—l—ly!"

"Man!" Billy Preston's head popped up in his own window, less than twelve feet from hers. At seventeen, he was still young enough to be embarrassed. No doubt he'd been lying on his bed, beating off to the lyrics. "I thought you were gone!" he exploded at her.

"Well, I'm back."

"Man, some white folks like this shit."

"I doubt that very seriously," she told him. Then she laughed. "One of my friends thinks rap is a plot to infuriate white people." Dale had said that, of course, in her laconic voice, a slight grin on her face.

Billy's father Robert threw open his own window, one down from his son's. "Turn down that damn noise!" he snapped at Billy. Marcia and Billy glanced across at his angry dark head and both shut their windows in an unspoken pact to avoid an argument. Since Robert had retired from his position as an Army staff sergeant a few years ago, he tried to impose order on their little corner of Lewell Street. Unfortunately for Robert, neither his family nor Marcia had enlisted in his army.

She wandered back into the kitchen and sipped her tea. The phone rang. It was Lydia. Marcia told herself she'd known that Lydia would call all along. That didn't stop her heart from becoming erratic. She thought about Lydia's fawn-colored eyes while they chatted. She wouldn't let herself look at her wrist. She thought about the stream, but it slipped through her fingers, lost in their small talk, in their careful treading around each other. Mr. Cool, Marcia cautioned, determined not to to be engulfed by something she couldn't handle. No hanky-panky about love and marriage, just good, clean sex.

Lydia was saying she wanted to go to a movie. Marcia hemmed and hawed. Evidently Lydia hadn't believed Marcia's I-am-not-interested-in-anything-but-recreational-sex speech, because why else would she be asking about movies? Finally Marcia told her she didn't have time for movies.

"Only for fucking?" Lydia said.

"That's right," Marcia laughed. "I've got it on my calendar, 'Fucking, nine to eleven, Sunday night.'"

"Well, then I guess I gotta be there." Lydia wrote down Marcia's address and hung up.

Marcia sat there drinking her cooling tea, not sure what to think. Had Lydia been as frightened as she by how easy it was to be with each other? What if Lydia were offended that Marcia didn't want to go to a film? She might believe she wasn't being taken seriously. But it's not that kind of relationship, Marcia assured herself. I don't want that kind of relationship. I can see a movie with Dale or Sarah. I want to fuck with Lydia. What's wrong with that?

She thought of making more tea but abandoned the idea. Instead she crossed the kitchen into her tiny living room, farthest from Billy's rap music, and sat there in the dark, pondering conundrums. She was afraid to hope but also afraid to accept what it meant to give up hope. After her last lover, she didn't trust her own judgment, yet she didn't know what else she could trust either. And what she'd assumed would put the issue on hold—telling people she was only interested in a sexual relationship—didn't work either, not if she were lying, which in Lydia's case she probably was.

It's way too early for this sort of soul-searching, she told herself, and not much use anyway. Sometimes she felt her own motivations were as formless as sands shifting in the wind. It was safest to hide out in her backyard, with its handmade bench overhung with ferns and azaleas, or on her front porch having meandering conversations with Billy and his uncle Lucas. She'd never considered herself a recluse, yet that seemed to be what she was becoming, just as Reba was getting more obsessive and Dale more iconoclastic. The harmless quirks of their twenties—when she had fantasized about living in the country—had rigidified into the eccentricities of their forties. Which might be why Sarah was dating a twenty-two-year-old, trying to use the powerful medicine of youth to break through the scar tissue of a few decades of increasing inflexibility.

Lydia's three years older than I am, Marcia thought, just as stultified as me. How can people our age, so set in our ways, bend enough to let each other in? Besides, there was plenty more happening in her life than meeting Lydia. If their group actually bought a house, as unlikely as that seemed, any plans Marcia had for being a hermit would be dashed for good. I'm not going to do anything crazy, she promised the fates in the sky. No risks, no regrets.

# CHAPTER 2

Tall, stark Reba, dressed entirely in black, was standing on the sidewalk talking to the listing agent when Dale and Marcia arrived at the house on 62nd Street. The agent was an attractive woman in her early thirties who told them how fascinated she was with their rehabbing scheme. This property, she said, would be perfect for them, because not only were its problems chiefly cosmetic, it was also cheap—only $197,000.

Marcia already didn't like it. There was a school nearby, which lowered real estate values. In normal towns a school a few blocks away might be an asset; in Oakland, the upscale folks who would buy their refurbished house either had no kids or paid for a private education for their offspring. They figured a school in the neighborhood was nothing more than a magnet for noise, litter, and vandalism.

The other bad point, number six on their "Prejudices of Prospective Buyers" sheet, which Polly had written up as a joke one evening, was that there were too many people of too many ethnicities out on the sidewalk. This spelled chaos to their buyers. Marcia had eavesdropped enough at Open Houses to know their most likely prospects, although supposedly anxious to live in what they termed "a multiculturally rich neighborhood," wanted all that richness to take place inside four walls, where they need not witness it. Marcia remembered one would-be buyer shaking her head as she watched a bare-chested Vietnamese man sitting on his porch rail, smoking a cigarette. "It's the middle of February!" she'd told Marcia, her voice shaking with outrage or fear.

Reba, who seemed always about to fly off in ten directions at once, told them she was really excited about the potential of the house, which was, as Sarah had said, nothing more than a stucco box. Dale and Marcia glanced at each other; Reba had never not been excited. "An overactive imagination," Dale had suggested to Marcia, who agreed, thinking Reba would see great potential in a child's sand castle. "She just needs something to focus on," Marcia said, and that was true as well; the longer they dallied out of the market, the more set Reba's jaw became, the more anxious her eyes, the less able she was to control her frustration. Thinking back on it as she walked through the house, Marcia was sorry they hadn't gotten the two places they'd put offers on in February, undistinguished as they were, if only to cool Reba off.

Dale returned from poking at the foundations. So far she had said nothing, merely jabbing a screwdriver here and there. Finally she stood in one place, craning her neck as she looked around her, as if she were reminding herself of all the factors before she rendered a verdict. "What do you think?" she asked Marcia.

"No," Marcia said. "The yard's too small, the school's too near, the street's a beehive of activity, and the house itself is nothing special. Besides, it has a captive bathroom."

"For crissake—"

"They won't like it," Marcia warned, referring to the yuppies they planned to sell to.

Dale shrugged. "I can see certain advantages to it. It's close to us, it's easy to drag shit in and out of the back yard, and it's got a garage. But on the whole, I'd say no too."

"Then *you* look," Reba snapped. She had proposed eight houses since they'd been outbid on their early offers, and been turned down by the group on all of them. Marcia could understand why she was sick of it. "I'll go out this Sunday," Marcia promised. She wondered if she would. Her CD was gathering more than cobwebs in the bank.

The agent joined them again on the sidewalk, smiling in advance. "Undervalued, right?" she asked. "Didn't I tell you? A few cosmetic..." She broke off at the stormy look on Reba's face.

"Thanks so much for meeting us," Marcia told her. "Maybe you could let us know—" While Marcia was talking, Reba walked off in a huff, and Dale waved a cheery and somewhat sheepish good-bye. Marcia, the most polite, was left to explain to the agent that they had qualms that ran deeper than cosmetic.

The agent shook her head. "Look, I like the idea of women making money in this market, which is why I called you before this house got listed. But prices are rising ten thousand a month, fifteen in some neighborhoods. If you don't get in soon, you'll never get in. It almost doesn't matter what you buy."

Sunday at noon, on a hazy but bright day that offered no relief from the drought that was steadily shriveling Northern California, Dale and Marcia continued the search. *Chronicle* Open House guide on the car seat between them, Marcia and Dale crawled through likely neighborhoods—North Oakland, Emeryville, West Berkeley, though many of the latter had to be eliminated because of the rent laws.

"Incredible how many houses are 'vastly undervalued,'" Marcia said after two hours of looking. They were staring glumly at a North Oakland two-bedroom stucco with a $22,000 termite report which carried a price tag of a quarter-mil.

"'Perfect for rehab' means a shack in someone's backyard."

"If it has a structure at all. Remember that sliver of land someone offered us for $65,000?"

Dale laughed. "It was probably a good deal at that." They piled into Dale's red pickup, and Dale began cruising down Alcatraz towards the bay. She turned on Martin Luther King and then scooted ahead of traffic to turn left onto Harmon, forgetting about the barricades the police had recently installed to discourage drug traffic (dealers were afraid of being gunned down by the competition, not trapped by the cops).

Her car phone buzzed.

Dale had won a car phone by being Customer Ten Thousand for 1989 at a lumber yard in El Cerrito. She said she'd almost given it to Number Ten Thousand One but she'd never won anything in her life so she thought she should keep it. It didn't mean, however, that she would get an answering machine.

"Hang up," she said by way of greeting.

Marcia could hear Reba's excited voice on the other end. She stretched out as far as she could in the tiny cab. Pickups were rattletraps. She preferred being low to the ground in her Ranchero.

"We're only a block away," Dale said into the phone. "Be there as soon as I get out of these goddamn barricades."

A block from what, Marcia wondered, Drug Central? This neighborhood even had resident cops ensconced in a big RV with red and blue strobes mounted in tiger stripes along its fat yellow body. The lights kept the neighbors awake but didn't seem to deter drug sales. Dealers moved around the corner or down the block. The RV had an affectionate name, though: Cop Hotel, reminiscent of the product for roaches.

Dale hung the phone on its holder and turned to Marcia. "Reba was talking to a guy at the hardware store. He owns a place on Fairview he wants to sell."

Marcia groaned. Fairview Street was not only Drug Central but Murder Central. "Dale."

"He said he'd sell it for maybe one twenty-five. Two flats." She chuckled. "One twenty-five!"

She gunned the engine, zooming around the corner and running into another set of cement barriers. South Berkeley was crammed with barricades. The city was so serious about preventing drive-by shootings that they had prevented cars.

"They're meeting us at the house," Dale said, throwing her truck into reverse. She tapped Marcia's knee. "He says he'll *carry a loan*."

Dale and Marcia had gone to college together eons before. Marcia had been the first woman to make love to Dale, but Dale had not been in love with her, while Dale, the second woman Marcia had slept with, was the first woman with whom she'd fallen in love. Unraveling this distinction had taken them three years of periodic rambling rehashes fueled by many gallons of beer but it had resulted in an unbreakable friendship. "I don't like it," Marcia said. "Why's this guy willing to sell two flats for one twenty-five to someone he meets at a hardware store?"

Dale had to go all the way back up to Martin Luther King before she found a way out of the maze. They parked the truck beside a liquor store on the corner of MLK and Fairview, in front of a crowd of men who stopped drinking from bottles stuffed in crumpled paper bags long enough to stare at them with eyes hard as slate. Marcia resisted an urge to check over her shoulder as she and Dale began walking down Fairview Street, past faded gray houses with tall peaked gables which hadn't seen good days since the early '70s. Most of the recent home improvements were security-minded: affixing sturdy black bars across windows or erecting three-foot-high chain link fences to enclose a square of grass browning in the drought. "It's probably rent-controlled," Marcia said, trying to dampen Dale's uncharacteristic enthusiasm.

"No. Reba asked him that. He says he grew up in the house, and now his daughter and aunt live there. It's been in the family for forty-five years and never registered."

Marcia grunted. It began to make sense. The guy must not know present values, didn't know two flats should be at least one-seventy-five, even in this neighborhood, that renovated they could go higher than one-thirty-five per unit. If they really got the place for one-twenty-five...

They approached another set of barricades at the intersection of Fairview and Key streets. Fairview was blocked on almost every corner, with big yellow and black signs announcing the obvious: NOT A THROUGH STREET.

Nevertheless, Marcia spotted the local drug store in what had been a garage but was now something else, judging by the ugly sliding glass doors festooned with tattered rose-colored drapes which had replaced the classic entry. She could tell it was a drug store because too many cars of all makes and ages sat in front and the drapes kept flapping open and closed as people sneaked quick looks outside.

"This is it," Dale said, stopping in front of a rambling Queen Anne Victorian on a sun-blasted double corner lot catty-corner from the dope garage, on the other side of the barricade. Marcia dragged her attention away from America's newest cottage industry to boggle at the house, which was so large it dwarfed all the decrepit turn-of-the-century stick and row houses in its vicinity.

"Jesus, it's monstrous!" Marcia yelped, thinking with horror that it looked exactly like the Addams Family's. Complete with two round towers and a peaked witches' cap, it also sported steep gables decorated with sunbursts and plaster garlands. Instead of bats in the belfry, however, pigeons fluttered through an open ventilation hole in the attic. Yellow paint hung off the house in big swatches, like skin shed from a snake, and the window frames, enclosing grimy panes edged by small squares of colored glass, had eroded down to bare wood. The fancy front porch with its latticework arches and carved wooden posts sagged so far to the left it threatened to break loose from its moorings. A jumble of pickets had collapsed on top of some dead grass in the front yard.

"Sarah will love it," Dale said, nodding in admiration.

Marcia wondered aloud if the pigeons had registered with the rent board. Dale snorted.

They paced through browning weeds down the Key Street side of the house, examining a big bay which jutted out to within a few yards of another toppling fence and the sidewalk. The back door opened to a seven-foot drop. There was no sign that there had ever been steps or a landing. There was, in fact, no indication of human habitation. Marcia meandered through the backyard, mentally sinking a pond beyond some pavers to create a barbecue/patio area. On the other side of the house a wild tangle of morning glories camouflaged a twelve-foot high wall above which peeked the roof and upper-story windows of the more modest Victorian next door. Marcia decided she didn't want to poke her hand through the mass of vines to determine the wall's mysterious and perhaps unthinkable composition. Instead she fought past the clinging strands of bright green foliage and attained the front yard again. She was standing there shaking her head when Reba pulled up in her Land Rover with a skinny black guy who hopped out and shook her hand overzealously. "You must be Dale!"

"Marcia. Dale's over there." Marcia nodded to where she'd left Dale stabbing at the foundations with her screwdriver.

"I'm Matthew Foster," he said, trying too hard with his good cheer. Even in a used car lot, Marcia reflected, they'd tell him to tone it down. He stuck his hand in his back pocket and came up with a worn brown wallet which contained a purple and navy business card proclaiming that he was a specialist in floral arrangements. "Weddings, funerals," he explained.

"How nice," Marcia couldn't stop herself from saying.

He smiled. "Guess you girls don't go in for weddings."

Reba scissored her arms across her chest and jacked one hip up on the hood of her jeep. She was a half-inch taller than Foster and a lot skinnier. "Oh, I don't know," she said from around her toothpick. "My daughter's getting to be that age."

Marcia considered telling an astonished Foster that even dykes had trouble picturing Reba as a mother, which is why Polly got the cards that second Sunday in May, but Foster had already decided it was safest to gaze down the street and say how sad it was to sell his family home. Reba told a story about her grandmother selling her house in Missouri, while Marcia and Foster pretended to be interested. "Guess this area's got the last bargains in Berkeley," Foster put in when he could finally find an opening.

With that proclamation, Reba and Foster strode to the back to look for Dale. Marcia stayed on the sidewalk to try to apply their appropriate street definitions, but Fairview fell into another category altogether. The drug store was a detriment, as were two boarded-up houses down the block. On the other hand, there was no school to generate noise and litter, and BART was within walking distance. The block was almost deserted, but that was possibly because any moment thugs could drive around blasting Uzis out the windows, assuming the thugs could find an opening in the barricades wide enough to fit a car through. Sporadic gunfire, Marcia thought, had to be considered a significant downside.

The three of them went for coffee afterwards, "to strategize," Reba said. Foster, it developed, had tried to sell the house once before that summer, but the deal had fallen through when the buyer couldn't get financing. He seemed perfectly willing to sell to them for one-twenty-five. He'd sacrificed his own daughter and his aunt, dragging them from the bowels of the Victorian to inform them in front of the embarrassed threesome from the rehab crew that they had to get out "soon as these girls buy this place." The daughter was a model for an agency in the City and looked it. She started screaming at her father and kept it up on their entire hurried visit through the house, but the aunt just turned away. Probably she knew Foster inside and out.

"It's not our fault he's selling," Reba tried to reassure Marcia and Dale, both shaken by the scene with the female Fosters. "I mean, he offered it to me."

"How?" Marcia asked. "Was he standing out in front of Marcus Hardware with a sign saying 'Buy my house'?"

"No, I was just talking to him about looking. I mean, we were in line."

Marcia tried to imagine Reba turning to Mr. Foster and telling him she was in the market for a house. She couldn't. "But even if we ignore the thing with his family, don't you think we should advise him to call an agent and get an appraisal?"

Reba nearly spat out a mouthful of cappuccino. "Are you nuts?" She turned to Dale. "She's trying to kill our golden goose."

"But why is he willing to sell it so cheap?" Dale wanted to know.

Reba shrugged. "It's not our concern. Besides, all the violins about selling his family home was crap. *He* lives in Walnut Creek."

"Well..." Marcia sputtered to a halt. The new wisdoms about not being coercive or codependent seemed to collide with love your neighbor. Wasn't Mr. Foster a neighbor? Could she live with herself if she didn't let him know he was selling under the market?

"Don't be absurd," Reba growled at her when she'd galvanized herself to express some of this. "Maybe he's desperate. How should we know? He sees this as an easy way to do it. Y'know, no muss, no fuss."

"Sell it while you're standing in line at the hardware store," Marcia echoed.

"He must think he's putting something over on us," Dale surmised. "He figures there's something drastically wrong with the house that we're not seeing because we're women."

"Ergo, a sexist. Ergo, we're absolved from moral responsibility," Reba concluded.

"Well, *is* there something drastically wrong?" Marcia asked. She was beginning to feel lightheaded. At first she feared she'd gotten caffeinated coffee by mistake, but then she realized it was an anxiety attack.

"Well," Dale said, "it's almost a hundred years old, and they haven't done a thing to it in the last twenty. Sure, there's plenty wrong."

"But it's still a terrific buy," Reba insisted. "Two flats, one-twenty-five." She stroked her tall glass of milk-chocolate-colored cappuccino. "Wait until Sarah sees it. She'll flip."

When Marcia got home, she went out into her front yard to divide her irises. She worked quickly, using her three-pronged fork to pry them out and then a kitchen knife to separate the new rhizomes from the old ones. The withered old tubers went into one bag, the firm fledglings into another. Too bad the division of the Fairview house could not be so easily solved. It had been separated into two flats sometime in the '50s, and the divorce was not amicable. The downstairs had an enormous grand hall and kitchen, but consequently it had hardly more than a closet for a bedroom (the former pantry, Vernita Foster opined in the midst of screaming at her father). The upstairs flat had no living room, no dining room, a kitchen jerryrigged out of one of the five bedrooms, with the other four bedrooms marching railroad fashion along a hallway. Neither bathroom was captive, however, Reba pointed out.

Billy and a bunch of his friends flooded out onto Robert's porch. They arranged themselves artfully on the steps, better to attract passing girls, and turned on a boombox so loud the wooden stairs jumped at the low notes. Then they began shouting at each other over the music. Marcia ignored them even though they were only twenty feet away. Amazing what a waist-high fence could do—that and a twenty-five-year generation gap. She probably appeared to them as an exotic species of fauna, digging in the dirt for a purpose they couldn't imagine. If they noticed her at all, weird would sum her up.

After about twenty minutes Robert came flying out of the downstairs where he had his stereo and his 27-inch TV, crossed his beefy hands over his chest, and demanded that the boys turn down the volume. The boys obeyed, which was a relief, except that now, through the din of a couple other conversations, she heard one of Billy's friends talking about her. "Man, I don't see how Billy can stand to live next door to a fuckin' queer. Look at that shit every day, all that dyke kissin' and huggin'? Oooweee, gives me the creeps just thinkin' about it!"

Marcia sighed. She was far enough away that she might not be able to hear...or should she confront the prick? She was debating what to do when Billy evidently tuned into the discussion. "Hey, shut up, man. She'll hear you."

"So what, man?"

Billy's voice was strained and embarrassed. Marcia carefully separated another iris, cutting away the daughters from the mother. The mother went into the bag to be composted, the daughters to the other pile.

"'Cause she's my neighbor, man. And I like her, that's why. So shut the fuck up!"

There was a tense moment on both sides of the fence. Billy had been practically warbling at the end there, his voice slipping up into a higher register. "Oh, fuck this," said another voice. "C'mon, let's *do something*!"

"Like what?"

"Who the fuck knows? Let's go down to that market."

"Oh, *man*!"

And the tension was gone. Marcia went inside and took a bath. She lay in the hot water, enjoying the unaccustomed quiet, thinking about Billy. There was nothing more frightening for a kid than defying his friends, but he'd done it. For her.

Marcia was sorry her date with Lydia was for tonight. She was so worried about spending her fifteen thou for a monstrosity on the worst street in Berkeley, how could she concentrate on Lydia too? Though, she realized, not being able to obsess about Lydia might be a good thing. It was the first time in seven days she'd gotten Lydia off her mind for longer than a couple hours.

Of course, she could talk to Lydia about her potential Waterloo, but they didn't have that kind of relationship yet. And I don't want *any* kind of relationship, Marcia reminded herself, though perhaps telling Lydia she wouldn't go to a movie with her had skidded past blunt to dishonest, since she'd done little but replay scenes from last Sunday's chance meeting at the botanical garden.

Her favorite image was Lydia walking up to the crest of a hill, her students ranged around her like geese following the farmer. She had been wearing a short-sleeved maroon blouse, loose cotton pants, and her Reeboks, and she bounced when she walked, as if she were striding across a trampoline rather than a dirt path. She had abruptly stopped at the top of the hill to point out a species of salvia. Her light brown eyes were alive, her face half-amused as she'd leaned forward to hear the students' comments. Her tight behind made a crescent moon against the charcoal gray of her pants, and her breasts were not more than a promise under the too-large shirt. But Marcia could imagine them. She had wanted to saunter up the hill herself, the student-geese scattering in her wake, until she stood in front of Lydia and Lydia fell into her arms and Marcia began kneading Lydia's back and belly and breasts. This hadn't happened. But when the class was over, Lydia had appeared at Marcia's side and said simply, "Let's go for coffee."

Nine o'clock was fast approaching, and Marcia was getting more and more nervous. It was so terrific the first time, she thought. What if now it's awful? She prowled into her living room and hovered at the window. Just as she was about to turn away, Lydia's staid gray Volvo sedan pulled up to the curb. Marcia watched Lydia get out of her car and glance towards Robert's steps, where Billy and his friends had repositioned themselves after returning from their rambling. Lydia was wearing her black leather vest, jeans, and a sheer white blouse that probably showed too much to seven teenage boys. No doubt they were admiring her—Marcia certainly was—as Lydia fluffed out her long dark hair, jangled her earrings, then checked her watch, glancing at the house. Marcia resisted the urge to duck. Sudden movements are much easier to spot than a head at a dark window. Lydia evidently decided to risk being a few minutes early. She started up the front stairs, her steps light enough to make it almost all the way before the creaking began.

Marcia opened her door. "Hi," she said. "C'mon in." They kissed awkwardly after Marcia shut the door, nervous with each other. Marcia offered to take Lydia's vest, but Lydia wanted to keep it on. Lydia looked around at the living room, where she could see nothing since it was unlit. "C'mon," Marcia prompted, ignoring her front room—it was so tiny even two people felt claustrophobic. She led Lydia into the kitchen, which was much more homey. "I made some coffee," Marcia said. "And I have carrot cake. Would you like some?" Reggae music was blaring from the tape deck in her bedroom. She thought about shutting it off, but instead she indicated a chair at the oak table and began to walk towards the counter, which held both the coffeemaker and the carrot cake, conveniently laid out with two plates and a knife.

Lydia caught her wrist and pulled her around to face her. "I thought you only had time to fuck," Lydia said quietly. "Instead you offer me carrot cake. What's the matter? Lose your nerve?"

As Marcia stammered a denial, she admired the ploy. Lydia had leapt right to the heart of the matter, all right. Her eyes were flashing amused, kindly, reassuring, turned-on, all of it. Marcia felt herself starting to get wet. Fast. But what if she wanted some carrot cake? What then?

"I guess I should shove that carrot cake up your cunt. Then we can eat and fuck at the same time."

She didn't want any carrot cake after all. Lydia's eyes were drilling into her own. She would have to look down in a moment. She was being led along a path from which there was no escape. "I'm sorry," she muttered, half-sincerely. She did feel like an idiot. "I didn't mean to sound so uninviting."

The slap almost floored her. Lydia must have been practicing. Marcia rebounded from the wall, now glad she'd put on the reggae tape. Billy's constant rap music made her aware how easily sound traveled. She had no desire for Billy and his friends to hear whatever was going to happen next.

"You think saying you're sorry is enough?" Lydia's voice grated. She caught Marcia's wrist and pinned her arm behind her back. Marcia knew how to get out of the hold but she had no intention of escaping. "I'm really sorry," she said.

It sounded weak and pathetic. She wondered if Lydia were actually angry. Lydia was using her other hand to unbuckle her belt. Marcia, barely breathing, caught by Lydia's implacable gaze, nevertheless managed to follow the slow passage of the heavy black leather belt from the pantloops. "Get in there," Lydia said, stepping behind Marcia as she jerked her head at the bedroom.

Marcia moved fast, wishing she didn't have to break eye contact. Lydia moved faster, jerking her along by her arm. Marcia's knees were suddenly weak. Lydia took advantage of that fact by shoving her face forward on the bed. Marcia's butt was firmly on the bed, but her legs jutted out at an uncomfortable angle. Her arm hurt. Lydia was holding it far up her back, her hand nearly to the base of her neck.

The belt slammed into the bed next to her. Marcia jumped. Then she lay perfectly still as Lydia reached underneath her, unbuttoned her jeans, and yanked them down to her knees. "No underpants," Lydia observed with satisfaction. "I guess you really were ready to go."

Marcia kept her mouth shut. She'd said too much already. The belt hit the bed again, hard. Marcia cringed away from it. Her arm was really starting to ache now, and her legs were uncomfortable. She wanted to move either up or down on the bed. The belt smacked her lightly on the thighs. Surprised, she bolted forward. Lydia moved with her. Settled more firmly now, Marcia waited, aware of her breathing, of her cunt dripping, of the softness of the bedspread against her cheek, the bunchiness of the jeans hobbling her knees.

The belt fell lightly again, this time on her ass. Prepared, she didn't jump. She waited. Her cunt ached. The bed again, whoosh. Give it to me, she thought. She said nothing. The tip of the belt caressed the flesh on her behind, sneaked between her legs and came up wet. "I want to see how much you can take," Lydia said softly, leaning forward so she could speak into Marcia's ear.

Marcia stopped breathing. She wished she didn't have the music on. She wanted to hear every nuance in utter stillness. She wanted to hear Lydia breathe. She still hadn't started breathing herself when Lydia whispered, "I know how much punishment I think you've earned by your arrogance and rudeness. If you can satisfy me that you've learned your lesson, you'll get to go down on me. But I'm not going to tell you how much it's going to take to convince me. Maybe you'll give up when it was only a couple strokes more. You won't know."

Now Marcia thought she sounded like a steam locomotive. She seemed to have two modes: not breathing or panting. But she would never give up. Never.

"Oh, you will," Lydia assured her. "Just tell me when to stop," she added sweetly, her lips next to Marcia's ear. "But remember, a few more might have done it." Then she reared back and applied the belt with a smack, then another, gradually increasing her strokes in both speed and intensity. It hurt at first, Marcia gasping as each blow fell, but very soon she was transported by the smack of the leather against her ass, by the picture in her mind of herself lying on the bed, her behind being strapped with the heavy belt, until she was somewhere else entirely, in sync with the rhythm of the strapping, floating in space, and when she came back to herself for a moment she found herself wondering what this was, this incredibly high feeling, alpha waves or something. Then she told herself to stop thinking, stay on the wave, like surfing but no, not at all like surfing, too transcendental for surfing because surfing was in the mind using the body as a tool, this was in the body get rid of the mind, shit, now Lydia was doing it harder, faster, it hurt now, burn, burn, focus on the space where it didn't hurt but made her fly only now it was starting to hurt all over, she didn't know how much more she could stand, and once that thought came into her head it wouldn't leave no matter how much she tried to chase it away, the blows were raining down, and her ass, which had been rising to meet the belt, now was beaten down, exhausted, poor thing, the point was being lost, what was the point, hang on a little longer, oh yes, cunt flowing like a river, I want to be fucked now, want to go down on her, yes, that was it, the skin on her ass was on fire, bruises surely tomorrow, for sure bruises, stop. I can't stand anymore, stop, and finally she said it out loud. Lydia stopped. Let her arm go. Leaned close again. "Marcia," she murmured.

"I—I—" Marcia was shocked by the tears in her voice. She was nearly crying.

"C'mon, baby," Lydia said, and crouched on the bed next to her and drew her face first to her breasts, then down further to her belly, where there were fine hairs that tickled Marcia's lips. "You were very good, better than I suspected, yes, really very good..."

The wet on Marcia's cheeks could have been tears of relief or Lydia's sweat or Lydia's juices, she was that soaked, but whatever it was made a nice smooth slide down to her cunt, which was so open, so fantastically open, that Marcia didn't spend much time with her tongue. Instead she went to the crux of it, led off with four fingers, and when they went in easily, worked in her thumb, up a little on her elbow to get the right angle, careful, coaxing her hand along the channel, until her fingers folded into a loose fist, gently and gracefully as if she were cupping a baby bird in her palm. She moved her head up, rested her face against the flat of Lydia's shoulder, pumped, and gloried as Lydia started to howl above the boom-boom-boom of Black Uhuru coming to dinner.

# CHAPTER 3

The phone began ringing five minutes after Lydia skipped down the stairs to dash to her first class, having, with both tact and foresight, brought along a change of clothes in the Volvo's trunk. Before she'd left, she'd availed herself of the carrot cake after all, gobbling down two large pieces while Marcia alternately nibbled at her neck and sipped steaming hot coffee. Marcia was just wandering into her bathroom to take a shower when Sarah called. "Foster says he'll take twenty-five thousand down," she said. "He'll carry the rest. We're opening an escrow account this morning."

"This morning?" Marcia said. "But what about a contract? What about inspections? What about a termite report?" She paused a minute, her head whirling, and then bleated, "What about us deciding we want it?"

"Are you kidding? It's a Queen Anne! Whatta we care about inspections? He's selling it 'as-is,' and we're going to be renovating it from scratch anyway. Boy, it's so great! It's even got some of the original light fixtures downstairs! Did you notice?"

Marcia hadn't. Sarah hung up. Marcia wandered back into the bathroom, trying to convince herself that she hadn't answered the phone.

Her investment group's *Nightmare on Fairview Street* was no match for daydreaming about Lydia and how wonderful it'd been to sleep next to her, on top of her, under her, and all the other permutations they'd managed during an active but marvelously restorative night. She had just disappeared into a memory of their arms and legs tangled, her cheek lodged against the heavy sway of Lydia's breast when the phone jangled again. "Could you transfer your money into the business account today?" Polly asked, her voice trembly and fraught with import. "We need to give the checks time to clear."

"Already?" Gone were Lydia's breast and Marcia's peace of mind.

"Isn't this exciting? I'm so glad we finally found something. Sarah is just..."

Sarah's ecstasy at buying an historic house was apparently beyond description. Polly hung up and the doorbell rang. "Fuck it!" Marcia cried. She yanked on a robe, stalked across the living room, and threw open her door. Billy stood there wearing his new satin jacket, which his uncle, Staff Sergeant Thomas Preston, had gotten for him in the Philippines. "Like it?" he asked, pirouetting on her porch.

"Lovely," she said. "C'mon in. Want some carrot cake?"

"Ugh. You got anything else? I'll have coffee."

She poured him a cup and the phone rang again. "This is infuriating," she told him. It was Reba. "Did Polly call you about transferring your money?"

"Yes. But why are we doing this so fast? We hadn't even decided yet."

"Are you really undecided, Marcia? A Queen Anne for one-hundred-twenty-five?"

Marcia tried another tack. "Well, what about the division business? How are we going to keep it two units with that awful floor plan? I don't see how it's going to work."

"If we can't do it two units, we'll go back to one."

"No!" Marcia said, restraining her impulse to shout. "Forget it. No way. You can count my money out if we go to one unit."

"This is a democracy, Marcia. Majority rules."

"My money doesn't want a democracy. My money wants consensus. And I will block converting it back to one unit, Reba."

Silence on either end. Billy too had decided the carrot cake wasn't that bad. He'd gone through three pieces already. "You buying a place?" he asked.

Marcia rolled her eyes and covered the receiver. "On Fairview Street," she said. Billy made a big production of choking on his carrot cake and pretending to die.

Marcia turned her back on him. "I'm serious," she told Reba.

"We'll talk later," Reba promised. She hung up.

"You and Uncle Lucas," Billy said. "Both of you crazier'n shit."

"Yeah, well." Marcia sat down at the table and watched Billy separate off a fourth piece of cake.

"Your new girlfriend's really cute."

"She's not my girlfriend."

"She stayed the night."

"That she did. That doesn't mean we're married."

"She's cute, though."

They sipped their coffee. Marcia liked this time of day. It had been, she recalled, exactly this time that Billy had first knocked on her door. "Hi," he had announced. "I'm Billy Preston. I just moved in."

Marcia already knew that since she had watched the entire proceedings through various windows, but she treated it as if it were a big surprise. "Really! That's exciting. How old are you anyway? Twelve?"

He giggled. "Ten."

"Ah, ten. That's a good age. You want a cookie? Come on in. Did your mother send you over to say hi?"

"I don't have a mother. My pop don't talk to white folks but Aunt Esther said I oughta come."

"Well, that was sweet of her. Have another cookie. Was that your grandma I saw?" Marcia had marveled that the boy could support the elderly woman who leaned so heavily on him as she hobbled up the stairs.

"Great-grandma," he said solemnly.

"Wow. She must be old."

"*Really* old."

"What do you want to be when you get big?"

"An Army pilot!" He pantomimed sweeping the sky with a gun: "ACK-ACK-ACK-ACK!"

"I don't think it works like that anymore," Marcia mused. "I think you just push a button."

Billy shook his head. "No, no. I saw it in the movies."

Marcia nodded. "Probably I'm wrong."

Billy jumped up. "Thanks for the cookies!" he yelled, and he zoomed out the door. But he was back, the next day and the next. Sometime during that first couple months he announced that Aunt Esther had told him Marcia didn't like men.

"Well, she's wrong," Marcia said. "I do like men." Billy scuffed his feet. "Pop and Esther had a big fight. Esther said she wished she was queer like you."

"Why is that?" This was obviously disturbing to him, though Marcia thought it had nothing to do with the gay part.

"'Cause she says men are no good and she hates 'em. She says they're all rotten bastards."

"That seems kind of sweeping, doesn't it?" She watched him look away from her. "OK, Billy, I'm going to let you in on a grownup secret, but it's really complicated, so you have to listen closely."

"What is it?"

She handed him his usual plate of cookies and glass of milk. "Your aunt actually likes men a lot. That's why she says she hates them. Now I know that sounds stupid, but it's how adults think. It's like—well, take your sister, for instance."

"I hate my sister," Billy said.

"Yes, exactly. But if someone you didn't know was hurting your sister, you'd help her, wouldn't you?"

He grudgingly admitted that maybe he would, depending.

"Because you really love your sister. Now wait—don't have a fit. You do. Trust me. Your sister pisses you off, but she's your sister. Well, it's sort of like that with Esther and men. Men piss her off, but she still loves 'em. But— and here's the really important part—none of this has anything to do with how she feels about you. She loves you and Melinda most of all, above everyone else, whether you're a boy or a girl. Her being angry at men has nothing to do with you."

He pondered that for a long while, munching on a chocolate chip cookie. Then he looked up at her. "And you like men too?"

"Sure. But I can just say it straight out. I'm not mad at men so I can like them easier than Esther can."

Billy was back the next day. "Aunt Esther says I should take your word for it that it's easier for you to like men 'cause she says she doesn't know a thing about it. And she did say she didn't mean me." He smiled at her. "So you were right."

"Sometimes it happens."

"Guess what?" Billy announced, already on another topic. "Uncle Lucas promised to get me a bomber jacket for Christmas!"

Uncle Lucas was the other Preston family member who spent a lot of time at Marcia's. It was nicer, he said, giving her a wink, than hanging around at Mr. Big-Deal Sergeant Robert's house. "Only good thing that happened in 'Nam was I left when he showed up," Lucas said. "Place wasn't big enough for two heroes." Robert had stayed in the Army after his tour, but Lucas had gotten out and started drinking himself to death, a fate that was proving slow to come.

Every couple months Lucas asked Marcia how long she'd been sober. "Jesus," he always said. "But you're still crazy underneath. That's the only reason I come over here, y'know. Keep you straight." Then he would chuckle. "I'm not doin' much of a job, am I?"

At that point, Marcia still had not spoken to Robert. On Christmas Day, she went next door with a cake. Robert opened the door and looked at her. "I understand you don't talk to white people," Marcia said.

"Who told you an ignorant thing like that?" Robert snapped, crossing his arms across his chest.

"A little bird. Anyhow, I thought you might make an exception in my case."

"Why would I?"

"Because it's Christmas and I come bearing gifts."

Robert thought about it without, Marcia marveled, cracking a smile. Meanwhile Aunt Esther, taller than Robert by three inches, was looming over her brother's shoulder, her dark eyes twinkling. When it seemed Robert was anchored permanently in place, she edged him aside with her hip and held out her hand to draw Marcia in. "Never did care for that Trojan horse story," she said. "You're more than welcome."

Over the years, the Preston military trinity, Lucas and Robert and Thomas, got Billy Army Aviation wings, mirror sunglasses, and models of helicopters. Marcia teased Billy about wanting to fly around in multimillion-dollar eggbeaters killing people. She maintained he could kill people for much less if he stayed on the ground. Robert said Marcia was a bleeding-heart liberal and they always spouted junk like that. Billy no longer wore bomber jackets or aviator glasses but sometimes to annoy Marcia he swept the sky with his imaginary machine gun, as he was doing now, carrot cake crumbs tumbling down the front of his satin jacket. "ACK-ACK-ACK-ACK. Shot down, Marcia. You buy a house on Fairview Street, you gonna get it both ways. You gonna lose your money and maybe your life!"

"Ain't it the truth," Marcia said. She was starting to feel sick. She hoped it wasn't the carrot cake.


By ten she'd sped to her job as manager of Top Hat Catering, which served, the logo claimed, parties from two to twelve-hundred, though luckily they'd never come anywhere near the upper range. She cleared messages off her desk, scheduled half-a-dozen workers for events, and upbraided a bakery for shipping over five seeded baguettes instead of fifteen. At eleven she was in a meeting to discuss how they would handle the increased holiday load—an annual jump in business, everyone warned everyone else, which might surge earlier than usual, depending on whether the A's and the Giants continued to stay in front of their respective divisions. "World Series parties," Top Hat's bearded owner said, peaking his hands on either side of his nose in prayer. He had been a mover and a shaker during the 1969 battle over People's Park, once diving in front of a tank rumbling down Haste Street, but now he restricted his activism to defending his West Berkeley neighborhood from what he called "creeping industrialism," though most of Berkeley's industry had crept out of town in the last twenty years.

By three, Dale was the only member of the rehab crew who hadn't contacted Marcia (aside from Carol, of course, who didn't count), and the only person she really wanted to hear from. Reba had phoned several times—had she transferred the money yet?—no, she hadn't, she was going to do it tomorrow morning, that would have to be soon enough. She wanted to talk about the unit business first. Fine, Reba said, talk away, but she better make it fast. Foster had ordered a title search done on the house only a month earlier. Therefore the search would take less than twenty-four hours. "Since he's carrying the loan, the title company says this'll be the shortest escrow in history," Reba chortled.

"I want to have a meeting about the unit stuff," Marcia insisted.

"Fine, have a meeting. You call all the people."

Sarah agreed to come to an emergency caucus. Polly did as well, probably because Reba hadn't clued her in that she should refuse. Carol gave some trouble but eventually said she'd be there. Marcia still couldn't get Dale. "Where are you?" she crooned as the phone rang and rang. She hated it that Dale didn't have an answering machine. It was absurd. Everyone in California had a machine. She tried Dale's car phone though she'd promised her she would never, ever call it. No answer. Perhaps Dale had freaked out and taken her five thousand dollars to Mexico, or more likely run off to Berlin to join her girlfriend Renate, with whom she'd been having a long-distance relationship for the last nine years. They never saw each other for more than two months at a stretch. "Maybe it's the only way," Marcia had said glumly as she sat in a dyke fern bar in a dimly lit Berlin suburb last summer. Her seven-year-long marriage to Annie had ended only six months earlier and she was still in shock. Dale had dragged her to Berlin to recreate, she'd said, in every sense of the word. Renate was doing her part by directing a steady stream of women past their table, but finally Dale called a halt. "Can't you see she's devastated?" she scolded Renate, somewhat unfairly, since Marcia getting done in Berlin had been Dale's idea.

Marcia now thought she'd been attracted to Annie's rage for self-destruction because she'd sworn off self-destruction herself, sort of boozing by proxy, though Annie was much more creative in provoking disaster than Marcia had ever been on her sodden, predictable drunks. Marcia had spent the beginning of her thirties believing she was the glue that held Annie together, the middle feeling trapped by the role she'd defined for herself, and the end extricating herself from the trap by a series of painful and drama-filled talks that went nowhere. Once abandoned, Annie rescued herself handily by becoming an account executive at an advertising agency in the City, leading Marcia to walk around blinking for a few weeks wondering just who was crazy here, her or Annie. "Does it matter?" Dale had asked.

"Of course it matters!" It amazed Marcia that Annie had managed to disorient her more in her absence than in her presence, but then Annie had always been the champion of paradox.

Marcia hadn't gotten done in Berlin, but she'd come home to the Bay Area, gone on a whirlwind fuck-tour with any and everyone she could think of, then disappeared back into her house to recover. "Always the extremes," Dale said. "Why can't you just date a couple people?"

Marcia didn't know. It never worked that way for her. She was either monogamous with a lover, promiscuous with a crowd, or withdrawn, generally happily, at home. She'd been in the last stage and liking it when she'd run into Lydia at the botanical garden. Lydia worried her. She just didn't seem the type to be into sex for sex's sake, nor was her interest in Marcia limited—at least Marcia hoped it wasn't. Which meant Lydia must have a hidden agenda, though she hadn't put up a speck of fuss about Marcia's recreational sex rule. Marcia admitted that she too had a hidden agenda, but she had decided to ignore that part until she figured out what Lydia's might be. But maybe this mad fling with Lydia only presaged a return to her wilder days. "You're too old for that shit," she cautioned herself as her phone rang. Ted, her college-boy assistant, began a nasal commentary in her ear of why he hadn't come to work, something to do with windsurfing and an accident. She put Ted on hold and dialed Dale's number. Nothing. She punched Ted back in and told him to take plenty of Vitamin C. He sounded bewildered and she realized she hadn't heard a word he'd said.

Dale kept insisting that she and Marcia were the domestic type and therefore Marcia had to get married whether she liked it or not. Why, Marcia asked blandly, when all it brings is bitterness and confusion? Dale said the big secret was finding the right person which diminished the bitterness and confusion factor to a bearable level. Hah, Marcia thought, drawing up a food list for the Babakov's fiftieth anniversary bash.

"Don't kid yourself that you're doing anything but marking time 'til the wedding," Dale had told Marcia only a few days earlier. The nervous-making part was that Dale's perceptions were usually correct. All evidence to the contrary, Marcia knew herself to be a stodgy monogamist, and she would be happiest in a marriage that worked.

Think about something else, she commanded. For instance, how did she expect to complete a massive landscaping project in the fall, during the busiest season of the year at the catering company? Why couldn't their investment group wait until spring? Because they wanted to sell in the spring, they would say, and they were right. Spring was definitely when home buyers' hearts took a turn towards the romantic, and that's what they'd need for someone to plunk down money for their monstrosity on Fairview.

My god, she told herself, you've given into it. You're acting as if the place is already ours.

Just as she was about to leave, a woman called and asked for her personally. Marcia couldn't place the voice. "Fuck you," the woman said. "I'll make you regret this." It took Marcia a few minutes of pondering to realize her caller was Foster's model daughter. And Vernita Foster, joint tenant with her father, was, according to Polly, co-signing the loan papers.

Dale had evidently resigned herself as well. She had spent the day at the house, it turned out, poking here and there. The aunt had let her in, though Vernita had come home midday and screamed at her and then begun calling everyone to leave threats on phone machines. "Don't you think this is a little worrisome?" Sarah asked, scrabbling her fingers anxiously through her hair so it looked more like the bird's nest it had resembled for years. Her sky-blue eyes were ringed by purplish shadows. Twenty-two-year-old Marines evidently never slept.

"Naw," Carol said. "Once the papers are signed, what can she do?"

"Who's writing up the contract?"

That was Polly's job. Reba was too grand to bother herself with the nitty-gritty of legal dealings, but she wanted to keep it in the family. "We're just using one of the normal forms and changing things," Polly explained.

"I want to talk about the units," Marcia interjected. "How are we going to do the floor plans so they're not completely screwy?" Best go on the offense, she decided, and just assume there would be two units.

"That's what I spent all day thinking about," Dale said wearily. "Here's my idea. You know there's that dumb kitchen upstairs? OK, what if instead of a unit on each floor, we have a big front unit and a small back unit, both with an upstairs and a downstairs? The back unit's stair-case would be outside where that shed is, enclosed with a greenhouse structure. We make a kitchen in reverse downstairs, backed up by the other kitchen. We get rid of that stupid kitchen upstairs and turn it and the back bedroom into a master bedroom/bath for the back unit. We can use all the kitchen plumbing for the bathroom, and we'll have gained another bath for the front unit."

Reba shook her head with admiration. "Hey, what a gal."

"But wait," Sarah said. "I think we need to at least consider converting it back. We can restore it to what it should be, what it was designed to be, and sell to a large family. How many affordable five-bedroom houses are there?"

"None," Carol told her, "because nobody wants one. Why do you think all these Victorians were broken up in the first place? Great plan, Dale."

"Terrific," Polly agreed.

Even Marcia couldn't think of anything wrong with the idea. It was awfully clever, in fact.

"I guess it's all right," she said. She wished she didn't feel as if she were slitting her own throat.

Sarah pointed out that they were buying in a black neighborhood and converting a house to appeal to yuppies. "Exactly," Carol said combatively. Reba admitted that was so, but muddied the issue by telling her the front unit should be large enough for a kid or two. Polly said they shouldn't gloss over Sarah's concerns and that she personally would feel more comfortable if everyone's objections were addressed. Dale and Marcia said they were suffering from hypoglycemia and had to eat soon or no one would be safe. Both scuttled out the door before anybody could object.

On the way back from dinner, Dale revealed that she had not transferred her money either. Reba was now insisting they get cashier's checks so the money would clear instantly.

"I don't see why it has to be so fast," Marcia complained. "It's crazy."

"We all keep thinking he's going to realize he's selling it way under market," Dale said.

Marcia spun the Ranchero around a curve, at least insofar as the ancient vehicle could be said to spin. "Let me stop off at my house before I take you back to the truck, would you? I need to return a video."

Once inside, they decided to listen to the answering machine to see if Foster's daughter had left any more messages.

The tape ran back, on and on and on. "Oh-oh," Marcia said. "It must be Vivian."

"Who's Vivian?"

"She's this woman who fills in at work. She has this complicated schedule that changes every semester."

The answering machine had begun to talk. "Hi, Marcia, Vivian. I wanted to tell you about those hours you wanted me to do. I can do the eighth, but not at the time you scheduled. I can do two hours from six a.m. to eight, but then I have an appointment so I can't get back until ten-thirty. Then I have a class at twelve, but I can fit in an hour before. After my class, I can come back at three and work until seven. That only makes seven hours, but it's the best I can do. That's if I get that class. I'll know my schedule Wednesday, so I'll tell you for sure then. If I have a morning class, it's harder. I'd need to be to school at eight—"

"STOP!" Dale shouted, collapsing against the counter with laughter. "Give me a break. Does she go on like this?"

"For hours," Marcia said. "She can use up the entire tape." She too was laughing, but it had a rueful quality. After all, she had to listen to this crap.

"I can't believe it," Dale said.

Vivian was continuing to talk. "And then my other job starts on the thirteenth. I won't know my schedule there until Friday, but I thought I should call you and tell you all the possibilities so that if something doesn't work—"

"What *could* work?" Dale demanded.

"I should ask you over all the time to listen to my machine," Marcia said. She wandered into the bathroom and brushed her teeth and washed her face, the dull drone in the background occasionally interrupted by Dale's hoots of laughter.

"Now she's warning you she might get sick in October because she has a history of illness!" Dale could hardly speak through her convulsions, and tears were bulging out of her eyes.

"I know this is hilarious to you, but I have to deal with these people." Marcia tried to sound harsh, but she started giggling halfway through. Finally the machine clicked and another voice came on. Lydia.

"Hi, Mars. Just wanted to let you know how much I enjoyed the movie. Heh heh."

"Who's that?" Marcia pictured Dale's ears perked forward.

"Lydia is her name."

"Lydia? Lydia." Dale gave Marcia a significant look. "*And...*"

Marcia shrugged. "She's nice."

"Why haven't *I* been told?"

"You will be."

"When?"

"When the time's right."

"Is she nice?"

Marsha's voice turned querulous. "Yes, I said that already."

Dale looked unconvinced. "Why don't you want to tell me about her?"

"Because—" Marcia heaved a big sigh and then finished in a rush. "Because I really like her and I don't want to think about that now."

Dale nodded. "Okay." They started out the door but then Dale stopped halfway down the front steps. "Hey. How come she said 'heh heh' about the movie?"

Marcia opened her mouth to answer but then they both started laughing and she didn't have to.


Two days later, Marcia left a message on Lydia's machine: "Hey lady, wanta fuck?" After she hung up she remembered Cory, Lydia's seventeen-year-old son. "Shit," she said, whapping her forehead with the heel of her hand. She realized there was no more way to unleave a message than there was to unmail a letter.

Lydia called her at work later that day. Not knowing who it was, Marcia shouted over the intercom: "I'm on another line! Take a number, OK?" The receptionist didn't, or chose not to, hear. Marcia stabbed the red button, then flashing line three. "Yeah!" she barked.

"Jesus! You sound busy. Maybe I'll try later."

"Oh, Lydia. I'm going to put you on hold a minute. Lemme get rid of this other call."

It took her one and a half minutes to wheedle Lucy Prior, an obsessive-compulsive who could not leave her party alone once she'd handed it over, off the line. She pushed flashing three again. "OK, here I am," she said, heaving a deep breath.

"I love being on hold," Lydia said serenely. "You don't have to feel bad about doing nothing. You can meditate or just *be*, because something will start in a moment, but since you don't have control over when it will happen, you don't need to worry about it."

"Yeah, I never thought about that," Marcia mused. She hated being on hold. It infuriated her. In fact, she believed a good test of her spiritual well-being was seeing how equally she could manage waiting in lines or on the phone. If she were in decent shape, she could hum a little tune or amuse herself while she was waiting instead of seething. "I don't like not being in control," she confessed to Lydia.

Lydia laughed. "I bet. The way you answered, you're not exactly giving other people much space."

Marcia was abruptly tired of this conversation. "So, what'd you call about?"

"Your message."

Marcia had forgotten. Now it flooded back to her. "Oh, I'm sorry. The minute I hung up, I remembered your son. Did you—"

"Oh, he wouldn't have cared. He would have been happy for me, I think. But I got home first."

"Oh, good," Marcia said, relieved.

"But if you feel so apologetic about it, I suppose some sort of retribution might be arranged."

Marcia laughed. "Yes, I don't want my psyche damaged by all this unresolved guilt. When and where?"

"My place? Tonight? Cory's out until eleven."

"Great." People were swimming around her desk, thrusting papers at her. "I gotta go. See you at eight. Let's have eaten, OK?" She didn't wait for an answer.

By four o'clock, Marcia was champing at the bit. She kept glancing at the clock and drifting off into reveries centering on how Lydia had yowled when Marcia was fisting her and how Lydia could suck her nipples with such devilish abandon that Marcia thought she might slide away into a black hole of delight and never find her way back. Between her fantasies she worried she was becoming too attached to Lydia. It was easier to sit by herself in her house than be challenged by unanswerable questions, like how did you know if you've found the right woman? Dale was always insisting she forget about right or wrong and concentrate instead on what was real. So which was the telltale emotion she was supposed to focus on: the wonderful part or the fearful?

Maybe she should just stick to sex, which was supposedly what they were doing. But that rarely worked over time because one person fell for the other. In truth, there wasn't a whole lot of point to it otherwise. Thrills could only go so far; they didn't keep you warm on a rainy night and they didn't listen when you needed an ear. They didn't feed you chicken soup or help you water your yard. They didn't need what you had to give, either. It was like taking a Maserati on a bumpy one-lane road. So much was missing, so much held in check.

Lydia clapped her in handcuffs the moment she walked in the door. Marcia was surprised that Lydia even owned handcuffs, since she didn't seem to have a lot of paraphernalia—the belt, her vest, now the handcuffs. Maybe she had other stuff, but Marcia hadn't seen it. Maybe her toys would appear one at a time, scene by scene.

It was disconcerting that Lydia would fall into role so quickly, without even a polite conversation about their respective health and the usual forties' plaint about how they had no time anymore to glance at a newspaper or water their houseplants. Marcia had a sneaking suspicion Lydia was plunging right into it to please Marcia rather than herself, which led Marcia to assume Lydia was suffering from performance anxiety, an occupational hazard for tops and a turnoff for bottoms. But apart from all that, Marcia had hoped Lydia wouldn't start so fast because she really did want to talk first. They had to talk sometime, didn't they?

"Lydia," Marcia said, following her into the bedroom. "You wanta chat for a few minutes?"

Lydia pulled down the bed covers to reveal pale blue satin sheets. Then she sat on the bed and regarded Marcia. "I thought what we were about here was sex and no gab." At Marcia's protest, she waved her off. "C'mon, I'm teasing. What do you want to talk about?"

Marcia thought she should invent a few questions to ask Lydia to demonstrate that she wasn't just consumed with herself, but Lydia wasn't buying it. She finally waved her hand impatiently in front of Marcia's nose. "I'm listening," she prompted.

"Well, remember I told you about how my rehab group is looking to buy a house?" She had mentioned it to Lydia over their first dinner. Since then they'd been too busy fucking to expand on that kind of information.

"You found one."

"Yes. But we did this bizarre thing. We've been so careful." Marcia described their criteria for house-hunting, how they eliminated houses near schools, parks, or big apartment buildings. And she explained that living in Jesse Jackson's rainbow community was fine as long as everyone stayed indoors.

"This sounds unbelievably racist," Lydia said. "If all the people on the street were white, would your buyers mind them being outside?"

"Well...maybe. I was thinking just recently it's more classist than racist." At Lydia's skeptical look, Marcia hurried to add, "I mean, you're right. But it's not us thinking this stuff. We're just factoring in the preconceptions of the most likely buyers for the kind of rehab we're doing."

Marcia didn't mention that Sarah had spent one entire evening propounding that gentrification was race war fought with Skilsaws, and that their own conception of who their buyers might be was racist from the start.

Lydia plumped up the pillow behind her and then clasped Marcia's little finger, bringing it to her lips before she said, "By factoring them in, aren't you fostering them?" Yes, Marcia thought hopelessly, there was that problem as well. Lydia meanwhile was gazing at Marcia with glints of amusement in her shiny brown eyes. "Would you like those handcuffs off? Maybe you can argue better if you're not fettered."

"Who's arguing?" Marcia asked. She leaned back against the pillow, her hands resting on her slightly mounded stomach. "Anyway, we'll see how right you are because after months of looking and rejecting, we went and bought a house on a street so rotten no one goes outside."

"Well, that way you won't have anyone to offend your prospective buyers," Lydia told her.

"If we have any buyers," Marcia said gloomily. "I mean, listen, Lydia, we're buying a house on Fairview—eight drive-bys last winter?—from this florist who thinks he's putting one over on us and whose daughter leaves threatening messages on our phone machines. And these are the people who're carrying our loan." Marcia took a deep breath. "And the house, Lydia—Christ, the house is divided into two flats but in this horrible way, it doesn't work at all because there were originally five bedrooms on the second floor and they're arranged like railroad cars. It's horrible, except that Dale—she's been my closest friend for years, you have to meet her—has worked out this clever way around it, but that meant we had to get the house so I'm not thrilled about it. So I'm sinking fifteen thousand bucks into this boondoggle. How our clever group with our careful schemes came to this I really don't understand. It was the last thing we were looking for. It's way too big, for one thing. And there are pigeons in the attic. The whole place is full of pigeon shit."

While Marcia rattled on, Lydia had been rummaging in her bedside dresser drawer. Finally she emerged with a pair of scissors. "I was planning to cut off your T-shirt," she told Marcia.

"Oh no!" Marcia squawked. "This is my favorite shirt." It had a moose and "Royal Isle" on it in purple letters.

Lydia peered at it doubtfully. "Well, I'm flattered that you wore your favorite shirt to come see me. Are you sure you don't want the handcuffs off? They seem to be interfering with your ability to lament about the house."

"I think I'm doing pretty well. Fuck the house. I don't want to lose my money."

"Are you that fond of your money?"

"It took me fifteen years to earn it. I have a feeling it's going to take fifteen minutes to lose it Friday morning at the title company."

"But why would you lose it? You could always resell the house in a minute."

"Sure, right now. But what if things change? What if we can't stand working together? We're already arguing."

"Can't you get out of it?"

"No. It wouldn't be fair. We only have sixty-seven thousand bucks. My fifteen is part of that. We need that much. It probably isn't enough." Marcia paused. "Then there's a whole different issue. Gardening for me is like meditating. Don't you think there's a danger when you turn your avocation into a business venture?" She started drumming her fingers against her knee, and Lydia chuckled. "What's funny?" Marcia asked.

"You. You're determined to look on the dark side. You could have waltzed in here and announced how excited you were to buy a house with your friends, how you might make thousands, how wonderful it will be to do a project with other women—"

At the look on Marcia's face, Lydia burst out laughing. "Well, what I wonder is if this pessimism of yours affects your thinking on other topics."

Hah! Marcia thought, I *knew* she had a hidden agenda. "I'm not really pessimistic," Marcia said. "It's just—I feel stuck. When this rehab thing first started, I thought we'd buy house after house, and I would quit my job and do landscaping full-time. But that doesn't seem possible, so now I'm going to end up doing two jobs instead of one, and managing the catering company is demanding enough without tacking more stuff onto it. In some ways it's the perfect job for me because I'm such a control freak, but it's crazy to think I can do a big garden during our busiest season—" She stopped suddenly, aware of her own voice rising and falling. "Shit, I don't know why I'm babbling about this. You should come over for dinner next time, OK? I'm sorry."

"For what?"

"For being so insensitive."

"Are you trying to get back into role?"

"No, I'm being serious."

Lydia smiled. "You haven't been that insensitive. You've just been very singleminded about what you want. And you still are except this time you wanted to talk more than you wanted to get laid."

Marcia laughed. "That's true. Next time you choose what we do, all right? Or the next few times."

"I thought you were a control freak. Won't that be hard for you?"

"It'll be unbearable," Marcia said. "I guess I'll just have to suffer." She raised her cuffed hands. "Do you still want to make love?"

"Maybe later," Lydia said. "Let's just lie in bed. Are you sure you're that enamoured of that T-shirt?"

"No."

"Actually, I'm going to take the cuffs off because I want you naked and your arms around me."

"Sounds like a deal."

Once Marcia was freed, they both stripped, and Marcia stretched out on her back and pulled Lydia against her. They crushed together tight, trying to make contact with every inch of warm, vibrant flesh. Lydia, Marcia reflected, felt like ambrosia must taste, or heaven must look. Holding someone, she thought, was so simple and so profound; an act that made her thank God she was human and alive and in bed with this woman who nestled her nose into the hard muscles above Marcia's breasts and blew warm, wet air at her nipples. After a few moments of this, they both started to laugh, and then surprisingly they slipped into sleep.

She drowsily woke sometime later when Lydia drew her arm behind her, meanwhile shoving her from her side over to her stomach. Cold steel snapped around one wrist, and Lydia stuck her knee between Marcia's legs as she yanked Marcia's other hand to the small of her back and pinioned it as well. "Hey!" Marcia muttered, but before she had a chance to say more, she was being tipped forward over something—Lydia was shoving a pillow underneath her thighs. As her ass rose in the air, her head, seesaw fashion, plunged down into a big fluffy pile of satin. Marcia tried to knock the satin mound away with her chin but couldn't. It was another pillow, she realized, pressed up against her face. She was swamped in cool, slick fabric, with icy cuffs fastening her wrists.

Lydia began stroking her ass. Her fingers were light and feathery at first, but when she got to the thin skin under the cheeks, she started pinching gently. Marcia squeaked, tried to move the pillow under her nose again and failed. She was suddenly panting so much she thought she might suffocate. Instead she ended up nearly biting through the pillow case in an attempt to stifle her yell when she came.

It was only partly effective. Lydia was giggling. "Do you always do that?"

"Only with you, babe," Marcia said, Bogart-ing it.

Lydia switched on her bedside lamp and contemplated Marcia as if she were an exotic puzzle. Lydia's eyes were light and shiny as agates.

"Gorgeous," Marcia said. "You're gorgeous. Sorry I yelled. Is Cory home?"

"Yes, but he's probably got his headphones on. I think he sleeps that way." She grinned. "But who knows? Maybe tomorrow at breakfast he'll ask his dreary old mom for the secret."

Marcia nuzzled her face against Lydia's neck. Then she emerged to marvel, "Boy, I must feel really safe with you. I let you handcuff me while I was asleep?" She twisted around to look at Lydia. It was hard moving on the bed with her wrists locked behind her.

"You put up a minor struggle."

Marcia snorted. "Hey, good survival skills." She thought about how she'd squealed when Lydia was pinching her ass. She told Lydia she felt like a big mouse being played with by a cat.

Lydia shook her head. "Really? I think just the opposite. I'd say I'm the mouse."

"Why?"

"Because... I really feel *caught* by you, Marcia. I like you a lot."

Klaxons of alarm went off in Marcia's head. "Could you uncuff me?"

Lydia found the key on her bedside table and unlocked each cuff. Then she held Marcia's wrists in her hands. "I think it's significant that after I tell you I like you, you want me to take the handcuffs off. Feeling trapped?"

Marcia hardly heard the question. How could Lydia say she liked her? She knew nothing about Lydia. If she knew nothing about Lydia, how could Lydia know anything about her? They needed to find out more about each other, that was it. Lydia was practically a mystery woman. "Listen, Lydia, next time you should come over for dinner, OK? We have to stop just screwing with each other."

"Because I said I like you?"

"No, no. Listen, I insist. I'm a good cook. You'll enjoy yourself, I promise."

"You insist?" Lydia said, her voice brimming with amusement.

What the hell's so funny? Marcia wondered. "Yes, absolutely," she said.

"Good," Lydia concluded. "I didn't want you to suffer being out of control about our next date for too long. Now that that's settled, make love to me, Marcia, would you please?"

# CHAPTER 4

When Marcia pulled up in front of her house Thursday morning, two Oakland police cars were parked in front of Robert's. Glancing at the cruisers curiously, Marcia waved at Gra' Preston, Billy's great-grandmother, who sat in her usual spot on the front porch. Wrapped in her multicolored afghan, her head was inclined slightly so the thin white hair dotting her scalp looked like patches of snow on a dark meadow. Marcia didn't find out why the cops had been around until early Friday morning, when a grumpy Billy came over to ask if she could jump start their car.

"Sure," she said, following him down her front steps. "How come I haven't heard 'Roxanne' lately?" she teased, trying to get him to smile.

"Don't have time for that shit."

"Why not?"

He looked away, evasive. She unlocked her trunk, handed him the jumper cables, and started her car, docking it in front of Robert's boxy gray Volvo. She hopped out, lifted her hood, and helped him attach the cables. He shrugged as he walked away from her to get in his own car; he knew he hadn't answered her question, and he was courteous to the end. Once he got the engine going and had honked the horn to call Melinda, however, he opened up. "Well, ya know I decided to go to summer school?"

"Yes."

"Up at Skyline High, ya know, not where I usually go." Robert had refused to let either Melinda or Billy attend the general run of Oakland schools. Melinda was using Aunt Esther's address so she could go to Berkeley High, and Billy was enrolled at Oakland Tech in a special unit for gifted kids.

"Yes," she prompted.

"So..." He looked evasive again. "See, I saw this guy doin' somethin', and I thought it was dangerous..." He sighed. "Sellin' some shit, y'know, but not just drugs."

He would not consider drugs dangerous or even worth remarking upon. Weapons? "So I tell Pop, y'know, first mistake." He grinned ruefully. "Well, he told me to mind my own business. I didn't like that. So I tell Aunt Esther. Second mistake. She gets mad at Pop and he gets mad at her and they start arguin' and Esther calls the cops."

Marcia couldn't believe it. "Esther told the cops about this kid?"

"Yeah." Seeing her amazement, he looked worried again.

"Is he in a gang?"

Billy made a noise like he'd just spit out a rotten walnut. "Ain't nothin' more than a buncha assholes, know what I mean? They ain't no gang, no way." It always amazed her how he was able to effortlessly switch back and forth between languages. He spoke white to some of his pals in his classes; she'd heard him on the phone. To her he spoke half-black; otherwise she wouldn't be able to understand his references or his accent. She'd heard him talk black when he was playing football out on the street. It was unintelligible to her.

"So what are you going to do?"

"Nothin'. *Melinda! C'mon!*" He leaned in and honked the horn a couple more times. Marcia jumped at the sudden noise. "Sorry," he said to her. "Anyway, I don't gotta do nothin'. Turns out they were watchin' this kid their ownselves. I just gotta add my own piece."

Melinda came clattering down the stairs in her half-heels. A sophomore at Berkeley High, she lived in a world made up almost solely of her boyfriend Al and Al's golden retriever Pandy. She piled into the car and rapped on the horn. "C'mon, Billy, Daddy says we're gonna be late!"

Billy rolled his eyes at her—women—and Marcia laughed. "Take care of yourself," she said. She watched the Volvo pull away and then stowed her jumper cables. Hope he'll be all right, she thought. But a moment later she'd forgotten about Billy because Reba called to say Foster had jumped his price to one-twenty-eight. "The bastard," Reba said. "We shook on it. We had a deal."

"What about the contract?"

"We're signing it at the title company. So he can do whatever he pleases. I'd like to tell him to go fuck himself, but I thought I should call you first."

Reba was calling Marcia because she assumed Marcia wanted out of the house and would agree with her. "Reba," Marcia said, "you want to nix the whole deal which you maintain will double our money for three thousand bucks, which is all of five hundred apiece?"

Why am I saying this, Marcia wondered. Why don't I get enraged and say the guy's a crook? But she couldn't. Reba's irrationality infuriated her.

"You're right," Reba said after a moment. "I've let it become an ego thing. OK, I'll tell him we'll go for it. See you at the title company."

Jesus, Marcia thought, hanging up. I've just screwed myself.

The moment the papers were signed, Polly, Sarah, and Dale raced over to Piedmont to finish the addition they'd been working on for half the summer. Reba went to negotiate a five-month hiatus for their next scheduled job, and Carol had a house to paint.

Left on her own, Marcia dutifully pointed the Ranchero towards Top Hat Catering but turned down Ashby at the last moment. She was too early for work anyhow, and Top Hat was in the midst of the summer blahs... Even with the baseball playoffs, the real holiday madness wouldn't start until October.

As she pulled up at the corner of Fairview and Keys, she had an uneasy feeling that the rambling white Queen Anne, dismayed to find itself still standing each morning, was trying to accomplish its own destruction—dropping its Victorian curlicues to lie like beached starfish on the brown lawn, or shedding its paint and roofing so it could perish of exposure. "Let me go," it whispered to Marcia.

Turning a deaf ear, Marcia began strolling around the yard of this house she had just purchased, feeling a mixture of exhilaration and dread—pretty commonplace in the human condition, she supposed, though the poles of this particular experience seemed altogether too extreme. Back in January when they'd first formed their group, Marcia had been ambivalent as well. She'd almost opted out when Reba recruited truculent and sullen Carol, but then she'd persuaded herself that it wasn't as if anyone else were an unknown quantity—she'd known Reba and Polly for more than ten years, and they were upstarts compared to best pals Dale and Sarah, who had both overcome their own misgivings about Carol. Besides, Marcia had asked herself, did she want to get left out of the deal of the century?

Now, as she peered into the deep shade of the overhanging bay to discover a trove of tiny vials and burned-up matchbook covers, she worried not about Carol, who seemed negligible, but about Dale and Sarah. Would she start bickering with them? Would forced contact and tension at work make them distant where it counted? Sarah was already changing. Marcia sat down in the stubbly grass, shaking her head. How come she hadn't considered this before? Her friends were more important to her than anything. She'd heard all the work stories, of Polly and Reba's arguments, Dale's temper, Sarah's stubbornness. Always Marcia had been the outsider, the objective listener, occasionally the mediator. Now she'd become a partner in psychodrama.

Cut it out, she told herself. Focus on what you can do this moment, not what you should have thought of months ago. Unfortunately, what she could spy from her vantage point near the drug debris wasn't very encouraging. She hadn't seen such scorched earth since films of napalmed jungles in Vietnam. In fact, what had happened to that rose?

She got to her feet and walked towards the back, remembering a half-thought intention to base one of her patios near that big Cecile Brunner, since it would stay well-leafed for almost the entire year. Now the bush was hacked to bits, broken-off canes littering the ground. Clearly an axe attack by the vengeful daughter. If Vernita Foster were so pissed off about selling the house, why had she signed the papers? Not your responsibility, Marcia told herself. She stared at the remnants of the big rose. It would come back, probably better than ever. She wished she could say the same for the house.

With Lydia gone for the weekend delivering a paper at a convention in Denver, Marcia occupied herself by devising a landscaping plan for what the group was now simply calling "Fairview Street." Steps from a deck off the dining room bay led to the main house's section of the yard, while lacy bamboo created seclusion for the rear unit. Both gardens looked out on a small pond where tall reeds and Japanese iris did double-duty, hiding the gravel of the driveway beyond.

She presented her plan at the rehab team's interminable Tuesday night meeting, but no one paid attention. Polly, already doing demo, had uncovered a large area of dry rot at the back of the house. "That shed's dead meat anyway," Carol said. "The stairway to the rear unit goes on its slab."

"The rot's not limited to the shed," Polly told her.

Sarah interrupted them by holding up a copy of *The Old House Journal* with a photograph of a house like theirs on the cover, except the *Journal*'s Queen Anne wasn't trying to commit suicide. She told them they had a moral imperative to return the Fairview Victorian to its original and intended configuration, which was a magnificent five-bedroom mansion. She had already gone through the files at the Berkeley Architectural Heritage Association and learned that their house had been built in 1897 by a Mr. Henry Able for the sum of $2,800, in the days when most houses cost in the $1,200-$1,400 range. In other words,

Sarah maintained, they had acquired a masterpiece. Did they really want to be barbarians as well as gentrifiers? Or would they commit themselves to bringing the house—and by extension, the street, the neighborhood, all of South Berkeley—back to glowing, vibrant life?

Carol made a rude noise. The others sighed. It was starting already, Marcia thought. Tension. Division.

"We can't afford it, hon," Reba told Sarah in a soft voice. The two had been lovers in the early '70s, and Reba still had a gentleness about her when she talked to Sarah.

"But why?" Sarah asked.

"First there's the restoration costs, which would be considerable," Marcia took up. "But even worse, we'd lose the potential of a two-unit sale." Marcia turned to Dale for a nod of agreement, but Dale was immersed in drawing an entire flock of Canadian geese next to her herd of buffalo. Reba, trying to be fair, admitted that yes, she could see Sarah's point, that she'd known all along they'd bought something really special—after all, that's why they'd bought it, right?—but if they intended to delve into this unit business thoroughly, it seemed to her that they really had to start with gentrification.

"We've already bought the goddamn place!" Carol shouted, her face blazing red and her teeth white.

Marcia clutched her chest and said she was about to have an episode of tachycardia, they were driving her that crazy. That startled Dale away from her geese but only until she ascertained Marcia was kidding. Sarah scowled, shaking her head of newly styled hair, which only contributed to Marcia's feeling they were sliding off the edge into the Twilight Zone. Polly, perhaps fearing complete breakdown, yelped in an overwrought voice, "Hysteria is not the answer!"

This brought Ruth, Reba and Polly's fourteen-year-old daughter, flying down the stairs from the loft which extended over the living room. Hands planted on her hips, dressed in her usual costume of leotards, leg warmers, earrings, bright red lipstick, and a lot of scarves, Ruth said if they were driving each other crazy, what did they think they were doing to her? Marcia was struck again by how uncanny it was to see Reba and Ruth together. One could never imagine butch Reba wearing lipstick, for instance, and yet there was the result, standing right next to her, looking completely feminine. Marcia had often thought the two should be subjects for a photo essay on gender-bending.

Trying to convince each other, the rehab partners set about convincing Ruth instead. What did she think, a five-bedroom fully restored Queen Anne or an historically deviant but attractive three-bedroom and one-bedroom on two levels?

Ruth twitched with annoyance during their recital. When they finished, she informed them that she didn't have time in her busy schedule to grace them with her advice, fresh, brief, and brilliant though it would be. Then she lambasted them for buying a house on Fairview Street in the first place. What had they been thinking of? This wasn't the '60s! Their fondest decade sounded like bitter swill cast from Ruth's cherry-red lips. They all sunk further in their uncomfortable chairs as Ruth paced the bird's eye maple planking that Reba had scrounged from a junior high school gym remodel. When Ruth reached center stage of this theater in the round, she halted. To answer their ridiculous and unnecessary question, she said, it was *beyond the pale* to consider a *five*-bedroom on Fairview. Were they *brain-dead* or what? Who had that many kids? *No one.* Therefore, who would buy it? Drug dealers? Uzi manufacturers? *No one.* Then she left, promising to be back by twelve.

"Doesn't she have to go to bed?" Sarah wondered. "I mean, it's a school night."

Polly rolled her eyes, and Reba shrugged. No one spoke until finally Sarah said, "Well, I guess that about covers it."

Carol strapped on a helmet and was gone in thirty seconds, her motorcycle trailing clouds of exhaust as she gunned it up the street. Sarah and Dale and Marcia stood uncomfortably on the front porch, the overhead yellow bulb casting deep shadows on their faces, aging them twenty years. Dale reached under her T-shirt to adjust the corset she was wearing to support her back. None of them looked at each other. This is terrible, Marcia thought. She had just decided she had to ask Sarah how she was feeling even though it would reopen the whole topic when Sarah pulled a cigarette from her shirt pocket and lit it with a flourish. Dale and Marcia's eyes grew to fish proportions while their mouths, equally fish-like, gulped air. "You're smoking!" Marcia bleated.

Sarah smiled thinly. "Haven't you ever done anything unexpected?" she asked. She took a long drag and let it out slowly, still not looking at them. Then she said, "I guess you should meet my friend." As Marcia and Dale fell all over each other assuring her that they would really love to meet her, Sarah gave them tight defensive hugs and then swept down the front steps on the last wave of their shouted promises to check calendars and coordinate possible dates.

Marcia drove home deep in thought. *Had* she ever done anything unexpected? Not until the last couple weeks, she concluded, when she'd met Lydia, whom she couldn't yet relegate to a nonthreatening category, and bought Fairview Street, which now seemed the apex of insanity. Hadn't her life before been pretty mundane? She honestly couldn't remember. Perhaps it'd all been risky and scary, though since Annie had left she'd felt like a cowboy riding on the open plains, wishing for company but sorry when it appears. Now she'd abandoned her independence and invested everything she owned for a blindfolded trip in a stagecoach crowded with her best friends. The possibility of losing her friends to this folly bothered her a lot more than losing her money. Funny, she thought, how you never find out what's really important until you're knee-deep in it and sinking.

# CHAPTER 5

At dawn the following morning, Marcia began enacting her landscaping plan, digging up a small area in the backyard the others had assured her would remain unsullied by their work. She attacked the hard, dry soil with a pickaxe, added amendments, and even managed to plant a flat's worth of Snow in Summer before she had to leave for Top Hat Catering. The Snow in Summer would make nice gray mounds at the rear of the pond, and it would go well with her most expensive tree purchase, a coral-bark maple whose red trunk would reflect on the water. On Thursday when she came by after work, she found a seven-foot high heap of haphazard lengths of lumber stacked on top of her plants.

She stormed in the rear door of the house, running up the board-ramp that someone had built. "Hey!" she yelled. "Who took that lumber delivery?"

"I did," Dale said innocently, looking up from where she was breaking away stained and crumbling plaster.

Distracted by the smell of rotting wood, Marcia peered in behind Dale. It was brown and musty as far up as she could see, which was further than one would hope, given that there were points of daylight far, far above her. "Oh, my god," she said. The house had been bleeding for years.

"It's pretty bad," Dale acknowledged. "Sort of like the entire rear wall." She had a sick look on her face. "We shoulda caught it. I poked in here, but I thought it was confined to that one area by the sink. It spreads all the way up to the other kitchen. I think there's a leak in the gutter and it's just been pouring down this wall for years..." She stood up, her face expectant. "What about the delivery?"

"Nothing," Marcia said.

She went out to pickaxe around some more, trying not to think about what she'd seen in that wall. Probably, she decided, it was only safe to put in paving stones and decks for the moment. As she hefted the pickaxe, she remembered the time she had picked up the ringing phone to hear Dale sounding very small on the other end. "Where are you?" Marcia asked. Dale was driving back to California from the East coast.

"I don't know. I mean, I guess I'm in a town in Texas." Dale seemed to be disintegrating as she spoke.

Marcia got very quiet. "Dale, tell me what's wrong."

"I asked these guys where I was—they're still looking at me like I'm the biggest weirdo they ever saw—I don't remember anything since I was in this gay bar in North Carolina. And now these guys say I'm in Texas. And I guess I am. It looks like Texas."

"Jesus, Dale." Marcia's heart started pounding. She wanted to reach down the phone line and haul Dale right into her living room. She had to think. "Listen to me. Would you do what I tell you?"

"Yes, I will." Dale was practically whispering.

"All right. No matter how bad you feel I don't want you to drink anymore. No more until you get back to California. Then we'll talk about what you want to do. But I want you to promise me that you won't drink again until you get to California."

Dale repeated it. "OK, I won't. Marcia, are you really all right not drinking?" Marcia had sobered up a year earlier.

"Yes, I am, and you can be too. But forget that. We're talking only a couple days here, just 'til you get back home. OK?"

"OK. I think I should split because those guys I asked are still hanging around. I'll see you soon."

"All right." Marcia heard the phone click. She put down the receiver and then realized with a start that she should have flown to Texas and driven Dale to California herself. She couldn't call Dale back; she didn't even know what town Dale was in.

Dale was as good as her word. She didn't drink until she crossed the state line. And she managed to keep her car on the road until she reached Berkeley proper, where she was apparently so relieved she rolled it down a steep hillside at the top of Ashby Avenue at three in the morning. She exited her car from the busted-out back window, brushed herself off, and walked down to Marcia's, arriving at five to collapse on the couch. A few days later, she went with Marcia to an AA meeting.

Marcia dropped her pickaxe and climbed the ramp into the house. Dale had demolished half the kitchen wall. A pile of plaster-covered sheathing lay in a heap on the floor. Dale was rubbing her hands through her short hair. "Don't try to move all that stuff," Marcia warned. "Not with your back."

Dale grinned at her. Fourteen years, Marcia thought. That phone call from Texas had been fourteen years ago, and both of them were still safe and sound. "It's a miracle," Dale said, pointing at the wall. "The gutter was the culprit, which means it's nothing to fix. But we do have to replace this whole section."

"Oh, well," Marcia said, "that's the way it goes."


Marcia took off work on Friday to spend her whole day at the house. She was on pins and needles because Lydia was back from her convention and coming over for dinner. Marcia had made a stew the night before so she wouldn't be distracted by cooking. She wished she hadn't orchestrated this date where they would be forced to talk to each other for an entire evening. The way they fell into each other when they were talking would at some point necessitate an acknowledgment that something beyond recreational sex was going on. When they were actually having sex, they had an excuse to be intimate—after all, that's what sex was all about. They could ignore the fact that it usually didn't work so well with someone you'd just met, passing ecstasy off as a singular perception or that they both had moons in psychic Pisces. Marcia couldn't understand why she'd been so frantic last time about getting to know Lydia better. Mystery was enticing, while knowledge was often either disappointing or demanding.

Polly outdid herself for lunch. She'd gone to Lucca Delicatessen on Piedmont and gotten Semifreddi's rolls, smoked turkey, thinly sliced Black Forest ham, and corni-chons. She'd also turned up with chocolate-covered espresso beans and biscottis for dessert. This was because she'd been sent to Peet's to buy coffee for everyone, in their special thermoses marked with permanent ink: MARCIA DECAF or DALE CAF.

They sat outside in the yard. Marcia had forgiven Dale for dumping the lumber on top of her Snow in Summer, so they hunkered down near the scene of the crime, perched on the paving stones Marcia had been hauling into the yard that morning. They'd all dug into their sandwiches when Marcia suddenly said, "Did it ever occur to you that straight women never get to fuck anybody and straight men never get to be fucked?"

Everyone stopped chewing. Dale stuffed her hand into the bag of tortilla chips but left it there, her fingers hidden under a chaos of blue triangles. "Jesus," Reba said finally. "I never thought of that."

"It can't be true," Sarah said. She obviously didn't want it to be.

Polly was shaking her head. "The poor babies."

But Sarah was up in arms. "No, it really isn't true. Don't you think straight women fuck their men all the time?"

Everyone shook their heads. "Umm-mm. I don't think so."

"I can't believe it," Sarah protested. "They're missing out on half their lives!"

"But they don't know it."

"No, that's ridiculous," she insisted. "I know one straight woman who fucks her boyfriend all the time."

"One," Reba grunted. She started eating again, and so did Carol. Neither cut too much slack for hets.

"But one out of one or two!" Sarah cried. "I don't talk with too many straight women about sex. So that's fifty percent at least."

"I'd say more like ten, fifteen percent," Marcia estimated. She privately thought even that was high, but Sarah was upset enough already.

"Or five," Dale hazarded. She had now withdrawn a few blue chips, but she wasn't eating them. They sat in her hand like monochromatic butterflies.

"There's always straight people at the dildo store." This information came from Carol. No one said anything again for a couple moments, since none of them had ever before mentioned dildos. They might not talk to straight people about sex, but they didn't talk to each other either.

"You mean Good Vibrations?" Marcia asked. What store hardly mattered, but she felt she should lend Carol a measure of support, if only as minimally as admitting she knew such an outlet existed. She excused herself on the grounds that she had more to hide than the rest, although it flickered through her mind that perhaps each of them felt her secrets were more taboo, and the ones who had no secrets believed themselves to be hopelessly naive, a fact worse than the most terrible secret.

Carol didn't bother to answer Marcia's pointless question. She chomped on her sandwich. Then she grabbed some tortilla chips and stuffed them in her mouth. As if by rote, Dale began to munch on hers. Butterflies disappearing into the maw of the great monster.... Marcia brought herself back to the present with a start. "I went to a meeting once and there were all these straight people, and the men were talking about getting fucked. I mean, by their girlfriends."

Reba looked faintly interested. "Yeah? What kind of meeting?"

Marcia didn't want to say what kind of meeting. Why had she brought this up at all? "It was a Society of Janus meeting," she said finally.

"What's that?" Polly asked.

"It's an S/M group," Marcia explained.

Dale looked pained. She hated it when Marcia talked about S/M. Her way of dealing with Marcia's sexuality was to avoid the subject whenever possible. They'd talked about it occasionally over the years, more or less depending on who Marcia was seeing and how adamant she felt at the time, but their conversations were always abbreviated and shot through with strain and embarrassment. Marcia knew that maintaining Dale's comfort level meant keeping her own mouth shut. When she couldn't, or wouldn't, Dale tried to understand, but it was obviously a real effort, and one Dale wouldn't have made for anyone else.

There was a longer silence this time until Sarah, who was a lot worse on the subject than Dale, finally figured out what to say. "See! I told you they fuck each other!"

"Some." Reba always had to have the last word.

An hour or two later, Marcia, digging around outside an open window, heard Polly chortle, "S/M and dildos. And this is only the first week! What do you suppose we'll be talking about in February?"

"Money," Reba answered. "We better be talking about money."

Marcia dashed home, put the stew on to heat, sliced a few hunks of baguette and threw them into a cloth, and then took a hurried bath. Lydia was arriving in half an hour, and she was not one who liked to be kept waiting. Marcia smiled, stalking around her bedroom naked. What to wear? The moose T-shirt, of course, she thought, pulling it on. It would amuse Lydia. Clean jeans, fancy socks.... Billy had evidently just gotten back because rap started blaring at ear-splitting levels from the street. Marcia slapped Tchaikowsky's Piano Concerto Number One on her tape player to try to drown it out. Her strategy was not successful. Van Cliburn merged into rap in the quiet parts, the rap slipped into the crescendoes, then the rap segued oddly into a thin, eerie scream. Marcia perked up her head. Nothing stopped, not Van Cliburn, not the rap, not the scream, not the shots. They were definitely shots. Before her thoughts had gone any further, she was surprised to find herself on the floor, sliding across her bedroom door jamb into the kitchen, away from the shots, but then she realized the screaming was coming from next door, so she continued out the back, crawling on her belly, approved combat-fashion, glancing to her right, toward Robert's—nothing, she couldn't see a thing over the fence—scrambled down the back stairs, ran hunched over across her yard, drawn by that thin, high-pitched scream, wishing the rap would self-destruct. Then there was a throatier wail from somewhere else entirely, across the street, perhaps. Marcia took a deep breath and jumped up against the fence, ready to plunge back down depending on what greeted her on the other side. Nothing ahead of her but the wood frame of Robert's house. To her right, towards the street—Billy, frozen, standing in his front yard, holding a revolver limply in his hand. Adrenaline pushed her up and over the six-foot redwood structure. She slid down, ran fifteen feet through a tangled mass of dusty ivy, and stared at what Billy stared at, his eyes lost and drowned.

"Jesus," she said. She was standing in it. Pools of blood, rivers of blood. A boy lying in the blood on his side, one arm between his legs, as if he'd tried to get into the fetal position before he died. Yes, he had to be dead. Couldn't be anything else with that much blood. The hand that wasn't between his legs held a revolver. His finger was crooked around the trigger. Up on the porch, Gra' was almost out of her chair, one claw-like hand grasping the wrought iron railing, her mouth so wide the eerie scream seemed to be coming from her belly. The deeper wailing was from Mrs. Kingston across the street. Someone yelled about ambulances. Police. Fire department. Marcia told herself she had to check. No matter how much blood. No matter how hopeless.

She knelt next to the boy and put her fingers against his neck. Nothing. Then she wondered if she had only felt her own pulse. But she had felt nothing, so how could she have felt her own pulse? She put her fingers under his nose. No whisper flicked across her fingertips, no matter how hard she prayed. She remembered once spotting Sarah's kitten lying in the gutter. As they ran towards it, she had sworn she saw it twitch. But when they got to it, they found it'd been dead awhile. She had so much wanted it to live that she'd willed it to move. But the boy did not breathe. Not a hint. Not a breeze.

How could a human body hold so much blood? It was like scarlet silk splayed across the boy's dark skin, as if it clothed him against death. It hadn't. It was turned around, his insides outside, and it could not be put back.

The door slammed open from the downstairs flat, where Lucas had a curtained-off alcove near the washing machine and Robert kept his books and his TV. Robert peeled out and swiveled on his heel to stare up at Gra', who just then mercifully stopped screaming. He started around the porch stairs and saw Marcia inexplicably crouched next to Billy. Then he saw the blood and the boy. Marcia thought it had been a long time since the shots. She could hear the TV from the flat below, loud. Robert had also been trying to drown out Billy's rap music. Instead Billy himself had drowned. He dropped the revolver. It landed in the blood. Marcia wondered if that were a good idea. She didn't know anymore what constituted a good idea. Tires squealed outside. People were arriving who knew about ideas, people who would want to talk. She wiped her hand on the front of her T-shirt. The blood smelled like molten copper. It shone in the fading western light like it'd been polished and polished. She tried to catch Billy's eye. She wanted to tell him something, but he was lying in a stream two feet deep, the water slipping over him, his eyes staring out at hers unseeing. He had drowned.


Later a man asked her if Gra's screams or the shots were first. She tried to think. Lydia was sitting on the couch beside her, holding her hand. A bloody handprint was still on the front of Marcia's T-shirt. Marcia could only remember Billy's eyes. "Where is Billy?" she asked. She had wondered that before.

"Maybe this should wait until tomorrow," Lydia told the man. She squeezed Marcia's hand.

"When did you say you arrived, Miss?" the man asked Lydia.

"Soon afterwards. I was going to have dinner with Marcia."

Marcia was trying to remember if the screams came before the shots. It was all mixed up with Tchaikovsky and rap. A beat with gunfire. But which was best? Yes. That was the real question. She had to decide what was the right answer for Billy. The boy was dead. She was on Billy's side. Someone else could be for the dead boy. So which was best, screams or shots? It seemed imponderably complicated. She couldn't figure it out. She wished she could talk to Lydia alone for a moment. Maybe Lydia would know. The detective kept staring at her. He was making her nervous. But surely, yes, screams should be first. The other boy had a gun in his hand. Screaming, Gra' being threatened, Billy defending her. Billy defending his great-grandmother. She couldn't see the fallacy in it.

"I think the screaming came first," she said slowly. After she said it, she thought it was true. In fact, hadn't she heard that unearthly scream first? Yes, she had. So she was telling the truth. "Yes, the screams were first."

The detective wrote it down. He left. Lydia made her take another bath. She took the T-shirt away. She said Marcia wouldn't want it anymore. Marcia had no idea what she might want. She got into bed with Lydia and let Lydia hold her. She lay in Lydia's arms and thought about Billy's eyes. Billy had no one to hold him, and he was the one who had drowned.

# CHAPTER 6

When Marcia spotted Robert and Lucas pulling up in the Volvo at ten the following morning, she bounded out of the house and joined them on the sidewalk. "How is he?" she asked.

Robert seemed to have shrunk overnight. The skin sagged around his jowls, and his eyes bulging above his slab-like cheekbones looked as if they'd sucked up all the liquid from his face. Marcia was trying so hard not to stare at him that she jumped when Robert started talking. "He looks at the floor. He keeps saying, 'I don't know how it happened.' He wants to take it back and start again. He never meant to kill that boy."

He didn't focus on her while he spoke, instead staring into the street or up at the porch, where Gra's chair was empty. Then he heaved a sigh and started up the steps, leaving Lucas on the walk with Marcia. All of them pointedly avoided looking at the grass where the boy's body had crumpled, at the mud hole Lucas had made washing away the blood the night before.

As he marched up the steps, Robert held his head steady, the soldier on parade. Burning with a hundred questions, Marcia wanted to follow him, but she couldn't accompany him uninvited into the house. He disappeared inside but was back out in less than twenty seconds, just as Marcia was asking Lucas when Billy could come home.

"He can't come home," Robert answered. He descended three stairs and stood there. Marcia took his re-emergence as an invitation and perched on the bottom step, while Lucas leaned against the front fence. He was wearing a tie and he hadn't been drinking. It was remarkable how good he looked. Billy couldn't come home, Robert explained, because of a small matter of a murder one charge and a bail of $200,000. "My attorney says it's got to be a mistake," Robert assured Marcia and thus himself. "A crazy mix-up."

"So they won't let him out," Marcia marveled, stating the obvious. She couldn't understand it. "The other kid had a gun. Besides, this all has to do with Billy being a witness, right?"

No one answered. The phone rang inside the house, and Robert disappeared. Lucas and Marcia talked about the Giants' amazing surge towards a National League West title. Lucas pushed away from the fence and came to sit next to Marcia on the bottom step. His hands trembled as he loosened his tie. Robert returned from his phone call. "No mistake," he said. "There's a bail hearing Monday morning." He looked desperate. "He has to sit in there all weekend. I gotta get him out of there. He just stares at the floor!"

"We'll get him out," Lucas said faintly. He didn't sound convincing.

"Of course we will," Marcia said in a stronger voice. "They'll realize they've made an error, for one thing. Maybe they'll let him go tomorrow when they figure it out."

Robert shook his head. "I don't think so. The lawyer said the best we could do is get the bail reduced a whole lot, like to twenty thousand. Then I could pay a bail bondsman."

Marcia had a question, but she wasn't sure how to ask it without offending anyone. Finally she just blurted it out. "Whose gun was it?"

"Mine," Robert said heavily. "I've got that gun shelf in my bookcase downstairs. Had it for years, both kids know it. He ran in while I was down there watchin' TV and then back out again like a mad dog was after him. I never saw the gun. Fact is, I didn't think a thing about it. You know how they are."

Teenagers, Robert meant. Marcia nodded. "Was it registered?"

Robert wrinkled up his face. "You kiddin' me? Why the hell would I have an unregistered weapon?" Undone by Marcia's gaffe, they stared out at the street. Miguel Fernandez, who lived across the way next door to Mrs. Kingston, drove by in his souped-up Chevy with the bass booming. He turned it off and went inside. Later, Marcia knew, he would flag Lucas down and find out what was happening. He refused to talk to either Marcia or Robert, both of whom had called the police on him several times about his car stereo system.

"Then I don't get it," Marcia said. "The kid was waiting for him, right? He was going to threaten Billy about testifying. That's what the detective said yesterday."

"Kid was parked across the street waitin' for Billy to get home," Lucas verified. "Buncha people saw 'im."

"Then he comes over with his revolver when Billy gets back." Marcia picked up the story. "Billy runs downstairs to get the gun. He runs back outside. They argue. He shoots the kid. Self-defense."

"He shouldn't have gotten the goddamn gun," Robert said. "He should have come inside and stayed there."

"Gra'," Lucas said.

"She was outside on the porch," Marcia echoed, beginning to feel like Lucas' straight man. "What's he supposed to do, leave his grandma out there with an asshole with a gun? Anyhow, he knew Melinda was coming home in a minute."

As she *had* done, walking down the street with Al and his dog, Pandy. Horribly, Pandy had bounded into the yard with a big grin and begun nosing at the kid lying on the ground.

"He should have gotten me," Robert insisted. "He should have gotten me, not the gun." He put the heel of his hand against his forehead. "Man, this headache is *bad*!" He stood up and went into the house.

Marcia thought about how Billy should have enlisted Robert's help, how he should have called 911, how he should have done about twenty other things. "But he would never have involved anybody else," she told Lucas. "He's a kid. He can't be perfect. A lot of adults wouldn't be perfect. He was probably scared to death." I'm preaching to the choir, she thought. She bid Lucas good-bye and went to work.

By Saturday, no one had recognized their mistake. Robert's attorney said the DA's office was closed-mouth about their intentions. They had announced, however, that they would oppose a lower bail. "I don't understand this!" Marcia cried, beset by images of Billy slumped catatonic on a filthy mattress in a freezing-cold cell. She was supposed to have gone sailing with Lydia and her son Cory, but she knew she couldn't be good company, so she'd opted for a quick breakfast with them and then returned to her house while they went off for a breezy day on the bay.

She had begun weeding in her back yard when she heard, "P-s-s-st!" over the top of the fence. It was, she saw, her other next-door neighbor, the prick lawyer, standing on his tiptoes. "What happened?" he asked.

She explained, briefly. She could hardly stand to talk to the man. He and his wife had only been there four months, having displaced Mrs. Pettison, who had moved back to Arkansas to be with her sister. The first thing he'd done was to build an illegal rental unit right up against a section of Marcia's side fence. When she complained, he informed her that he'd bought off the city inspectors so if she didn't want trouble she'd better keep her mouth shut. A week later he told her she was a racist for calling the cops on Miguel, and three days after that he said, "Boy, you must be so relieved we moved next door," and he was serious.

"Bad news," he commented now.

"But why?" Marcia asked. "The DA's office knew he was going to testify."

The lawyer tried to look wise and inscrutable, though Marcia knew he was uninterested now that he'd gotten the story. As he walked away, she stabbed her weeding tool into the soil and sank to the ground, clutching her arms around her knees.

A lot of people like the lawyer were moving in, fixing up their houses and strolling around the street as if they were in Paris, talking about the cultural advantages of living in an artists' community (except they were chasing away the artists), a black community (except they'd bought out the blacks), a neighborhood that was *changing*. Change was the operative word. It meant they were living here now, and wasn't Marcia glad?

Whenever asked, Marcia responded that she wasn't glad, that actually she was depressed about it. The parking had dried up as every homeowner who bought at elevated prices rented out basements and closets, the noise had increased, and no one knew or cared about each other anymore. Those subjected to her honest assessment guffawed anxiously as if she'd told a hilarious joke they didn't quite understand but would think about when they got home. The few who knew she meant every word considered her fanatical and possibly dangerous. They could not believe that a white person living in a black neighborhood would not fall down on her knees and thank god every time another house was sold to whites.

She wished they could have seen the neighborhood in its heyday, before the Reagan years, before crack had fallen on such fertile ground, on families weakened by increasing unemployment and poverty. Almost everyone had owned their homes; most had bought in the late '40s or early '50s and raised their kids there. Early on, there were scout troops and clubs, then football teams and dances, then garage bands and entry-level jobs for the girls.

As the nation galloped into the trickledown '80s, there was less and less for the boys. But weekends still meant barbecues to which anyone could come, and the entire block showed up for weddings and funerals.

Now just a couple blocks away, on the other side of Market, was an area where the quiet streets lined with small, well-kept homes had turned into a war zone, and older residents looked on in horror as helicopters hovered nightly over their rooftops. It was as if an already compromised immune system were under attack; the dissolution was sudden, shocking, but not really surprising. In the absence of an economy one will arise.

The elderly on Marcia's own block were glad they could escape the nearby drug wars by selling to yuppies, but it meant leaving a neighborhood network which had sustained them for years. At the moving sales, lifelong friends held jelly jars up to the sun and remembered sending their own kids to the first day of school; women hugged each other with tears coursing down their faces. They should have been allowed to grow old together, Marcia reflected.

Of course, her rehab group was introducing the same plague to Fairview Street; in a house where there had been two residents and one car, there would now be four to six residents and four cars. She could justify it as progress— or, if she needed more ammunition, urban infill, the darling of environmentalists. Funny how what looks good from one side can look so rotten from the other.

The next morning, as she was crawling out of bed with Lydia, Billy's lawyer called her and asked if she would testify at the bail hearing in Billy's behalf. Bail really had been set at two hundred thousand. The defense was going to try to get it lowered to ten thousand.

"That'd only cost Mr. Preston a thousand," the lawyer explained to Marcia. "Two if they drop it to twenty."

"But why are they doing this?" Marcia wanted to know.

"The kid Billy shot wasn't the kid he was going to testify against. But both of them were in the same gang, a fact which the DA's office is ignoring. I'm sure we'll find out more at the bail hearing. Will you come?"

"Of course," Marcia said. She got the courtroom number and the time and then went to stand in front of the mirror. Two images stared back at her: a good-looking rough-suave butch with knowing eyes and a tipsy smile, or an awkward woman with hair that was too short, a face that was too angular, and a manner that could best be described as confrontational. Which image one saw, Marcia realized, depended entirely on who was doing the viewing.

"Lydia," she called out. "I have to testify in court at Billy's bail hearing tomorrow. Can you think of a way for me to look less—less like me?"

Lydia appeared in back of her, holding two cups of steaming coffee. She handed Marcia one and examined her critically. "No," she finally concluded. "I'm afraid anything you did would be fake." She sipped her coffee. "You weren't thinking of wearing a dress, were you?"

"Are you kidding? I'd look like a bad drag queen. No, I was thinking—I don't know, something with my hair or..." Her voice trailed off as she stared at herself in the mirror. She tried to brush her hair up into what she fancied was a style, but all she achieved was middle-aged dyke trying to look punk. It was not an improvement.

Lydia hugged her from behind and smoothed her hair back down. "Baby, you're damned handsome. Go as yourself."

Marcia didn't give up the idea entirely. She considered an early-morning appointment at a hairdresser's. In the end, however, she simply put on her best clothes and went downtown. She sat outside in the hall with Lucas until it was her turn. Since Billy was a juvenile, it was a closed hearing. When she was called into the court chambers, Lucas came with her, since he was a relative. He had, she realized, just been keeping her company. Marcia winked at Billy, noting that he'd lost weight, and that he seemed dazed but eager. No doubt he was looking forward to coming home.

She took the oath and gave her testimony quickly. Billy's attorney was black, of course—Robert would never hire anyone else—and he seemed good, leading Marcia past generalities into specific incidents where Billy had proven himself trustworthy and considerate.

Then he handed her off to the prosecuting attorney, a white guy in his mid-twenties with an ill-fitting suit and the look of a starved carnivore. As he approached the witness stand, he tried to stare her down as if she might suddenly blurt out that she knew she had to tell the truth, the whole truth, and yes, Billy was a real bastard. Instead, Marcia gazed at him calmly, a slight smile on her face. If he were going to get her to admit anything, he was going to have to ask her a question first. Finally the judge told him to get going. He began by hassling her about being gay—"How'd you feel about living next door to a teenage *boy, Miss* Lanier," but the judge told him to move on, so he asked her what she knew about drug sales at the grocery store up on Market. She shook her head, mystified. The prosecutor smiled a shit-eating grin, as if to say, see, she's a fool, but the judge ignored him. He leaned over from the bench to ask her if she'd actually seen the shooting. She shook her head. He dismissed her and she went back out into the corridor. The prosecutor's aide tapped her shoulder and asked her if she'd wait to speak to the prosecutor. "Sure," she said. She sat down on a wooden bench.

Soon Robert and Lucas pushed through the doors. Esther came a couple steps later, dabbing at her eyes with a handkerchief. "They want me to talk to the prosecutor," Marcia said quickly.

Robert looked suspicious. "Why?"

Marcia turned up her palms. "I have no idea."

Esther tapped the heel of her Italian shoe on the wooden leg of the bench. "Couldn't hurt," she decided. "Marcia's not going to say anything bad."

"There's nothing bad to say," Marcia pointed out. Robert grunted, in either assent or distress.

Esther announced she had to get back. "Big doings at Health and Human Services," she said. She was a liaison between the Alameda County Board of Supervisors and the many-armed system of clinics and hospitals. She click-clacked down the hall while Lucas went to stand near an open window for a smoke. Robert was the one who finally divulged the news: "They reduced it to a hundred-twenty thou."

So the judge had only dropped the bail request by eighty thousand. Robert would have to pay—to lose—twelve thousand dollars if he wanted Billy out of jail. What the hell was going on here? It's self-defense! She asked the prosecutor the same question, minus the swear words and the attitude, in his office fifteen minutes later.

"Well, I think there's some things you don't understand," the prosecutor said, shoving a big lock of blond hair out of his eyes. He seemed ridiculously young to her, plus he had a way of tipping back his chair and putting his feet on the desk that made Marcia want to grab his ankles and dump him on his head.

"Such as?"

"That Billy Preston is not really a nice kid."

"He is a nice kid."

"We'd all like it to be so, Miss Lanier. Believe me we would. I think you'll find he's in a gang."

"He is not in a gang," she said, exasperated. Why were they torturing Billy like this? Maybe this was this jerk's first big case. But it wasn't a big case. It was Billy and it was self-defense. "He was helping the DA's office, for heaven's sake. That's how the whole thing started." She had a moment's self-doubt. What if that were a story? But no, the prosecutor was nodding.

"Very tricky, that. A complicated scheme indeed."

"What are you talking about?"

"There was a gang contract out on Billy."

"Yes, because he'd agreed to testify."

"So he says." The man smiled. "But it also turns out there was a contract on the kid Billy killed. Billy stands to collect ten thousand dollars. Get it now? Billy's already got a contract on him. He points the finger at this kid for selling automatic weapons. He figures he's off the hook."

"No, I don't get it. The kid Billy shot is not the same kid he fingered. And he wanted to keep his mouth shut. It was his Aunt Esther who spilled the beans. Do you think Aunt Esther is in a gang? Besides, there's probably a gang contract out on half the kids in Oakland."

"Let's not be naive, Miss Lanier..." His smug assurance infuriated her. You self-satisfied pig. You ignorant prick. Staring at his face, she realized she hated him for being so smug, so white. How could black people stand the constant humiliation of being defined by vipers like this man, of being told every day that who they were and what they thought was not really who they were? She'd never felt more keenly the disadvantages of being a woman, that this twenty-five-year-old twerp just out of law school sincerely believed he knew more about Billy than a bright forty-two-year-old who'd lived next door to him for ages.

Or worse, that he didn't care what he knew or didn't know—that Billy was dog meat, a black kid who had to be in a gang and who wanted money enough to kill for it. He couldn't be what she knew him to be, a kid too trusting to know you shouldn't go to the cops.

And come to think of it, why was Mr. Blond Hair telling her all this crap? Why wasn't he telling Robert or Esther? Because *she* was white? Because he felt he owed her an explanation for the prosecution's baffling behavior that he wouldn't give to Billy's own relatives?

"That business about the store," he continued. "You know they sell drugs there. And then there's the car detailing lot further up. That's a drug front too."

She boggled at him. Whose reality was this? "You don't know a damn thing about our neighborhood—" she stared at his name plate—"Mr. Ricklin. Besides, what does that have to do with anything?"

"I've asked around. Billy's been seen at the car lot frequently. It's in that gang's territory. Conflict." When Ricklin smiled, it was completely humorless.

"Billy goes up there to collect his Uncle Lucas," Marcia said. "Lucas polishes cars for spending money. Billy also takes care of his great-grandmother, his sister, his dad, his aunt, and even me half the time. He's a good kid, Mr. Ricklin. I really think you shouldn't make assumptions when you obviously know so little."

"Oh, I know plenty," Ricklin assured her. "Plenty enough, anyway. I'm sure you're well-intentioned, Miss Lanier, though I wonder just why you're so involved with this teenage boy."

He winked at her. Now had he decided she was making it with Billy?

"I've lived next door to him for seven years," she told him, her voice controlled. "He's my friend."

He shrugged.

"Furthermore, I've lived in my house for seventeen years. I know everything that's happening on that block. I'm much more familiar with the neighborhood than you are, Mr. Ricklin."

Ricklin smirked at her. "Thanks so much for your help, Miss Lanier."

She left his office feeling defeated. When she turned the corner and saw Robert looking at her, she felt even worse. I'm no more capable of dissuading white men from their folly than you are, she thought at Robert.

"So," Robert said. His lips had tightened, as if a bad card had suddenly popped up in the draw for a winning hand. An anomaly, not a portent. He couldn't afford to lose.

Lucas touched Marcia on the shoulder. "Best to talk later," he suggested. He walked her to her car, warning off panhandlers, nuts, and just garden-variety passersby with a hard look. When they got to Marcia's Ranchero, Lucas nudged the near tire with the toe of his shoe. "This here's a shitkicker's car, lady," he said.

Marcia laughed. "I suppose it is," she answered, looking at the rusty piece of junk with new eyes.

"But it'd be good for fishin'. See ya."

Marcia had driven nearly the whole way home before she realized that Billy's "hit" had come to Billy's house with a loaded gun and sat outside for forty-five minutes waiting for his assassin to arrive.

Billy came home on Tuesday morning. He was exhausted, he told Marcia when he appeared on her porch. He thanked her for being a character witness but he wouldn't look at her while he said it. She invited him in and gave him some coffee, trying to make him comfortable. "Well, it sure didn't do much," Marcia protested, trying to move him beyond his embarrassed gratitude.

Billy waved his hands in denial. "My lawyer said it was really important." He sighed then, sipping at his coffee. Robert, he explained, had managed to get instant cash for the bail bondsman from his employees' credit union. Like so many military retirees, Robert had gone into security, working nights as a guard at a San Francisco museum.

He had been kept separate from the rest of the inmates, Billy said, and they hadn't sent him to juvie. Aunt Esther had managed that bit of business, and she and a couple of supervisors were keeping a steady pressure on the district attorney. Someone should wise up pretty soon, Billy maintained.

"I hope so," Marcia said. She was thinking that apart from not having a mother, Billy had a lot of advantages. He was bright, motivated, in a good program at school, and he had connections. If the DA's office treated Billy like this, what did they do to an average kid from West Oakland? "Are you all right?" she asked him.

"I feel bad about that guy. I guess I shoulda called my pop. But I—I don' know, I just didn't. I didn't think of it."

Marcia nodded. He'd always been a kid who'd solved his own problems. "Did you figure you could scare him away?"

Billy shook his head. "That's the worst, Marcia. I keep going over it. I don't know what I was thinking. I hope I didn't mean to kill him. I really hope I didn't. But he was gonna kill me. He raised the gun. When he did that, I had to fire. But maybe he wouldn't—if I hadn't come out with the gun—"

Marcia nodded again. "Yeah," she said.

# CHAPTER 7

"Marcia has a new girlfriend," Polly informed the group Thursday morning—minus Carol, who was, as always, off on other painting jobs. Marcia should have been at Top Hat Catering herself, but she had set Ted up with a full schedule and a promise to call him at noon. Polly had an irrepressible grin on her Madonna's face, and Marcia half-expected her to power up into the air and shout, "Gimme a G, gimme an O, G-O MARCIA!"

How staggering it must have been for Polly, Marcia thought, beatific cheerleader of her White Plains high school, to discover she was a lesbian; that Pretty Polly, perfect in every way, was so terribly imperfect in this, the most important. How could she marry, have kids, satisfy her big Catholic family? But Polly didn't opt out; she had guts. She'd cheered on gay liberation in the '70s, met Reba in '79 during the one summer Reba played softball in the bar league, and quickly became the bouncy foil to her tall lover's dark fanaticism. Throwing herself into learning carpentry, keeping the books, raising Ruth, growing a backyard vegetable garden, for years she matched Reba's bluster with earnestness, certain life would work out if she'd only try harder. But as Reba's surges of energy fizzled out more and more into obsessive short circuits,

Polly had been forced to step into the void, to be more directive and insistent. When she came upon a situation that promised the innocent fun of her adolescence, like romantic intrigue, she leapt at it with the fervor of a kitten greeting a litter mate. "She's really cute," Polly reported to the rest, who had stopped whatever they were doing to listen.

Marcia rolled her eyes. She'd been expecting Polly to trot out her big news ever since Polly had run into Marcia and Lydia over an evening cappuccino at Just Desserts. Dale had an expectant grin on her face, while Reba was torn between get-to-work and curiosity. Sarah looked puzzled and hurt at hearing this momentous news from anyone but Marcia.

"She's not really my girlfriend," Marcia explained, mostly to Sarah. The five women were in Fairview Street's decimated kitchen—sink torn out, stove shoved against the far wall, counters pried loose from their moorings. Dale had set up her chop saw and table saw in the center of the room, and she stood there, hour upon hour, ripping boards. She was ripping so many boards because Reba, in order to save money, had ordered a bulk load of lumber—the same odd-sized pieces that had been dumped on top of Marcia's Snow in Summer. After listening to the steady whine of the table saw through the open back door for half the morning, Marcia had come inside to point out to Dale that Reba's cost-cutting efforts were labor-intensive and therefore self-defeating, but instead she found herself defending her status as a single woman.

Sarah still looked dismayed. "She isn't," Marcia insisted.

This was perhaps strictly true, but the situation was becoming more muddled by the moment. Marcia had, for instance, reserved two spaces for her and Lydia to go to a sex party in San Francisco that coming Saturday, on a weekend Cory was staying with his father in San Jose. The party was supposed to be a more elaborate version of a sex date, with additional players to add to the fun. But from the moment she'd made the reservations, Marcia wasn't sure she wanted to romp with anyone else, and she was entirely certain she wouldn't want to watch other people with Lydia. But did that mean she wanted Lydia to be her girlfriend?

Marcia had also noticed she was spending a lot of time telling herself how happy she was to be alone, free, and unfettered. Before Lydia, she hadn't needed convincing. On the other hand, once burned, twice shy. Annie was still too present on Marcia's emotional horizon, like a malevolent sun which refused to set so darkness could spread its healing balm. Reba was speaking to her. "What? It's hard to hear with the saw."

"What's her name?"

Hadn't they finished this subject? Sarah had even unstrapped her tool belt and gone outside, her shoulders drawn together.

"Lydia," Polly answered, arms crossed, eyes dancing.

"Lydia...Lydia..." Reba trilled. "Lovely. Is she a birdwatcher? Sounds like a birdwatcher name."

"She's a plant biologist," Marcia muttered. "She teaches at Cal."

"Umm, then you two should have a lot in common. So when do we meet the lovely lady?"

"*I* haven't even met her," Dale complained.

"Heard from Renate, Dale?" Marcia cut in with a thinly disguised change of subject.

But Reba was not to be deflected. Eyebrows raised, she demanded, "How come you haven't introduced us?"

"I've gotta get back to work," Marcia said irritably.

"Marcia's having a traumatic time, girls," Dale told them.

Polly nodded solemnly. "Yeah, I heard about your next-door neighbor, Marcia. That must have been awful. I'm sorry."

"Thanks," Marcia said, meaning it. Besides Dale, who had already participated in several conversations about the shooting, no one had mentioned Billy to her.

"He's that kid I've seen you with a couple times, huh? Kid on your porch or his porch? Kid on the boards." Reba chuckled. She had what Marcia considered an eclectic sense of humor. "You wouldn't expect him to murder someone."

"It wasn't murder," Marcia said. "It was self-defense."

"Pardonnez-moi. It was simply a figure of speech."

"Murder is not a figure of speech."

"Whatever. Anyway, he seemed like a nice kid."

"He *is* a nice kid." Maybe she should have it emblazoned on her chest: Billy Preston is a nice kid.

"So what happens now?" Polly asked.

"Everybody waits," Marcia told her.

"He doesn't have a court date yet. It's a form of bureaucratic torture. How would you like not knowing from day to day if you were going to be convicted of murder?" She wished, in fact, that she could talk to Billy about how he felt, but she'd hardly seen him. He was always on the run with his friends. She sighed. "I'm going back outside," she told them. Polly nodded regretfully. Her little bit of fun had fallen flat.

Sarah was sitting over by the morning glories, a cigarette dangling from her fingers, shadowed by the twelve-foot-high mystery wall. In spite of her hair and her ever-younger wardrobe, Sarah looked more drawn and haggard every day. "How come you didn't tell me?" Sarah greeted her, grinding the butt into the dirt next to her.

Marcia thought she could have framed the same accusation, but she shelved her resentment at learning about the nameless Marine secondhand and repeated that Lydia was not her girlfriend.

"Then what is she?" Sarah asked, a good question the others had not come up with.

"I don't know," Marcia said honestly.

Sarah dropped her head to rest the bridge of her nose on two fingers. "Marcia," she said, "what the hell are we doing here?"

"What do you mean?" Marcia asked, startled. She had been gathering her courage to part the thick curtain of morning glory vines and solve the mystery of the wall; now as Sarah raised her head, Marcia gazed into her friend's anxious blue eyes.

"This," Sarah said, throwing out her arm to encompass everything around them. "We're building units for yuppies, not for people who live in this neighborhood." She turned to Marcia with a baleful look. "You never used to be interested in money."

"I'm still not interested in money," Marcia said, "but at some point you realize you have to have some."

Sarah rubbed her hands on the knees of the Army fatigues she often wore when she worked. "I know these young lesbians who do construction. They couldn't do this. The market's out of sight for them."

"It was almost out of sight for us," Marcia said. "Maybe we're the last generation who can buy anything. If so, then the prices'll come down 'cause no one can afford them."

"Exactly. And that's why it's bad for us to participate. Everytime we buy or sell something, we're supporting this kind of price structure."

"Sarah, come on! We're just planning for our retirement."

"You were never like this, Marcia. You've lived in a rental house in a mixed neighborhood for years."

"Exactly. And now I have to figure out what to do because my neighborhood's gone yuppie and pretty soon my landlord will believe those dumb postcards and realize he can make a bundle by selling the house."

"What dumb postcards?"

"Oh, you know. 'Sell your house today, your profits will never be higher.' I get three a week, so he must be getting them too."

Sarah hauled herself to her feet, her face disturbed. "You know what happened, Marcia? We're decided we can no longer afford to be principled. When we can only be liberal from a place of power, we've had it." She stalked off across the hard earth, pacing like a cat, her—Marcia couldn't help noticing—LA Gear hi-tops too young, too wannabe, poking out turquoise and pink from the legs of her olive-drab fatigues.

"You look like an idiot!" Marcia wanted to shout at her. But she didn't. There was plenty else to yell about, like if Sarah was so fervent, why'd she thrown her own fifteen thousand into the pot? Besides, trying to look after your own future had to be positive, even if she herself had gone about it in this weird way, buying a moldering Victorian with her best pals. Did all these kids who couldn't afford houses want, in their middle-age, to support an entire top-heavy generation of decrepit boomers who'd been too politically correct to provide for themselves? Anyway, Sarah was a minority of one, so why am I so pissed off? She was prevented from answering by a scream coming from the attic.

Polly, it seemed, had been on pigeon duty, scooping up shit in garbage bags. By the time Marcia had scrambled up the single ladder into the attic, Reba was already stroking Polly's shoulders anxiously, while Polly's face was oddly flattened, as if fright had turned her two-dimensional. Leaning on a rafter, she pointed into a corner and croaked, "Bats!"

"Oh, I love bats!" both Dale and Marcia cried at once. They grinned at each other, surprised; after all these years, this was one liking they had not known they shared. They climbed past a paralyzed Polly to scrunch near some old boards which had probably stood in the attic for decades. A number of bats hung in the narrow spaces between the boards, tightly folded like dark envelopes. "So this place does have bats," Marcia said. "Perfect."

"Put a light on them," Reba advised.

"No!" Dale protested. "That might hurt them."

Reba crossed her arms. She did this before she was about to deliver a pronouncement, which according to Dale, she did nearly every morning. Dale put her foot lightly on the tips of Marcia's toes to alert her to the imminence of what they had both come to refer to as Reba's bowel movements. Dale maintained that Reba could not start work before she'd unloaded on them. Today it was the bats, tomorrow it would be something else. "We gotta get rid of them."

"Why?" Dale asked.

"We can't sell a house with bats in the goddamn attic! Besides, we screened off this ventilation space. They won't be able to get out."

"We'll build a bat house," Marcia said. "We'll put the house up here and bait it with fruit, and then take the boards away at night. Then when they go into their house to sleep, we can move them."

"To where?" Polly wanted to know. She had recovered some color.

"Somewhere nice."

Offhand, none of them could think of any place nice. "They can come to my yard," Dale finally offered. "I'll put the house under my eaves, and they can fly around my apple tree and catch insects."

Sarah spent an hour building the bat house and Reba put a few apple and orange slices inside. Dale and Marcia promised to return after dark to open the ventilation screen and cart off the boards. Hopefully when the bats came back from their night out on the town, they would zoom directly to their fancy new house. And hopefully in the meantime the pigeons, always watchful, would not notice that the barrier which had kept them from their roosts had been removed.

They worked through lunch. For a half-hour period, Marcia drifted around, watching what other people were doing. She was becoming concerned about Reba's penchant for demolishing everything in sight. "Don't forget that everything you rip down has to be rebuilt," Marcia reminded her.

Reba turned around and looked at her. "You want me to leave rotten areas?"

"Of course not. But are you speaking figuratively or literally? We only have a limited amount of money. We can't overbuild."

Dale and Polly drifted up behind her. They too had been concerned with Reba's precipitousness. Reba glowered at the circle of faces and said she agreed with Marcia's warning in principle.

"Cosmetics are often better," Polly told her lover. "We're going to have to spend a lot of money on tile and oak floors and fancy plumbing fixtures to appeal to the yups."

"All right!" Reba snarled. "I said I agreed."

But the following day, Reba tore out an entire passably tiled wall in the upstairs bathroom while the rest of them were off at a hamburger place for lunch. She said she'd decided making a more shallow closet in the adjoining bedroom would add a foot to the bathroom so they could fit in a double sink. "Yuppies like double sinks," she told everyone who came up to stare at the busted-up wall and the broken tiles littering the hallway. Marcia said nothing. She was tired from coming by late to let out the bats and then arriving very early to chase away the pigeons before Reba got to work. Compulsive Reba arrived at six-thirty in the morning and left twelve hours later. Marcia wondered why she'd ever thought it would be fun to work with her friends.

Marcia picked Lydia up at nine o'clock on Saturday night. When Lydia had first heard they were going to a sex party, she'd been dismayed. "An orgy?" she'd said. "Is it dangerous?"

"You mean will a giant ape burst through the wall and crush you? Not likely."

Marcia now wished several things: that she had never made the reservations, that she had not been her usual surly self when Lydia had expressed irrational, but understandable qualms, and that Lydia would drop her savior act and allow them not to go. But since Lydia had become convinced that going to the party was Marcia's fondest dream, she refused to listen to any of Marcia's entreaties that they go to a movie instead, go to dinner instead, fuck themselves into oblivion instead. No, they were going to the party.

Lydia slid into the Ranchero wearing a sheer blouse which did not hide the dark grapes of her nipples one iota, leather pants (another addition from her seemingly never-ending store of hidden fetish items), boots, and her leather vest. She carried a small purple gym bag which held god knows what. Glancing over at Marcia, she raised her eyebrows. "I thought we were going to the party."

"We are." Marcia pulled away from the curb and headed for the bridge.

"Then why are you dressed like that?" Marcia was clothed in Low Prep—a red and orange rugby shirt from Lands' End, brown cords, a cotton military belt in a contrasting orange, and her usual running shoes. Her own leather jacket was in the back seat, but it was clear she did not intend to wear it unless the weather took a downturn into the 'teens.

Marcia shrugged. "Perversity." Silence until the toll plaza. "I mean, here we are, about to do something fairly bizarre, right? How bizarre can it be when we all look like a herd of black Angus cattle?"

Lydia plucked at her pants. "Moo," she said.

It was a complicated business getting in the door. They had to knock, identify themselves, go up one flight of stairs and then down another, then re-identify themselves to a woman whose arms were covered with blue tattoos. As a first-time attendee, Lydia had to sign a waiver absolving the party-givers from any responsibility. They were finally waved through the long gray curtain that separated the party area from the hall entry.

A crowd of close to seventy women looked them up and down. The two of them were, as they instantly saw, on the upper end of the age scale; not the oldest by any means, but certainly in the top quarter. "They're so young," Lydia whispered.

"Do you know anybody?" Marcia asked, her lips next to Lydia's ear as they scanned the crowd, variously attired in leathers, uniforms, corsets, and slinky dresses.

"No. Oh... the one in the shades and the bomber jacket? I think she's my vet's assistant."

"We don't have to whisper," Marcia said. They wandered around the space, checking out the various apparatus: two slings, a leather-covered horse, a cross with attached wrist and ankle cuffs, several medical examining tables with stirrups, three mattresses with rubber covers. "Why the rubber?" Lydia asked. "It certainly doesn't look very comfortable."

"Blood," Marcia said. "You can't splash blood around anymore."

Lydia looked faintly censorious, and Marcia shrugged. "You know, some people are into cutting."

Lydia was watching her. "Sometimes I worry that you're heavier than I am."

"Really?" This had the earmarks of an interesting discussion. It was almost impossible to talk, however, over the music which was three times louder than Billy had ever turned up his rap tapes. "Come on, let's go over here."

Marcia cleared a space for them to sit on a wooden bench. In front of them, a woman strapped to a medical examining table was being steadily whipped by two other women; all three had blank, unreadable expressions. At first Marcia and Lydia kept looking everywhere else, mostly because the women were so close to them it seemed like eavesdropping. But after awhile, their eyes were drawn in morbid fascination. It was like watching a porno movie where the woman being fucked was so patently bored she could hardly keep her eyes propped open.

"This *is* bizarre," Lydia said.

Marcia turned up her palms, unable to disagree. "S/M always *looks* weird."

"But they don't look like they're feeling anything."

"No, you're right."

They were whispering in each other's ears again, despite Marcia's prohibition. "Do you want to leave?" Marcia asked.

"We just got here."

"Lydia, I really don't think I'm any heavier than you are."

Lydia took her hand. "No, I guess that's true. It's just—well, I would never have come here, for instance."

"But you're into S/M."

"Just because I watch TV doesn't mean I want to be on *Wheel of Fortune*."

"We don't have to do anything," Marcia assured her.

"No, of course not. Marcia, relax, OK? I'm fine."

I'm not, Marcia thought, but she didn't say anything. She was even more sorry she'd been so dismissive when Lydia had tried to discuss her nervousness about coming. Now Lydia was determined to be a good trooper no matter what. She wished Lydia would just tell her to fuck off sometimes. It was too easy to be mean when there were no repercussions.

They watched people for an hour or so. Several women were doing such extended scenes it was difficult to see how the bottom could stand it. Marcia found herself wincing as butts turned purple and breasts were festooned with clothes pins and tit clamps. Not too many people seemed to be fucking. Marcia remembered parties from the late '70s that were full of women screaming from orgasms. In fact, sometimes people seemed to orgasm in waves, coming from hearing other women come. Not now. Safe sex had created barriers more impenetrable than latex.

Occasionally someone glanced in their direction. Marcia met all such feelers with a flat, surly gaze. Finally Lydia said, "Marcia, I don't think people are going to come over here if you look at them like that."

"I don't want them to come over," Marcia explained.

Lydia stuck her tongue in Marcia's ear. "Don't you want to get fucked by six women *and* me, like a gang rape? Don't you think that'd be fun?"

"Not really," Marcia grumbled. Then it occurred to her that Lydia might want to play, but she could be nervous about topping in front of a crowd. "Do you want to switch?" Marcia asked her.

Lydia made a helpless shrugging motion. The music had risen louder than ever. Marcia put her mouth close to Lydia's ear and said, "Do you want me to top you?"

Lydia pulled back in amazement, shaking her head, and Marcia chuckled. She might have gotten a better response if she'd asked Lydia to jog across an eight-lane freeway. "A woman who'd rather fight than switch," she quipped, but Lydia couldn't hear her, and she didn't repeat herself. Instead she shifted around on the bench until Lydia was sitting inside her legs, with her arms draped over Lydia's shoulders, as if Lydia were inside a Marcia envelope. They did that for awhile, until Lydia announced she wanted something to drink and left for the refreshment area. After a good fifteen minutes, Marcia was starting to get anxious. She had risen to her feet when Lydia strolled back into the main room. "Where were you?" Marcia asked, regaining her spot on the bench.

"Talking to my vet's assistant."

"Hey, look who's here." A stocky redhead named Toni, dressed in a San Francisco cop's uniform, slung herself down next to Marcia. Marcia had once done a scene with her and two other women at a party at someone's house. Marcia didn't find her particularly attractive, but she seemed nice enough. Lydia sat on Toni's other side and Marcia introduced them. Across the way, on the always busy medical examining table, someone was finally getting fucked, and she moaned every time her partner's hand slid into her. "You still work at Peet's?" Marcia asked Toni.

Moan.

"Yeah, I hate it."

"Why?" From Lydia.

Moan.

Toni wrinkled her nose. "It's not very good pay, and when it's busy it's just crazy. I don't know. I can't afford to live just on my hours."

Moan.

"Are you a therapist?" Lydia asked.

"Isn't everyone?"

"I'm not." Pointing to Marcia. "She isn't."

Howl. Things were coming to a head now. The three glanced over at the woman, who was starting to flush, then went back to each other.

Toni was looking openly at Marcia, while Lydia watched both of them covertly. Toni put her hand on Marcia's knee. Marcia didn't want it there, but knocking it off seemed a considerable over-reaction. Instead she covered Toni's hand with her own, then carefully lifted it up and stuck it back into Toni's lap. "Like that, huh?" Toni said, smiling at her. "There's a nice horse up there on that stage I bet you'd like to feel under your belly."

"Not tonight," Marcia said. Not any night, she realized.

The woman getting fucked was shrieking now. They all turned to watch the denouement. Her hips moved like castanets, slapping up and down on the table. Her partner leaned into her and licked a wet trail up the slight rise of her stomach. The woman screamed once and then seemed to faint, coming alive an instant later to convulse hard, twice, three times. Then her breath came back and her breasts heaved, slick with sweat. Toni turned again to Marcia. "You sure?"

"Certain," Marcia said.

Toni stood up and smiled at Lydia. "Nice meeting you," she said. She took off across the room.

"It's exciting seeing people come," Lydia said, a wistful edge in her voice.

Marcia stood up. "Let's get out of here."

Lydia looked almost pathetically eager. "Now? But it's so early—"

"So what? We're older. We deserve an early night." They stepped outside into the cold, crisp air, Lydia shivering in her sheer blouse. Once they were in the car, Marcia wrapped her in her jacket and drove quickly across the bridge. "Was it fun for you?" Lydia asked when they were home in bed.

"No," Marcia said.

Lydia was quiet for a moment. "Let's talk about it tomorrow, all right?"

Marcia lay awake for a long while, listening to the even rise and fall of Lydia's breathing. I'm falling in love with this woman, she thought. It felt like the best thing that could have happened and also the worst thing, a dizzying mix of exhilaration and dread.

Maybe there was no such thing as recreational sex, at least not between Marcia Lanier and Lydia Fitzpatrick, not in the fall of '89. Maybe we should meet some other time, she thought desperately, when I'm over Annie, when I'm not involved with the house, when Billy's safe from that nest of great white sharks down at the courthouse. But she had the uneasy sensation that she'd already been walking up a path for some time without being aware of it. Everything was connected, from spending her savings on their nutty rehab scheme to meeting Lydia that day in the gardens. More than anything, Marcia wanted to be in control, and this felt exactly the opposite.

# CHAPTER 8

By the next morning Marcia was feeling just as confused but more courageous. As they sat in the kitchen
sipping the last of the coffee, Marcia decided she had to
dip beneath the ice of small talk which, because all else
was forbidden, crept in like a glacier to paralyze their
conversations. She started with, "How does Cory get a-
long with your girlfriends?"

This was her way of asking whether Lydia's seventeen-year-old son, whom she'd only glimpsed in snatches
apart from that one breakfast after Billy's arrest, was
always so closed-mouthed. Her question was also supposed to signal that just maybe she had a stake in how
Cory treated Lydia's lovers.

V-lines scored the bridge of Lydia's long nose as she
regarded Marcia, her agate eyes curious. Apparently she
decided, however, to take Marcia's query at face-value.
"Well, he's not very good. When I came out to him, he was
fourteen. He spent days screaming at me that I was sick."

Marcia smiled. "The poor kid doesn't know the half of
it."

"Nor will he," Lydia said. "I figure who I sleep with is
public knowledge, but what I do in bed is my business."

"Seems sensible. So how does he act with these female lovers of yours? How many have there been by the way?"

"Only two."

"Jeez, practically a virgin."

Lydia poked her in the side, and Marcia wrestled with her until Lydia caught her breath and continued. "He says he could have lived his life in perfect bliss if only I hadn't come out to him. He says he didn't want to know, and that I was really selfish for telling him. I felt bad about that for weeks."

Marcia sighed.

"Anyway, what he does is he's rude. He acts like the person's not there. With both of them he announced, 'She'll be gone in a month or two. Why should I bother to get to know her?'" This sentiment was too close for comfort, so they gazed across the kitchen at the wall stencils Lydia had copied from *Country Life*. Pigs had big blotches for legs, where paint had seeped under the stencil, and cows were black and white and pink, the latter color an escapee from the pigs. "It looked a lot better in the magazine," Lydia had explained. Now she said, "Sometimes he picks fights."

"Sounds fun."

"Once he threw a pillow."

"Violent."

"But, see, no one really has been important." She didn't add the word *before*, but Marcia thought it must be choking her, she wanted to say it so bad. "So in a sense he's been right." Silence. And now that Marcia had thawed the ice, it was hard to go further. Afraid even to gather their dishes, they continued to stare at the pink-spotted cows. Was it presumptuous to imagine they might want to spend the day together? "Do you have anything you need to do?" Marcia hazarded.

Lydia smiled. "Not really."

"Then let's get outta here, OK?"

They wound up back at the botanical gardens where they dazzled each other with knowledge the other had never considered. Lydia described what she did with her yams, which Marcia found difficult to understand, tuning in and out as she observed the interplay of leaf colors and textures in the tentative light of fall, so different from the immutable blaze of a California spring. "You see germplasm and I see art," Marcia finally said. "It couldn't be more different."

"Yes, that's true," Lydia said. "Gardens are so creative for you, while I don't even think of plants as plants. Would you like to see my lab?"

Since it was Saturday, they could drive on the narrow campus roads and park in front of the new concrete slab and glass complex that housed the department of genetics and plant biology. "Most people haven't even moved in yet," Lydia confided. "The idea was to combine several disciplines under the term genetic research." They climbed steps still littered with bits of Sheetrock, while yellow and orange extension cords hung like streamers from the third floor. "Reminds me of Fairview Street," Marcia said.

That resemblance ended as they walked into Lydia's lab, which seemed filled with enough equipment to stock a chemistry lab plus launch a jet liner on the side. "So where're the yams?" Marcia asked, joking as she felt increasingly at sea.

Lydia leaned over a petri dish. "This tiny dot contains most of what you'd need for a yam plant. But I'm not growing anything here. I'm mostly gene-mapping and then experimenting with vectors to see how we can transfer the sequences we want. I may never get to the whole plant stage."

Marcia followed Lydia around as she described the uses of equipment that looked both space-age and oddly primitive. Her voice quickened, her face became animated, and she began hauling Marcia from one table to another to "see what I mean."

Marcia had no idea what Lydia did mean—Lydia's technicality accelerated with her passion—but instead wondered what kind of mind made sense of all this, much less found it so electrifying. It was puzzle-solving, she decided, the ultimate acrostic, in which Lydia might contribute three definitions in a lifetime of work but never glimpse a solution. Of course, Marcia thought, the best puzzle is never solved, and life was surely that. Meanwhile about all that was getting a workout on this mini-tour was Lydia's vocal chords. "Hang on," Marcia said, "you lost me a while ago."

Lydia shook her head. "I'm sorry. Honestly, there're only a few people in the world who have a clue what I'm doing, and I'm convinced we're the only ones who understand each other. I should give up trying to explain it."

"But you're a teacher."

"A rotten one. I think I've really moved people, and then I get papers back that show me they haven't gotten a word. But I don't do much teaching now." She smiled. "Sometimes I feel guilty. It's like being paid to meditate."

"I'm impressed," Marcia said, gazing around the lab. She was also a little intimidated. Her sense of who Lydia was needed restructuring.

Lydia came forward to stroke Marcia's bare arm and rub her cheek against Marcia's. The smooth down on Lydia's face sent tingles of pleasure across Marcia's shoulders and up the back of her neck. At least there was something about Lydia she still knew. "I don't want you to be impressed," Lydia mumbled against her chin.

"Why?"

"Because it makes you distant." Then she thought a moment. "Even though *I'm* impressed by you."

Marcia drew away from her, astounded. "Me?"

"Your job is like running a war. It's funny, because you're so private, and I'm so extroverted, but what we do is just the opposite."

"I would never have picked my job," Marcia protested.

"You could be a landscape gardener anytime you wanted something more contemplative."

Marcia made a face. "I've been scared to do that," she confessed. "What if I didn't like it?"

Lydia laughed and took her arm. "Always looking on the bright side. Want to have lunch with a rotten teacher?"

"I didn't like the party," Lydia said later that evening. She was lying on her couch in front of the woodburning stove, which was consuming oak firewood from the supermarket at a rapid clip.

"I'm afraid I have to agree with you there," Marcia said. She sat on the floor, her head against Lydia's thigh. After lunch they'd spent a lazy afternoon, hardly speaking, at the Little Farm in Tilden Park. While Lydia read a murder mystery cover-to-cover, Marcia had plied the geese with lettuce.

"Would you have had a better time if I hadn't come?" Lydia seemed to be steeling herself for an unwelcome answer.

"If you hadn't come, I would have left about two hours sooner than we did, which would have given me a good fifteen minutes for my twenty bucks."

The muscles in Lydia's leg relaxed. Marcia hadn't noticed before how tight they'd been. This worried her—both Lydia's anxiety and that she hadn't been aware of it. "I didn't like it because it wasn't intimate," Lydia continued. "I don't see the point of sex if it's not intimate. But that didn't even seem like sex to me, not most of it. No one looked as if they were having fun. It's almost as if it's for show, but it's not. I guess I really don't understand it."

Marcia nodded. "It was different than ones I've gone to in the past." But she was wondering how much of that was due to seeing it through Lydia's eyes—and how she had changed over just the past few weeks. She had not expected to feel so protective of Lydia as she had at the party—she had practically encased Lydia in a cocoon. It would be very difficult now to lose her.

But what did Lydia mean by her contention that sex had no point for her unless it was intimate? Why had she agreed to a relationship that promised nothing more than recreational sex? Yet, Marcia admitted, from the start, sex between them *had* been intimate.

"Also," Lydia said, "and the extent to which I felt this surprised me, I really didn't like seeing other people look at you. Or touch you." Lydia dropped her hand down to lie on Marcia's shoulder. It felt good, and the good feeling worried her.

"I didn't do anything with anyone else," Marcia said idiotically.

"Still," Lydia said. She flipped on her stomach and ran her hand between Marcia's breasts and down across her midriff to rest at the top of her pubic bone. "Still, I didn't like it." Her hand roamed down further until her fingers found the seam of Marcia's crotch. "I want this. For me. C'mere. Get up."

Marcia swung onto her knees and then stood, facing Lydia and the couch. Lydia reached forward and unbuttoned Marcia's jeans. She pushed them to the floor and helped Marcia step out of them. Then she ran her fingers between Marcia's lips. "You're wet already," she told her. Marcia said nothing. "Did you hear me? You're soaking wet. What do you think that means?"

"I like you?" Marcia hazarded.

Lydia chuckled. "I think it means more than that. You want me to take you, don't you? You want to be mine as much as I want you to be."

"Yes." Admitting it was simple as a leaf falling off a tree. She felt dizzy and swayed on her feet. Lydia put a hand on her hip to steady her.

"C'mon, hon, lean forward, that's right, along the couch. There's room for two... No, you're not high enough. Get that pillow and put it under your thighs. I want your ass way up here. Good. Now spread your legs. Further. You can do better than that."

Lying face down on the couch, her T-shirt twisted under her, her bare behind sticking up like an offering, Marcia listened as Lydia left the room, padded somewhere—the bathroom, she thought—then returned. She heard something untwist, a lid. Lydia's fingers, now encased in a thin surgical glove, applied a cool, slick substance down the crease of Marcia's ass. Marcia turned her head to one side, resting her cheek against the cotton couch cover. The wing of a parrot grazed her eyelashes. Lydia had flamboyant tastes in fabrics. When Lydia's fingers touched her asshole, Marcia told herself to stop thinking about interior decorating and concentrate on being open. That was her task here; she had nothing to do but be open.

Lydia's hand was very slippery. "Relax," she said.

Marcia thought telling people to relax was the surest way to make them tense up. Nevertheless, she actually did relax. She was tuned into Lydia's lead, obeying what Lydia said to the letter. "We'll start with two fingers," Lydia told her.

Marcia felt loose. She pulled Lydia's fingers in like the ocean sucking up a piece of driftwood. Lydia laughed. "You want this, don't you, baby? You want it all. You want my whole hand."

Marcia got scared. "I don't know if—"

Lydia's voice turned hard. "Did I tell you to talk, Marcia?"

"No," Marcia muttered.

"Then shut up." Lydia pinched the skin at the base of Marcia's thigh and Marcia yelped. Her ass closed tight. Lydia withdrew carefully. "Marcia, you can do better than this. I know you can. Do I have to give you a spanking to convince you to open up for me?"

"No," Marcia moaned. "I will. Please, Lydia."

"All right, we'll try again. But this is the last time. Otherwise I'm unbuckling my belt."

The threat worked wonders.

Marcia told herself she had to really concentrate. She tilted forward another half-inch, raising her ass higher, spread her legs further. She felt Lydia's fingers coming down the crease, willed herself to open, felt the ring of muscle relax, felt Lydia slip in. Lydia didn't move much, just wiggled her fingers a little to let Marcia know she was really there. "That's three, Mars. Two to go. You've got to open a lot more."

Marcia moaned and thrust up against Lydia's hand. "You want it, don't you? You want it even though you're scared... four fingers," Lydia announced.

Marcia felt she was being split apart. "It hurts," she muttered.

Lydia stopped moving her hand. "Hurts real or hurts good?"

"Good. Full."

"Fine. OK, baby, now here we go. I want you as open as you can be."

There was a sensitive place inside that either got into it or stopped it. Tonight that place was asking for more, for bigger, for deeper. Marcia's cunt was engorged, juices dripping down her legs.

"There's a large part of my hand," Lydia informed her. "Sort of where everything comes together. You know my hand pretty well, don't you, Marcia?"

Gasped. "Yes."

"It's spanked you and strapped you and fucked you and now it's going up inside your ass, baby. Just let that big part slide in, and then you've got it made..."

But Lydia appeared to be stuck no matter how open Marcia tried to be. Marcia started to get nervous. "Marcia, you're closing up again. You really want that spanking, don't you?" Lydia withdrew in a rush, and Marcia cried out, "No, no, I—" She felt absurdly disappointed, on the verge of tears.

As if sensing that Marcia's upset was real, Lydia leaned forward and kissed her shoulder, then nibbled at her ear and said softly, "Don't worry, babe. We'll try again." Then she straightened up and let her voice go harsh. "So get ready, Marcia, you've earned a good one this time." She pulled off the glove and inserted her leg in place of the pillow, hauling Marcia across her knee, holding Marcia's hand behind her back. Marcia's head was below the couch seat, her chin resting on the edge. Lydia's hand rose and fell with deadly precision, not hard, not fast, but steadily, until Marcia was begging her to stop and twisting to escape. Lydia halted and told Marcia if she didn't quit jumping around she'd just have to start again from the beginning. Marcia took a deep breath and stayed still for the remainder of the spanking. The pillow ended up on the floor with the discarded glove as Lydia levered Marcia on her back and squatted over her, her thighs clasping Marcia's ears, her hands pinning Marcia's wrists. Too bad, Marcia thought, she'd wanted to play with Lydia's nipples. But it hardly mattered, not with Lydia doing the death grip with her legs, rocking against Marcia's mouth, or when she turned the tables, sending Marcia screaming halfway over the arm of the couch. "Don't flail so much," Lydia complained.

"Don't do it so good then," Marcia countered. She pulled Lydia up beside her, opening her arm to draw Lydia close. Lydia snuggled in, settling her palm over Marcia's breast.

After a few minutes, Marcia asked hesitantly, "Did you mean what you said? About wanting me?"

"Did you mean it when you said yes?" Lydia responded. Her body had stiffened at Marcia's question, and Marcia wished she could reassure her. But reassuring her meant saying things she couldn't promise. Or wouldn't promise. Still, the ease with which she'd told Lydia she would be hers had startled her. She couldn't just put it off to bottoming. They'd been in that nether world between conscious time and fantasy time where defenses are stripped away and they hadn't yet fallen into the roles that would clothe them in something else.... Marcia felt Lydia waiting for an answer. She licked her lips. Dry. Maybe she should go wipe herself off. She felt sticky between her legs.

She got up from the couch and spent two minutes in the bathroom. She tried not to think. She realized she was scared. When she came back into the living room, Lydia was sitting in front of the woodstove, damping down the fire. She turned towards Marcia. No answer still. In Lydia's eyes was not disappointment but resignation. "It's cold," Marcia said. She went into Lydia's bedroom, pulled the quilt off the bed and brought it back into the living room. She spread it on the floor in front of the woodstove and wrapped them both inside the quilt. It seemed like camping, like pretend. She took Lydia's fingers in her own and pulled her close. They kissed while Lydia tried unsuccessfully to stifle a yawn. "I'm sorry," she apologized. She buried her face against Marcia's breast.

Marcia smiled. She told herself they needed to talk soon. Maybe when Lydia wasn't so sleepy.


The next morning Lydia turned from the stove and said, "So tell me about Annie," in a voice normally reserved for questioning the doctor about an illness one fears is terminal.

Marcia was determined not to be so gloomy. "Well, it was dramatic. We had a lot of excitement around drugs and alcohol even though I was sober. Then we had arguments about politics and terminology. And we fought about sex."

"Sounds like your normal garden-variety marriage," Lydia observed.

"Our main assumption," Marcia continued, "was that no matter what Annie did, I was at fault."

"That must have been pleasant," Lydia said, gazing at Marcia from under her long eyelashes. Then she turned her back and cracked two eggs against the lip of a bowl covered with long white streaks where all the orange had faded away.

"It was pretty miserable," Marcia admitted to Lydia's shoulders. "I got tired of apologizing for her and cleaning up the messes she'd made everywhere in her life and being told I was an ideological dunce." She smiled. "Even though I probably was. Am."

"So why didn't you leave?"

Marcia didn't answer for awhile, not until Lydia had cracked a couple more eggs, added cream, and beaten them into a yellow froth. "I don't know. I guess I thought we were married so I was supposed to stay. And I loved her. That means something."

Lydia spilled the eggs into a pan, then grated cheese over them. "I stopped loving Jeff. Maybe that made it easier for me."

"It would," Marcia agreed. "But you had Cory, and that'd be a lot worse."

They were silent for a moment while the omelette cooked.

Finally Lydia turned around to face Marcia. "What I'm trying to get at here is why you're so deathly afraid and I'm not. I haven't found many answers beyond that you got yourself into an ugly situation, and instead of admitting you'd made a mistake and getting out, you decided life was to blame. Now you're expecting life to zap you again when really it was just you not taking responsibility for your own shit."

Marcia instantly became so defensive her skin felt stiff. "Yeah," she snapped, "and then again maybe I'm just sick of being wrong, wrong, wrong."

Lydia shoved a plate of toast and eggs under her nose. Marcia sliced off a piece of the creamy omelette with her fork. They ate for a moment, until Marcia's skin loosened, and she decided she should be fair. "Of course," she admitted, "it takes two to play that game."

Lydia stopped spooning apricot preserves on her plate and looked into Marcia's pained eyes. "No, it doesn't, babe. It only takes one. You."

# CHAPTER 9

Marcia had just stretched as high as she could and tipped a giant box of Grape Nuts from the top shelf in the supermarket cereal aisle into Lydia's waiting hands when Dale, appearing from nowhere, stuck a finger into the naked space between Marcia's shirt and the waistband of her pants and tickled. Marcia nearly shrieked but managed to control herself. Then she introduced Dale and Lydia.

"Glad to meet you," Dale said. She had been triumphant at playing her trick on Marcia; now her grin widened and then gradually faded, as if the muscles of her face had suddenly developed a nervous disorder that glacially slowed their ability to function. Marcia stared at her, bewildered; what was the matter? Dale was also staring, now that she'd finally rid herself of the grin—she was mesmerized by the legend on the breast pocket of Lydia's T-shirt: "S/M = Sexual Magic."

It was enough to make a person homicidal, Marcia thought. Enough to make her want to grab Dale by the shirt collar and shake her, except you don't do that to people you love. Lydia, who had been making polite conversation about the progress of the Fairview Street house, ground to her own confused halt, sensing not only that something was wrong but that whatever would happen next would involve her only peripherally. "I'm going to check out the wines," she told Marcia. She left, wheeling the cart along the aisle.

Dale's face had reddened. She was looking everywhere but at Marcia.

"Don't be embarrassed for me," Marcia told her. "I'm not embarrassed."

"I don't know what you mean."

"You know exactly what I mean."

Dale abandoned ignorance and went on the offensive instead. "You didn't tell me anything about her."

Marcia leaned against the shelves lined with multicolored boxes of cereal. She felt sick to her stomach. She hated confrontations. So did Dale. They weren't supposed to do this to each other. "Why should I tell you? You should have assumed. You should have assumed because of me, not her."

Dale sighed. "I didn't think about it. I don't *want* to think about it."

"That's what straight people say," Marcia said, then instantly wanted to take it back. Low blow. They were both rocked by it. But it's true, goddamnit, Marcia thought. Doesn't matter. Still shouldn't have said it. Dale's eyes had clouded over. Marcia reached out and took her hand, and Dale stepped forward and hugged her awkwardly. "OK," Dale said. It was not OK. They just couldn't stand being at odds with each other for more than thirty or forty seconds.

"Come have dinner with us," Marcia said.

"No, I've got too much to do."

Marcia began to argue until Dale added, "I've really got to get going. I told Reba I'd help her pick up the french doors at the Home Depot tonight and I'm already late. I'll talk to you later." She gave a brief wave and rushed down the aisle towards the front of the store.

Marcia turned in the other direction. She ambled along, touching bars of soap here, toilet tissue there. The wines were all the way over on the other side. She was in no hurry. But Lydia met her halfway, near the dairy products. She bounced the cart up and down with her toes, watching Marcia, until Marcia irritably took it away from her and wheeled it into the deserted area by the oil and transmission fluid.

"What happened?"

Marcia didn't want to talk about it. "Nothing." Then, "She was freaked out by your attire."

"My attire..." Lydia stared down at herself, as if expecting to see something disastrous: she'd worn her pajama bottoms to Safeway, or her breasts were hanging out. Then she realized. "You're kidding. She's your closest friend, Marcia."

"I know." There was nothing more to say, except Lydia found something.

She was shaking her head, her eyes worried. "I can't deal with this too."

Marcia licked her lips. She knew exactly what Lydia meant. Lydia couldn't be expected to handle being perceived as a wedge between Marcia and Dale in addition to Marcia's ambivalence about their relationship. "Yeah, you're right," Marcia said heavily. She'd never felt more alone.

That Wednesday Reba came to work with her dark hair dyed auburn. Apart from the fact that her hair had no highlights and therefore lay on her scalp like something dead, it wasn't a bad color. Seen from a distance, it was amusing and cheery. Reba magnified the effect by wearing a dark green bowling shirt with "MAGARD TRUCKING" and a little devil embroidered on the back. She received a lot of compliments.

Thursday Polly and Sarah jumped into the fray. Polly had set her long dark hair on rollers, so it pouffed out around her head, circa high school 1965. Sarah had stayed more current by spot-coloring streaks of magenta in her blond clouds. Both wore shirtwaist dresses, pumps, and very dark red lipstick.

Friday Carol, still looking as if she crushed walnut shells between her molars for fun, arrived with her steel-gray hair in a Mohawk. She also wore one earring, a silver skull with grinning teeth, and she had painted her fingernails as maroon as Polly and Sarah's lips.

Monday arrived. "We're waiting," Reba said to Marcia and Dale at lunch.

"Well, prepare yourself for a long one," Dale told her. She was lounging on a blanket sunning herself. Marcia was also lying in the sun but was not enjoying it. It only made her sweaty and in a bad mood. Reba grabbed her ankle and she jumped half a foot. "How about you, sport? You going to surprise us?"

"Don't count on it."

"Bet you two were a barrel of laughs in college," Reba complained.

"We were unconscious most of the time," Marcia said. She moved out of the sun. "How can you stand it?" she asked Dale. Dale smiled, shading her eyes, and then lifted a weary hand in acknowledgement.

"Oh yeah," Reba said, "it's been so long I forgot. The ex-alkies. Sober, dumb, and glum." She stared off moodily into the middle distance, where a group of seagulls fought with their own house's pigeons over some scraps of food that someone had thrown in the street. "Our little Republicans," she continued fondly, patting Dale and Marcia's calves, conveniently within reach. Then she stood up and stretched. "Off to work, me hearties." Everyone moved but the Republicans. They still lay on their backs, knees up, one in the sun, one in the shade. On some level, Marcia thought, what Reba said was true. She and Dale were the conservative old stick-in-the-muds who would never dance, never wear a costume on Halloween, never leap up at a talent show and burst into song. Together, the two of them probably spent less than three hundred a year on clothes, shoes included. They'd each changed their hairstyles once in the 23 years they'd known each other.

The next day, Marcia cornered Dale by the table saw. "Dale," she said, "I know why you can't stand my being into S/M."

Dale finished her cut and then pushed up her safety glasses, leaving the saw running.

"It's not that you think it's horrible or revolting," Marcia continued. "It's just that it makes us different." She drummed her fingers on the metal surface of the saw bed. Dale looked at her with her soft, quiet eyes, pursed her

lips, and raised her eyebrows quizzically. Marcia waited
for perhaps a minute. When Dale still said nothing, Marcia
turned away and went into the side yard to ready the area
around the butchered Cecile Brunner rose for the pavers.
A couple hours later, Dale came up behind her and caught
the pickaxe on its upward track. Marcia almost toppled
over backwards. She was exhausted. "Oh!" Dale said. "You
look so tired."

"I am." Marcia collapsed to the ground. "My back
hurts like shit. I really shouldn't pickaxe for more than an
hour a day."

"Yeah, I know." Dale handed her a can of decaffein-
ated diet iced tea. The stuff was lethal but Marcia liked it.
"I get sick of doing the cuts all the time." Because of Dale's
slipped disc, she did most of the measuring and the
sawing, standing for hours in front of the saw. The others
came down from their various perches and hauled away
their precut pieces. It was efficient but boring for Dale.

Dale snapped open a Coke and they drank in silence
for a few minutes. "It's funny, huh? You're right about it
making us different. I never thought about it being revolting or anything like that. I mean, I don't think about it at
all." Dale glanced at her. "And don't say that shit about
straight people again."

"No. I won't."

"Even though it's true."

Marcia laughed. "Even though it's true."

They finished their drinks, draining the cans. Dale
crushed her can to silver-dollar size. "Look, let's go to
dinner tonight after the meeting, OK? Ask Lydia."

"OK," Marcia said. "That's good. She'll like that."

"She probably thinks I'm a jerk, huh?"

"No. She thinks I'm a jerk, but she's got plenty of
reasons for that."

"I bet," Dale said, then scrambled away from Marcia's
punch. "Ciao."


Unfortunately, Lydia had an important meeting of her
own. "The yam people," she explained. "Remember?
They're the only ones who can understand me."

"I'm having better luck in that department," Marcia reported. Now, sitting on a couch in Reba and Polly's living room, she remembered how Lydia had looked earlier that evening as she'd sat meditating on Marcia's porch, how her hair fell across her shoulders like dark rain and the setting sun cast a pinkish glow to her skin. Her face had been so quiet she'd seemed not to be breathing, and it was all Marcia could do to not leap to her feet to holler her pleasure at being with Lydia against this glorious apricot sky.

Marcia was smiling still when Reba began a mock-chiding lecture: "Three days to put in two french doors is on schedule for finishing in the spring of '92, girls... And when're we going to see some progress in the yard, Marsh?"

"When everything I do doesn't get trashed," Marcia said.

"But when are you going to start on the deck? I want to see a skeleton," Reba insisted. She craved results without problems, Marcia thought, like what they were going to do about the dozens of stacked-up wooden packing crates Marcia had discovered hidden underneath the tangle of morning glory vines. Mrs. Jackson in the smaller Victorian next door was already forbidding Marcia to demolish the wall unless another barrier was put up immediately. "I'm not havin' them drug people cut across your yard to get to mine," the spry octogenarian had vowed, hanging out her upper-story window.

"If we're all going to sit around complaining," Sarah broke in, "I want to add that I'm sick of doing everything on the sly."

"What do you mean?" Marcia asked, eager to get Reba off her case.

"Our marvelous make-believe plans," Sarah muttered. "I hate doing this kind of stuff."

"I don't like it either," Polly seconded.

Dale looked guilty, Reba like a bulldog. Carol and Marcia wallowed at sea. "What are you talking about?" Carol asked.

"We faked the blueprints," Sarah explained. "Since they probably wouldn't have let us move the upstairs kitchen downstairs, we had to pretend it was there already, and then we had to pretend that the access to the upstairs was at the back and not the front, and we had to pretend that the other bathroom was already there as well as the wall separating the two units—"

Carol rubbed her hand across her mohawk. Thankfully she was letting it grow out; the sides looked like the gray fuzz on a peach. "We didn't get permits for any of this?"

"Certainly not," Reba said. "We would have had to go through months of shit with their goddamn architectural integrity department, and they could still have turned it down."

"Well, wait," Dale amended. "We *do* have permits. We have permits to do renovations on things that don't exist, on things that won't exist until we build them. In other words, we did a set of plans of the house as we found it, and then we did a set with all the renovations. Except the first set is a figment of our imaginations since it shows the backing kitchens and the extra bath and the rear entrance."

Marcia thought for a moment, and then shook her head. "But I don't see what else we could have done. What if they *had* forbidden us to move the kitchen? They don't have records of the renovations the Fosters did in the '50s. We had to change that floor plan or it wouldn't have been financially feasible."

"But that's always our excuse," Sarah said. She was so exercised she was bouncing in her chair. "We can't go to one unit, we have to gear it to yups, we had all those racist rules about what we can buy and what we can't... Do we even care what we're doing to this neighborhood?"

"We're doing something good," Carol said. "We're rehabbing a piece of shit."

Sarah ignored her. "And how do you think *I* feel? I'm a consultant to the Architectural Heritage Association, and I'm ripping apart a landmark! Do you realize there's been something illegal about every job we've done in the past few years? "

"We're anarchists," Reba told her with a grin. "Not subject to the whims of petty bureaucrats."

"Dyke subversives," Marcia expanded.

Sarah's disgust was palpable. "Oh, it's really subversive to fuck over everybody else out of greed. Kind of like trading in junk bonds or sinking your neighborhood S&L."

Dale glanced up from the fox, which was now eyeing a disheveled-looking chicken. "Well, those things have been pretty disastrous to the status quo, though I grant you, subversion probably wasn't the intent."

Before Marcia and Dale went to dinner, they paid eight dollars each to soak in a hot tub at Grand Central, and then wandered wet-haired into the Rockridge Cafe and ordered hamburgers and fries and double cafe lattes. Marcia was on a conversational roll. "The point is, we should have seen it. I don't understand how we could have been so stupid."

"Seen what?"

"Reba. We should have realized that someone so obsessive, someone who proposes eight houses and does all the research on them and gets shot down every time but still finds this place, is going to be a compulsive who will drive everyone else nuts."

Dale sighed and then ripped into her hamburger.

"The thing that kills me is that all this was so predictable. Why did I think I could add another full-time project in the middle of the holiday season?" She patted the beeper she'd begun wearing a week earlier. "I'm working constantly, I don't have a dime, and frankly I think we're going to have to spend more on the house. And please tell me why I thought working with other lesbians would be so wonderful? All it does is make everyone's stupidity and irrationality more personally offensive." Marcia sipped at her latte. "We had opportunities to get out of it. *You* could not have advanced your two-unit plan."

Dale had her mouth deep in the burger but she signaled comprehension with her eyes.

"And *I* could have raised a stink when Foster wanted to raise the price. Right there Reba was ready to can the whole deal. And I argued her out of it. I have brought this shit on myself, every bit of it. What am I, some kind of masochist?" They chewed dourly on their burgers until Marcia clapped her hand to her chest and burst out laughing. "Jesus, Dale, I asked myself that question in all seriousness. What on earth is the matter with me?"

"Nothing," Dale said, putting down her burger. "Besides, it's different."

"You *know* that?"

Dale looked offended. "Just because I don't like to talk about it doesn't mean I'm an idiot."

Marcia sighed and ate a fry while Dale polished off the remainder of her burger. Marcia's was sitting on her plate, hardly begun. "I know you don't like to, but *can* we talk about it for a couple minutes?" Dale rolled her eyes but rocked her head back and forth, which Marcia took for a yes. "Why do you think people care? What's so awful?" She really wanted to ask why Dale found it so hard to talk about, but she couldn't do that.

"No one likes that stuff, Marcia. People see you and they think Fall of the Roman Empire."

"Thanks heaps," Marcia said, laughing. She glanced around at the other patrons, none of whom were paying them any attention. Nevertheless she said, "You're not exempt from the social deviant category." Butch women, she thought, particularly those who look confident and demanding, aren't popular almost anywhere, even in lesbian circles where "straight-appearing" was a priority.

Dale anchored her head at a leftwards tilt. "How true. Just yesterday a woman grabbed her kid away like I was going to kick him."

She poked her tongue out of the corner of her mouth to lick up a speck of mustard and then grinned at Marcia. "'Course I might have, who knows? Anyway, to answer your question, people get freaked out for a lot of reasons. It's sex, for one thing."

Which was a good reason she and Dale didn't discuss it, Marcia thought. They didn't talk about what Dale did in bed either. Dale picked up a fry and waved it in Marcia's face. "And then you bring it into the street with your clothes. Bad enough there's all these dykes and fairies all over without freaks wearing leather. You'd think sexuality was part of the human condition."

Marcia was finally eating her hamburger, so her laugh was muffled.

"Then there's the violence argument," Dale continued.

"Oh, god," Marcia said, coming up for air, "that's so ignorant. Just because something looks similar doesn't mean it is. That argument makes consent irrelevant. It's like saying all sexual intercourse is rape."

Dale drummed her fingers on the table. "People do say that, you know."

"Nut cases," Marcia decreed.

"Hate to tell you this, honey, but plenty of people think you're a nut case."

Marcia raised her eyebrows. Unfortunately she'd never mastered hoisting just one aloft, so it was a pale imitation of Dale's classic look.

"Oh, well," Marcia said, but it hurt, and both of them knew it. "Anyway," she continued with a shrug as she met Dale's eyes, "here's one good thing. I really do like Lydia."

Dale nodded. "That's the most important. Here's another. Don't worry about the house so much. It can't get a whole lot worse."

Marcia worked all day at Fairview Street on Saturday, finally escaping at four. On the way to Lydia's, she picked up a deep-dish Chicago pizza. She had arranged with the elusive Cory to join him for a TV date to watch USC trounce Notre Dame. When she arrived at Lydia's, however, she discovered that Cory had gone off to see a friend and wouldn't be back for hours.

Her face fell. "Am I suddenly a pariah for teenage boys?" she asked Lydia. "Billy's avoiding me, Cory acts like I have the plague... And me, the soul of understanding." She plunked the pizza on the counter, wishing she'd been able to predict what a burden of gratitude her court appearance would land on Billy. But if she hadn't testified, wouldn't he have felt she didn't care?

Lydia was standing with her arms crossed over her chest, a la Sarah. "Did you come to visit me or my son?"

"Well, you, of course. I would like to watch the game, though."

But Lydia had other ideas. She had gone to Stormy Leather, bought fleece-lined black leather wrist cuffs, and affixed them to two rings which were, in their turn, screwed into her bed frame. "Very nice," Marcia said, stroking one with her index finger.

"This will take your mind off work," Lydia informed her.

"My mind is on college football."

"Nonsense. Go take a shower."

So Marcia ran in and out of the shower, annoyed at Lydia for being so damn environmentally conscious, with not only the requisite reduced flow shower head but the water heater set on barely tepid. She stalked into the bedroom, gracelessly fell on the bed backwards, and allowed Lydia to cuff her wrists. "Your mind is definitely on work," Lydia diagnosed, stroking Marcia's side with light fingertips while Marcia squirmed, trying not to be ticklish. "And you're in a horrible mood. Sex is the only answer."

"Television," Marcia countered.

"Television rots the mind."

"This doesn't?" Marcia yanked on the cuffs. Lydia had done a good job with her electric drill. "I'm totally helpless," she reported.

"Thank god," Lydia said. "If only I'd remembered to buy a gag." Instead she gagged Marcia with her tongue, which tasted good and felt even better. They began to grind against each other, and Marcia started getting excited despite her longing for Notre Dame vs. USC. She pinned Lydia's leg with one of her own, and Lydia's breathing got ragged. Because Marcia's hands were fastened behind her head, her breasts were upraised, like, Lydia informed her, swollen fruit.

Lydia had just begun to sip the nectar of that fruit when Marcia's beeper went off. "Oh, please!" Lydia said, glaring at it as if it were a cobra poised to strike.

Marcia sighed. "It's probably nothing. Now that they've got me on a beeper, they call to ask what they should have for lunch."

Lydia mashed off the beeper, picked up the phone, and dialed Marcia's number at work. Then she nestled the receiver between Marcia's neck and her shoulder. As the phone rang, she returned to Marcia's nipples. "Hey, let me talk to Ted... It's Marcia. Look, he just called me on the beeper, he's gotta be there.... Lydia, for god's sakes... Well, who else would have called? Yeah, I'll hold. Lydia!"

"What's wrong?" Lydia asked impishly.

"I can't think when you're doing that." Marcia twisted on the bed, trying to move away from Lydia's sharp teeth and devilish fingers. This was impossible, since the cuffs gave her very little play, particularly with Lydia lying half across her.

"Ted. What's the trouble?" Lydia tickled her and then ran her tongue in a long wet swoop down Marcia's side. Marcia began laughing. "No, nothing, Ted." She listened for a moment. "Well, I don't think Bruce is scheduled for the Parkers. Judy Inman is. Lydia! Why don't you look on the board? It's your imagination that I keep all this stuff in my head... Lydia, seriously..."

"You know how to make me stop if you really want me to," Lydia said. She licked down Marcia's belly to her pubic hair and nuzzled her chin in the curly, coarse bush.

"But why is he on there for the Parkers? They only want one person. Well, that's the problem. Somebody moved him from the Jekovichs to the Parkers. Whose handwriting is it?" When Lydia's tongue touched her clit, the phone slipped. "Sorry, Ted!" she called. "Lydia, for chrissake—"

Lydia snaked her hand up and resettled the phone. "I already told you what to do."

Marcia had never used a safeword in her life.

"Iceberg," she said. "No, Ted, I'm talking to someone else." Lydia kept sucking on her clit as if it were a popsicle melting in a desert sun. "Lydia!"

"That's not it," Lydia told her.

"What?"

"I said that's not it."

"Ted, I have to call you back. In five, all right? I *know* it's important."

Lydia plucked the receiver away and hung up the phone. "It's ice cube, not iceberg," she said. She was giggling.

"It is not ice cube," Marcia said. She had started to laugh too.

"I'm sorry, but it is."

"Lydia, I made up the damned thing, all right? It's my safeword. It's to protect me."

"Oh, really," Lydia said. "I thought a safeword was for me too. What if I'm not having any fun here, huh?"

It was astonishing, Marcia thought, how quickly a conversation could turn into a fight. Perhaps if they'd gone back to square one, the situation could have been salvaged, but Marcia, with the temperament of an enraged bull, leapt instead to square seventeen. "Is that what you're trying to imply?"

"Oh no, I love fucking a beeper, a phone, Ted, the house, your job..." They glared at each other.

Marcia suspected they were arguing about something entirely different, like the fact that Marcia avoided any promise of commitment beyond next night's dinner. Lydia now raised herself up on one elbow, causing the phone to crash to the floor. "Do you really want to fight about this? Do you realize how stupid it is?"

Flash fury. A million answers spun in Marcia's head. Who started the argument? Who escalated it? Are you calling me stupid? It *was* stupid, a sensible part of her said, but once Marcia was committed to battle, she found it hard to stop before she'd expended every weapon. If she'd had nuclear capability, she would have long ago bombed everyone she knew back into the Stone Age. "I would love to argue about it," she told Lydia in what she considered a mature, measured response.

"Well, I wouldn't," Lydia snapped. Her back was stiff, her usually graceful movements jerky.She hopped off the bed, threw on a pair of jeans and a shirt, and stormed barefoot out of the room.

"Lydia!" Marcia yelled.

She yanked on the wrist cuffs. No give whatsoever. "Lydia!" The front door slammed. "Unbelievable," Marcia said. "Un-fucking-believable." She lay there staring at the salmon-colored ceiling. Lydia admitted the paint job hadn't turned out the way she'd intended, but she resisted Marcia's every effort to change it.

"I have to have something of my own," Lydia had told her. "You can be awfully controlling, you know."

"But you don't like it yourself," Marcia had said reasonably. "How is that my being controlling?" This discussion, Marcia recalled now, had gone nowhere as well. Perhaps she was too controlling. In fact, any doubt remaining in anyone's mind about that conclusion would have to be measured in micromillimeters.

She pictured Ted sitting by the phone, waiting for her to tell him what to do. The idiot had all the information he needed to handle it himself. She sent him a psychic message: figure it out, bozo. When no acknowledgement came back through the ether, she considered kicking apart the bed frame. No, she should just lie here and relax. She remembered Lydia's comment about enjoying being on hold. Nothing to do, nothing to think about. She could practice meditating, she thought. She was always meaning to do that. Sober for fifteen years and she'd meditated maybe four times. Her beeper went off. "You little animal," she told it. She knocked it from the bedside table, swung her hips off the bed, and creamed the bastard with her heel. She sidled back on the bed and lay there. She dreamed of a river flowing to the sea. She lay on her back on the river and floated, surrounded by flowers and singing birds.

She was almost disappointed when she heard the front door open. Then she came to life when she realized it could be Cory. She examined the blankets. She could probably shove the pillow enough with her chin to hide her cuffed hands and pretend to be asleep. He would give plenty of warning before he barged into the bedroom. She was just planning her concealing moves when Lydia poked her head around the door frame. "Hi," she said. They stared at each other. Then Lydia said, "You're smiling."

"I'm reestablishing contact with my higher power. We haven't talked much the last ten or twelve years, so I thought this was a good opportunity to say hi."

Lydia looked suspicious. "How come you're not mad?"

Marcia shrugged. "How could I be when I've found Nirvana?"

"I knew I'd have to let you loose eventually," Lydia told her as she crossed the room and sat on the bed, "but

I was sure that the moment I did you'd strangle me. It's been a difficult ethical decision."

"And?"

"And in keeping with current doctrine, I've decided to choose me. But I did bring you a scone from the Cheese Board which I will feed to you at intervals."

"That's considerate. What if I promise I won't strangle you?"

"Why wouldn't you?"

"Who else would tie me up and leave me to die of starvation?"

"There's that," Lydia agreed. "Marcia, we're sort of tense with each other, wouldn't you say?"

"A little," Marcia admitted. She chewed on a piece of scone Lydia broke off for her. "Delicious. Well, there's way too much happening. I'm at the end of my rope. So to speak."

"It's hard to talk to you when you keep making dumb jokes." Lydia fed her another piece of scone. "Am I part of the too much that's happening?"

"No. You're a relief from the too much."

"Really? I'm trying not to be demanding."

It was bad, Marcia thought, when people told you how free they were letting you be. "That's wonderful," she said insincerely, then reminded herself that lying was a sure death knell to a relationship. So she added, "Of course, there's no better way to be demanding than to assure me you're not being demanding."

Lydia's mouth got tight. "Love is never fair, is it? And don't tell me not to talk of love."

"I would never, ever, tell you not to talk of love," Marcia said. "It's just that I'm trying to go day by day, while you're going year by year."

"I'm going moment to moment if you want to know the truth."

Marcia bit her lower lip. "Come lie down next to me, all right? Let me hold you." Lydia undid the cuffs and curled up in Marcia's arms. "Is there any way to resolve this?"

"Not now," Lydia said. "Now we wait."

"For Godot?"

"For God."

"Well, good, because God and I really did have a nice chat while you were spending the bank at the Cheese Board. God said go for her, Mars."

"Yeah? And what'd you say?"

"I said I'm scared."

"Then what?"

"Then God said fear's real and you can't just wish it away or say it isn't what you're feeling, that you have to accept it if you ever want to go beyond it. And that being honest puts you halfway there."

Lydia said nothing for a moment. Then Marcia felt her smiling against her shoulder. "Thanks for telling me, Marcia. It's so comforting to know God's on my side."

# CHAPTER 10

Sarah ground on the brakes at a yellow light, nearly sending Dale and Marcia through the windshield of her truck. Their calendars had finally executed a merger, so they were on their way, over Dale's groans, to a one-night-a-week dance club in the bowels of downtown Oakland. "Why are they going to let him finish school?" Dale asked, returning to the subject of Billy and his manslaughter plea.

"Isn't that crazy?" Marcia said. "If he's so dangerous that he needs to be locked up, how can they leave him in school?" She wished Sarah had invited her Marine over for dinner; she was as disgruntled as Dale about being dragged out after a packed day at work and at Fairview Street. "And of course if he's not dangerous, then—"

"Punishment," Sarah put in, shifting the gears past Marcia's thigh as the old truck lurched to a start. "They want to punish him whether it makes any sense or not."

"Robert's attorney heard the DA's office used Billy's case as part of their new push to get tough on black-on-black crimes. Robert says he doesn't need our help, thank you."

"Oh, right," Dale groaned. "Robert thinks we have some sort of in with white men?"

"White men seem to think I have an in," Marcia said. It still angered her that the prosecutor had called her to his office to explain the facts of life to her. He had done the same with Robert's attorney, it turned out, but why her? She was a very minor player in this whole incident, not worth anyone's attention except as a character witness.

"They wouldn't be doing this crap to a white kid," Sarah said.

"Even if he were a white kid who'd killed another white," Marcia agreed. "Well, it's all over with now. All but the punishment. All but the medieval part."

Dale was gazing out the window at the dark night. "Yeah, send him up to learn to be a crook."

"He won't. He's too good a kid. But we could have had an Army flyer and instead we get a warehouseman."

Sarah snorted. Hypocritical, Marcia thought, given the Marine. "Who knows which is better, world-wise," Dale said.

"World-wise I don't know," Marcia said. "Billy-wise I do. He should have gone into the military."

They sat silently for a minute, crushed together in the small cab, Marcia twisted against Dale's shoulder so Sarah could operate the gears. Then Dale muttered that going out on a work night was a travesty.

"Every night's a work night," Sarah retorted. All three were smarting under Reba's accelerated pace at Fairview Street. "We're going to see how normal people live—the ones who don't work twelve-hour days."

"I've heard about them," Dale said. "They've got pricks and they're called men."

"Men kill themselves working too," Marcia said in an attempt to be fair.

Both Dale and Sarah made disparaging noises through their teeth, so they dropped that topic and went on to Sarah's love interest. "Her name is Flame," Sarah confided, angling her truck back into traffic after Marcia shouted at her not to make a wrong turn on a one-way street.

Now Dale sounded as if she were being strangled. No wonder the lover had so far remained nameless, Marcia thought. "*Flame*?" Dale finally said, when it became evident that Marcia had decided no comment was best.

Marcia, who sometimes acted as if her sole purpose in life was to defuse loaded situations, adroitly leapt back into the conversation. "She's really a Marine?"

Sarah nodded. "The few, the proud. *Semper fi.*"

"The only real men left in this country are dykes," Dale said, but neither Marcia nor Sarah paid any attention because by then they'd pulled up in front of the club. "How come no one's here?" Marcia asked suspiciously, eyeing all the open parking spaces.

"It's too early," Sarah told her. "It's only ten."

They sighed, thinking that ten was past their bedtime, and then entered the club, which was exactly like an under-decorated bar with a cover charge but no pool table, and nothing to read like fliers or notices stapled on bulletin boards. Instead it deluged its patrons with music so loud people had to scream directly in each other's ears to be understood. Dale hated it at once; Marcia reserved judgment. She wanted to dance, she said, but since no one could hear her she wandered off by herself.

There were three levels to the club, the lowest a sunken dance floor, on which four couples and a single woman wearing loose cotton pants and nothing else gyrated. On the main floor was the bar itself, doing a steady business. Overlooking it all was a steel-railed open mezzanine furnished with tables and chairs from which one could view the action on the other two levels.

Marcia rambled around on the mezzanine for awhile and then descended to find Dale and Sarah at a table on the main floor as far from the speakers as they could get.

"Flame's not here," Dale reported as Marcia joined them.

"Where's Flame?" Marcia shouted in Sarah's ear.

Sarah didn't seem to care. She already had two empty glasses in front of her, and she was working on a third. Meanwhile she was making eyes at two younger women at the table closest to theirs. "Go ask the dark-haired one to dance," Sarah directed Marcia.

"Why?" Marcia wondered.

"'Cause I want the other."

Marcia shook her head and sipped at her Coke. She was annoyed that they only had sodas which meant she had to drink either caffeine or sugar. Dale was staring up at the ceiling. Marcia couldn't figure out why she looked like a rabbit until she realized that Dale had stuffed pieces of napkin in her ears.

"We should have taken two cars," Sarah now shouted at Marcia.

"Why?" Marcia wondered again.

Sarah rolled her eyes at Marcia's stupidity. "In case we want to pick someone up."

Dale came awake for that remark. "That's your domain," she said, indicating the two of them. "I'm married."

Marcia was stung. Didn't Lydia count for something? She bolted some Coke while she pondered Dale's treachery. Then she scooted her chair close to Sarah's. "Maybe you should call Flame," she suggested.

But Sarah hopped up from her chair, holding out her hand to Marcia as she sang an Everly Brothers' tune. "I'm through with romance, I'm through with love... C'mon, pardner, let's dance."

So Marcia stalked down the stairs to dance with Sarah, but she felt more like a washing machine on the spin cycle than Fred Astaire. Sarah, she decided, had entered a crazy second adolescence, smoking like a house in flames and drinking like someone on the slip from hell. She'd lost fifteen pounds in six months and her cheeks were sunken, her eyes dark-rimmed, her lips dry but somehow avaricious at the same time. She was always darting around seeking new prey; she'd only asked Marcia to dance so she could cruise the dance floor.

I'm not like this, Marcia told herself. I'm not looking for someone other than Lydia; in fact, I wasn't looking for anyone, Lydia included. Lydia had burst into her life with the force of a hurricane, and Marcia pictured herself as still trying to crawl out from under the wreckage. Wreckage of what? she asked herself. Yet surely it was significant that she considered Lydia a disruption.

The DJ slid seamlessly from one song to another. Pound pound pound. Sarah had her head thrown back, grinning like a death's mask at the spacy woman with no shirt. Marcia danced more and more woodenly. Twenty minutes more and she'd be petrified. Then a woman her own age with curly hair and an apologetic look stepped in front of her and began moving sinuously, like a cobra, her eyes half-closed. The sheepishness faded from her face as Marcia began copying her. The woman came closer, inviting Marcia to touch her. Marcia found it irresistible, reaching out to draw her nearer, until their clothes and then their flesh was charged with the imprint of the other.

She thought about stripping off the woman's clothes piece by piece—the woman shyly ducking her head with each new revelation—about laying her thumbs under the woman's cheekbones and pressing hard until the woman gasped, about barraging her with an avalanche of whispered questions and accusations until the woman was tongue-tied, helpless, her eyes like those of an animal caught in the headlights.

Top space, sinister, scary, cold, but underneath tuned in to the bottom's every nuance, any tiny motion that might indicate a seepage into something truly frightening, something not wanted, quick pull back into that which heightens, causes the breath to quicken, the skin to flush. It was so intimate, this exchange of psychic information, so often unspoken, intuited, a shred of DNA passing tongue-to-tongue, finger to nipple, hand to cunt. Top and bottom so different, bottom a surrender to being known, a reaming, while the top moves through a maze of clues to light, to knowledge, the bottom risking letting in the top, the top risking coming in, together tipping each other into that stream underneath consciousness where you know without asking. No wonder Lydia wouldn't bottom, Marcia thought—it was antithetical to her whole being. She was an investigator. And she did not let people in, no matter what she claimed.

Why am I dancing with this woman? Marcia asked herself. She glanced around wildly for Sarah, who had hooked up with someone Marcia had never seen, a kid with hair so short she could never be a Marine. How can you stop dancing when the song never ends? Drag your ass off the floor, that's how. She untangled herself from the woman, smiled her own sheepish grin, and waved good-bye. The woman's eyes went stupefied, a pleasurable sight only when those same eyes are about to darken with lust. Marcia wanted to crawl away but instead squared her shoulders and headed back to the bar area, where Dale was slouched over the table, bored, she said, out of her mind.

Marcia decided Sarah should have her fill of the girl with the crewcut and finished her Coke while Dale yelled in her ear about how she'd been given the run-around a week earlier by a lumber company which had made a billing error. "They wanted *me* to call the supervisor, *me* to find out who scheduled the run, *me* to call the truck driver who'd delivered the load. These are their own fucking employees! I told them I hoped the Japanese would be along soon to take them over."

When she started on Ronald Reagan and the national debt, Marcia hopped up to search for Sarah. She was not on the dance floor, nor was Crewcut. Marcia padded around, trying to avoid the woman she'd danced with. Finally she entered the women's room, where she found Sarah plastered up against Crewcut, or more accurately, Crewcut ramming Sarah into a wall, Sarah moaning past Crewcut's ear, which was, Marcia couldn't help noticing, almost purple with exertion.

This is pathetic, Marcia thought. Sarah's twenty-five years older than this woman, and she looks ridiculous, tawdry. You're too old to be making such a spectacle of yourself, Marcia wanted to tell her. Sarah's eyes fluttered open, and, with great presence of mind, she dug into her pockets and handed Marcia the key to her truck. "Good-bye," she mouthed.

Marcia returned to Dale and exhibited the key. Dale uncoiled her long body from the table in a single bound. "Hit the road, Jack," she told Marcia, and they were out the door into the chilly night, where Marcia wondered why it was so important to her to be different from Sarah. Because Sarah's running from herself, she answered. Maybe they were all just chasing rainbows. But goddammit, surely her life didn't need to be constrained to sitting on her porch with Billy and Lucas. When Annie had left, was that the end of life as she'd known it? Life As

Marcia Lived It, The End. I can't take another lousy relationship. I can't.

Dale interrupted her increasingly frantic thoughts. "Do you remember *The Killing of Sister George*?" Dale asked her.

Of course she remembered. They had gone to see it at a little theater right nearby, in downtown Oakland, sitting in the nearly deserted balcony. And although hardly anyone else was in the theater, Marcia thought whoever was must be staring at them, knowing they were dykes because they had come to see this movie about lesbians. Why she had cared about this, with her and Dale looking as they did back then, in workshirts and workboots and short hair and Levi jackets, was anybody's guess. She knew it must have been a long time ago because they were both smoking, and Dale was so mesmerized by the film that she kept dropping burning embers from her hand-rolled cigarettes on her jeans.

They went to the low-priced matinee on three successive days, and at each showing Dale set herself on fire at least once, causing both of them to leap up and pound at her legs with their open palms until they'd put out the burning cloth. "Yes, I remember."

"They were middle-aged," Dale said grimly. "They" were the protagonist and her rival, who eventually absconded with Sister George's younger lover, leaving Sister George to be killed off in her radio soap opera role as she'd already been decimated in real life.

"Well," Marcia said. She felt like pounding her head on the steering wheel.

"I'm sick of this mid-life crisis shit," Dale continued. "In our twenties we hated ourselves because of our classism, and in our thirties we hated ourselves because of our racism, and now that we're finally in our forties and could care less that we're white and middle-class, we discover we have no ethics or values and we were right to despise ourselves all along. It's really a fucking blow."

"I don't recall your hating yourself all that much," Marcia said drily. "I remember you telling me several times in the '70s about how you couldn't help it who'd put the sperm to the egg."

"Oh, good," Dale said. "Now I should hate myself because I never hated myself sufficiently."

# CHAPTER 11

When Marcia pulled up in front of Fairview Street early Saturday morning, country-western music was spilling from the house's windows. Remembering Lucas' comment about the shitkicker's car, Marcia wanted to throw a tarp over her Ranchero. She pulled her shovel from the back and waved at Mrs. Jackson, who was out sweeping her porch, receiving a cool nod in return. Turning the corner to the Key Street side, she shouted a "Hi!" at Mr. Thomas who, besides being the Neighborhood Watch block captain, kept the most meticulous yard she had ever seen, bolting from his house if a kid so much as dropped a gum wrapper on his lawn. Living so close to the drug garage was Thomas' downfall. Now he waved at her and then turned back to pruning the faded blossoms from his perfect roses, a hard commodity to come by in the Bay Area's foggy summer weather.

The twelve-foot-high wall of packing crates hadn't vanished in the night. But all the paving was in, and after Reba's chivvying, Marcia had made a good start on the deck off the dining room. Everything might be as perfect as Mr. Thomas' roses, except that worry was gnawing at Marcia's gut. During that slow week at her house, Marcia had studied a month's worth of real estate sections from three papers and conferred with her own sources. In this case, no news was bad news. Stories of price leaps had disappeared. The weekly count of houses sold at what percentage over last month's sales had also been quietly dropped. Houses that sounded decent in August were still for sale in October.

Underneath the resounding clap of media silence, Marcia could hear drums in the night, pounding recession, the deficit, real estate crash in the East. When the agents had said, "It can't go on like this forever" a year ago, they'd been laughing, ebullient. Now there was a thin edge of fear behind the words. Suddenly everyone remembered what they'd foretold in 1986, that prices couldn't just keep rising into the stratosphere.

Marcia tried to calm herself as she leaned over to position a dark-stemmed salvia whose red flowers would provide a counterpoint to the gray and purple of Spanish lavender. Reba had already been making noises about speeding things up. She'd intimated at their last meeting that they should sell in December, which every sane person knew was the worst time of the year. Marcia glanced around the yard, assessing how much she could accomplish in two months. Forget it, she told herself. If she were going to enjoy this at all, she needed to block out the pressure. Put her worries on the back burner. But it was hard not to reminisce about Saturdays in the past, lazing out on her porch with Billy, pre-murder rap, pre-Fairview Street—but not pre-Lydia.

Why *had* she been avoiding Lydia these past couple weeks? Letting past disasters with Annie sour her present with Lydia was nothing more than a coward's way of ducking chances. Nobody gets a guarantee. Instead of lamenting the universe's policy of no warranty and no returns, she should be kicking up her heels. Lydia was the first person she'd met in ages she could really talk to. Even better, Marcia thought, brushing sweat from her forehead as she knocked a rose bush from its container, she and Lydia could be quiet together. Marcia set great store by this indicator. If she couldn't be at peace with someone, no matter how smitten she was, she knew the relationship wouldn't work. Had she ever been at peace with Annie? Ever?

After Marcia had made her announcement about visiting her own life, Lydia had not phoned her, letting Marcia initiate contact. She was probably afraid of being too coercive or demanding, none of which meant, Marcia knew, that they weren't thinking of each other every minute anyway. Marcia had lately noticed that Lydia never mentioned her women lovers before Marcia but only compared Marcia to her ex-husband Jeff. Omissions can be the most telling, Marcia thought, using the shovel handle to lever herself to her feet. Then she swung around to see Lydia crossing the new flagstone path. "Oh, Marcia!" her love greeted her.

And of course she *was* her love, Marcia thought with wonder, then amazement at her own blindness. How can I think of you every minute and not know that I love you? "Lydia, I'm so glad you dropped by—"

But Lydia was shaking her head. "You're filthy!" she accused. "And you forgot, didn't you?"

Lydia's lips had shrunk dangerously thin. At least, Marcia thought nervously, she was mad and not tearful. Marcia glanced down at her dirt-stained jeans, her sweaty T-shirt, her hands black with grime. She could only imagine what her face looked like since she had spent the first half-hour ripping dusty vines from the wall of crates. "Oh, Jesus!" Marcia said. "We're going to Chez Panisse for lunch!" How could she have forgotten? Lydia had reminded her when Marcia had finally called this morning.

"You blew it," Dale cruised over to say helpfully. Sarah came out on the ramp, gazed at Lydia, and then disappeared back into the house, no doubt to alert the rest that Lydia the mystery woman had arrived. Lydia, ignoring all this byplay, said, "Go do something to yourself, Mars. Our reservations are in fifteen minutes."

Dale gave Marcia a wink while Marcia flushed red. "Ah—Dale, introduce Lydia to everybody, okay?" She dashed up the ramp past Reba, Sarah, and Polly, who were now gathering politely, waiting to be noticed. Luckily Sarah had reconnected the water to the upstairs bathroom. Marcia tore off her clothes, jumped in the shower, ran her fingers through her hair, scrubbed her face with the palms of her hands, and toweled off with her filthy T-shirt. "Dale!" she yelled out the window. When Dale appeared, she said, "Give me your shirt."

"It's not much better than yours," Dale protested, though she began unhooking her overalls.

"It is now," Marcia said, tossing her the soaking wet garment.

"Charming." They exchanged shirts, Dale with distaste, and then clattered down the steps to meet Lydia in the hallway, who examined Marcia critically before concluding, "Somewhat of an improvement. Now come on. We can take your car if you want."

"Bye, gals," Marcia said. "Thanks, Dale."

Ten minutes later they were sitting in the upstairs dining room at Chez Panisse, examining their menus. "I'm really sorry," Marcia said, tearing herself away from promises of grilled lamb chops with rosemary and pomegranate glaze or baked brie with herbs. Lydia had hardly spoken on the drive to the restaurant.

Lydia looked up, her eyes guarded. She was hurt, that much was clear. "I was just surprised," she said neutrally.

Even Marcia, who considered herself a devotee to the arts of denial and subterfuge, could not swallow this. "Honey, look—"

But Lydia waved off her excuses with a quick hand, her eyebrows mounded in a V of annoyance. The man at the next table looked up from his *New York Times* long enough to glare at Marcia balefully. When the waiter came Marcia ordered the lamb chops, figuring she needed sustenance. Lydia opted for some kind of white fish with lime salsa. She also wanted a salad with enoki mushrooms and the baked brie. "Appetizers," she informed both Marcia and the waiter. When she ordered a bottle of wine which cost seventeen dollars, Marcia wondered if Lydia had decided this was to be a good-bye lunch. She swallowed hard. If only she weren't such an idiot. But what control did she have over her unconscious? She hadn't forgotten on purpose.

The waiter left, and Lydia smiled at Marcia. "At least we can eat well," she said.

That could mean anything. "At least," Marcia agreed. They sat in a state of suspended animation until the flower-strewn brie hit the table, when amusement surplanted anxiety. Lydia insisted Marcia try a blue pansy, so Marcia insisted Lydia try a yellow one. They began picking through other flowers, handing each other half-eaten petals, proclaiming each one the best yet. Finally they were feeding each other the sloppy brie and then the enoki mushrooms one by one. By the time the main courses arrived they couldn't keep their hands off one another and they were rubbing legs under the table. "Come sit over here," Marcia said. "Then I can reach you better."

"It might be dangerous," Lydia demurred.

"Only if you resist." The man with the *New York Times* liked this remark.

Lydia came to sit on Marcia's side and rubbed her arm against Marcia's. "You're so commanding today," she said as Marcia fed her a piece of lamb. "Changing sides?"

"Butch on the streets, bottom in the sheets," Marcia told her. "But if you're interested, I'm very switchable."

"You are? I didn't know that."

"I love to top," Marcia said.

"Oh." Lydia looked surprised and not happy. "Well." She applied herself to her fish for a moment while Marcia watched her. She didn't look up so Marcia stole her hand into Lydia's lap, laying her palm open invitingly until Lydia dropped her free hand down to squeeze Marcia's. "Do you think this is a problem?" Lydia asked her plate, her hand clutching Marcia for support. "I just never liked it. Is that bad? Sometimes I feel like I'm avoiding something."

Marcia smiled. "Honey, it's fine. Some people are one, some another, some both. It doesn't really matter much anyway. It's just opposite ends of the same thing. Whatever we're doing we're doing together. Here, have some more lamb."

"You have fish." Lydia was keeping her hand in Marcia's.

"I hate to tell you this, but I'm not very fond of fish." She grinned at Lydia. "Do you think that's a problem?"

When they walked out of the restaurant, they had to step around three street people who had set up camp in the middle of the sidewalk. Two of them were refugees from their usual panhandling stations outside the espresso bar across the street, guys whom Marcia called her coffee klatsch pals because she often sat on the bench with them and chatted while she drank her cappuccino. Now she handed them each a dollar bill and introduced them to Lydia. Lydia seemed disconcerted at being presented to two men who had draped their sleeping bags against Chez Panisse's fence, so after smiling a greeting, she strolled off to stare in the window of a dress store. As Marcia prepared to join her, another man showed up, big as a football player and huddled in a brown poncho as woolly as his long curly hair. Marcia reached again into her pocket, pulled out a dollar, and watched him come towards her, shambling like a grizzly bear. When he saw her looking at him, his face lit up, warmth flooding into his pale blue eyes, and she smiled at him. He seemed astounded by her. "Hey!" he said, opening his big bear arms wide. "Give me a hug. Give me a hug!"

She was suddenly frightened and shrank away from him. He was so enormous, his need bigger yet. "No," she told him. "No, please leave me alone."

"He won't hurt you," one of her coffee buddies reassured her.

The bear-man stopped, his shoulders drooping with disappointment. "I'm not bothering you. I won't bother you."

"It's all right, I'm sorry," Marcia said. She waved a shaken good-bye and then walked the few paces to the dress store. Lydia fell into step and they continued on to the car, Lydia slightly tipsy, carrying her corked bottle of wine. Marcia unlocked the passenger side of the Ranchero, opened the door for Lydia, and then crossed to her own side, slipped into the seat, and sat there, her chin resting on the steering wheel, staring sightlessly through the cracked windshield.

"Marcia," Lydia said. "What is wrong with you?"

"That guy," Marcia said. "All he wanted was a hug." She explained what had happened. "Why would someone wanting a hug scare me? That's really fucked."

"Oh, Marcia! Don't wreck things."

"Wreck things? Look, we're coming out of there after eating pansies, for chrissakes—"

"We seem to be having trouble today," Lydia said.

"Why?" Marcia flashed. "Because I feel bad about the homeless and you won't bottom?"

"Because you forgot our lunch when it was something really special to me and now we can't even have fun without you attaching all kinds of doom and gloom meanings to everything." Lydia bit her lower lip, blinking anxiously at Marcia. "Maybe we really aren't very well-suited to each other." After she said it she sat there waiting for the Golden Gate Bridge to fall on her head.

Marcia, the strong-man, knew she was supposed to hold up the bridge with a single finger. She was supposed to leap into the breach with a dozen reasons why they were entirely perfect for each other, but she couldn't make herself do it. Instead a roaring began inside, as if she were off skimming waves, but she knew those waves happened only when she was telling someone she couldn't be what that someone wanted or needed.

But Lydia had miraculously survived, was in fact stroking Marcia's palm with her warm, strong fingers. "Marcia, you're so far away, baby."

Marcia looked at her in astonishment. I didn't kill you? You didn't die? The warmth from Lydia's flesh sent ripples of pleasure through Marcia's body, and she couldn't stop grinning. She turned to Lydia, put her arms around Lydia's waist, and drew her close. "I'm here," she told her. Lydia rested her cheek against Marcia's collarbone and Marcia felt caressed, not only by Lydia, but by air so soft and fresh it sparkled.

They had driven to Lydia's, not wanting to go back to Fairview Street to pick up Lydia's Volvo. "Cory won't be home for awhile," Lydia said.

"Great," Marcia told her. She was feeling slightly guilty about Fairview Street—after all, at least according to Reba she was supposed to be working all weekend—but she decided to throw it aside. As she trailed after Lydia to the bedroom, however, she wasn't certain she wanted to make love. Shouldn't they talk about intimacy and how their bodies fit together but sometimes their minds gave them trouble? Lydia was turning down her comforter to reveal wine-red satin sheets. "Do you like my sheets, honey?"

"Not really," Marcia admitted. "I'm kind of old-fashioned."

Lydia peered at her. "Is that how you think of yourself?" She shook her head. "Let's say I have a very different image of you."

Marcia wanted to protest but didn't know what to say. They were strangers, she thought. Lydia has burgundy sheets and a salmon ceiling and she's a scientist. She tried to form a picture of herself but she couldn't get it to stop moving long enough to bring it into focus. Since she'd met Lydia and started the damned house, she felt exhausted by the effort of following the traces of her own footsteps, trying to catch up with herself before she got so far ahead she'd disappear entirely. She swallowed. "I like flannel."

Lydia smiled. "Really. My sex fiend has a thing for flannel." She opened her dresser drawer, pulled out a set of fuzzy blue sheets, and tossed them on the bed. "Put 'em on, babe. And then take off your clothes. You have a date with my belt."

Marcia performed as directed while Lydia watched her, then held out her wrists so Lydia could click on the handcuffs. "You know how you've screwed up," Lydia said.

Marcia mumbled something. She did know how she'd screwed up, and she didn't want to think about that now. The Marcia who'd forgotten their date was terrified and a fuck-up and spent a lot of time kidding herself that she knew what was going on when she couldn't even see what was in front of her face. "Ah, Lydia—"

"What, baby?"

"Maybe—" The thing about doing S/M around real things, Marcia thought, was that you had to be ready to give up the fear or the anger, to eroticize it, thereby letting it go. So wasn't she ready to give up her fear, for god's sakes? Besides, Lydia was really getting into it, her eyes misty and sensuous, and she kept stroking Marcia's shoulders as if she could make her purr.

"Maybe what, hon? You want something special?"

"No," Marcia croaked, knowing she needed to say something now and unable to do it.

"Then c'mere." Lydia yanked on the links connecting Marcia's wrists and pulled her forward, kissing her gently, lolling her tongue in Marcia's mouth, then licking the side of her cheek all the way up to tickle her ear lobe. After a moment or two Marcia relaxed, letting herself be immersed in Lydia's scent, mouthing the soft skin at Lydia's throat, then the puckery skin around her nipples. When Lydia began pushing her thumb hard into Marcia's jawbone, Marcia slithered across the fresh flannel sheets. Lydia threw her leg across Marcia's to pin her to the mattress; it would work as long as Marcia allowed it.

"You feel so good," Lydia said. "How are you doing?"

"I'm all right," Marcia breathed. More than anything she wanted to be all right. If only Lydia hadn't drunk so much wine at lunch. Lydia was off somewhere on her own, and Marcia needed her, wanted her to know Marcia was in a jumble. Lydia began scratching Marcia's back, which Marcia loved, but not today, today it felt like Lydia was a tiger. I *like* tigers, Marcia thought. Then she threw off Lydia's restraining leg and flipped on her side, raising her cuffed hands in front of her face.

"What's going on?" Lydia asked. "You trying to hide from me?" Get it together, Marcia told herself, wanting it to be perfect for them, but her betrayal of their relationship was too real. To punish the Marcia that had fucked up made her present, and Marcia-in-love discovered with a spasm of disappointment that there was surprisingly little difference between the bad Marcia and the good; at base she was still ambivalent and frightened. This isn't going to work, Marcia thought frantically. It's too confused, too muddled. When Lydia dragged her out of her self-made cave by her hair, batted away her hands, and slapped her cheek, Marcia started sobbing.

Lydia stared at her in astonishment, then caught her by the shoulders and jerked her close, in her anxiety jamming the bridge of Marcia's nose against her collarbone, which hurt Marcia a lot more than the slap had. Marcia edged her cuffed hands up between them as if she were separating the glued flap of an envelope. Once she got her nose free, she could hear again. Lydia was asking, "Honey, what's wrong? Why are you crying?" in a voice verging on panic.

"Because—" Marcia tried to get her breath. "Because of how you must hate me."

"Hate you? I love you." It was the first time Lydia had said it. Marcia was feeling worse by the minute. "How could you think I hate you?"

She couldn't imagine how to explain. "I—I—"

"Baby, you're not crying because I slapped you, are you? I mean, you can't think I hate you—"

"No. I mean, yes, sort of. Sometimes the lines get all mooshed together. Like you're punishing me for being a rat, and we both know it's a game, I'm not really a rat, except I am. I'm a lousy, rotten rat. The reason I forgot our date is that on some level I can't handle our being together."

Lydia became very still. Marcia could hear her breathing slow to almost nothing, as if she were putting herself on ice to wait for a time when she could thaw out later, when what Marcia said wouldn't hurt so much.

"Tell me what you can't handle," Lydia said softly.

Marcia shivered, and Lydia drew the comforter up to cover them. "I'm afraid. Afraid you'll like me, afraid you'll get sick of me. I'm afraid I'll fuck you over, afraid we'll compromise in ways that are bad for us." Marcia sighed, then decided to go for broke. "I'm afraid I won't know who I am anymore, that I'll be different. It's like I have a new family with you and Cory, a new job with the house, and Billy's gone—everything's crazy."

Lydia was quiet for awhile. Then she said, "But nobody stays the same. Change means you're alive. Life *is* change."

Marcia closed her eyes. "Maybe I don't like life then."

Lydia lay next to her, pulling her close. It felt so wonderful to lie against Lydia that Marcia couldn't believe she wouldn't commit herself to anything this woman wanted.

Then Lydia said, "You've told me what you're afraid of. You haven't told me *why* you're afraid."

"I don't know. How do we really know why we're afraid?"

"Is it because of Annie? Is it you? Or me?" Lydia was smiling at her now. Then she leaned forward to nuzzle Marcia's cheek. "What's wrong, honey? Don't you want a wife?"

Marcia laughed. "To think you agreed to recreational sex. Why did you anyway?"

"I figured once I got you into bed you'd be hooked. But you're proving a harder fish to land than I expected. I'm not giving up though."

"God, what a manipulator! Here I am, being really honest—"

"Oh, oh, the hapless victim. I don't think you know how to be honest."

"Do tell."

"You're getting real smart-alecky, Mars."

"You gonna do something about it?"

"I will as long as you promise not to start crying again. Or only cry when I want you to, at least."

"I promise. Now that Miss Hidden Agenda has spill-ed—"

Then she stopped talking because Lydia had pasted her mouth over hers.

# CHAPTER 12

Marcia threw herself down in front of the TV to watch
the World Series pre-game show. She was wearing her
Giants T-shirt, and in a moment she would retrieve her
Giants cap from its hallowed spot on her living room
bookcase. She was watching the game alone because
Lydia and Cory were both A's fans and she didn't think
she could stand their fake solicitude if the A's blew the
Giants out one more time. Lydia thought watching the
games together was a fine test of character, but Marcia
pointed out it wasn't Lydia's equanimity that was under
scrutiny. Furthermore, after the drama of the weekend
and seven-hour days at work as well as three at the house,
Marcia felt she had so little strength of character in re-
serve she shouldn't squander any on consorting with the
enemy. Nevertheless, she did wish she had company.
She'd made a big bowl of popcorn, far too much for her
to eat. If Lucas dropped by, she decided, she would let
him in, but not Billy, because Billy was really obnoxious
about the A's.

The chair on which she was sitting rocked to one side,
dumping half the popcorn in her lap. Earthquake. A hand-
painted plate on the rail above her head flipped forward

to settle like a bird on the couch. She had risen without knowing it, showering popcorn to the floor. Now her shoulders loosened as it subsided. She had an instant to think, butter on my jeans, and then her floor began rippling as if she were standing on the surface of the ocean, and the TV went black. She burst out the front door and scrambled down the steps, hanging onto the bannister while she took the steps three at a time, low to the ground. The telephone poles across the street were not swaying in unison, but in opposition, so that the lines would alternately grow so taut she was certain they would snap, and then an instant later droop nearly to the ground. Her stomach got queasy as she watched the street begin to rise and fall in waves. A car down the block levitated up on one swell to land halfway across the sidewalk. The unsupported part of Mrs. Kingston's chimney collapsed brick by brick. The four art students who lived directly across the street poured out of their house, saw the telephone lines whipping around, and tried to funnel back in, but the two behind kept shoving the two in front. Then it stopped.

The students, who had been about to commit mayhem an instant before, laughed. "That was a big one," Marcia heard.

She looked over to Robert's house, but no one appeared to be home. Walking tentatively, as if the ground might open up to swallow her, she let herself in Robert's gate, went to the back, and peeked in the kitchen window. The stove was in place, and she couldn't see anything amiss besides some items lying on the floor, which apparently had fallen out of a cupboard. Then she retraced her steps and checked her own house, inside and out. All this she had done in an anxious haze, where everything was crystal-clear for that moment but forgotten the next. Had she checked her stove? She did it again. Robert's? She went back over and looked through Robert's window, then paced between the two houses like a sentry on duty, thinking only of Lydia. She wanted to see Lydia. Did she have to stay here to guard? Was there something else she should do? Finally she couldn't bear it any longer and hopped in her car to drive up to Berkeley. At the last second, as she was passing by Fairview on Martin Luther King, she jerked the wheel left.

The porch had half-collapsed at the front and right rear corner, and the weight of it was pulling the front windows out of plumb, so that gaps showed around the frames. One window and its frame had fallen out on the dead lawn, and there was broken glass everywhere.

Marcia went around to the back and entered through the ramp. The framing for the double wall that would separate the two kitchens was still standing, but a portion of the ceiling above it had crumpled. In fact, much of the downstairs plaster was now lying all over the floor. On the second floor, a similar scene greeted her. An enormous section of the upstairs ceiling was down, littering the hallway.

Marcia walked numbly down the stairs. She ran into Dale at the bottom. Dale turned her palms up and then burst into tears. Marcia threw her arms around her and held her, thinking that it was the only time that she had ever seen Dale cry. She rocked her back and forth for a few minutes and then said, "Dale."

"I know," Dale gasped. "Go on. See about Lydia. Polly and Reba will be here in a second. They already called."

Marcia kissed Dale's cheek and trotted through the kitchen and down the ramp. She scooted out to the Ranchero and took off. As she drove to North Berkeley, she passed a huge column of jet-black smoke. A couple radio stations were functioning but they seemed to know no more than she did. One said the main library was in flames. Another said the fire was on the campus. Marcia could see that part wasn't true. The Marina District in San Francisco was burning, though, everyone agreed on that.

Marcia tromped on the accelerator and gunned the car up Euclid. She left her car blocking Lydia's Volvo and dashed up the steps. Lydia opened the door and hauled her inside. "Thank god you're here!"

She seemed to be hyperventilating. "Marcia, I don't know where Cory is!"

"Where's he supposed to be?"

She apparently hadn't thought of that. "He was going to watch the game at a friend's house." Lydia ran to the phone. Marcia stayed out on the porch with Lydia's binoculars. She watched the fire in downtown Berkeley, which seemed to be putting out tremendous amounts of smoke but not spreading. The fire in San Francisco was much worse, and in less than an hour darkness would fall. "I can't get through," Lydia reported. "There's a dial tone, but it won't do anything."

"OK," Marcia said. "You know where the friend lives?"

"I have an address." They took the Ranchero, though it lugged badly on the hills, and drove up Spruce clear to the top. Then they had to backtrack along narrow, twisting roads before they found the friend's house. Cory was there, embarrassed that his mother had come to collect him. He trundled out to the car, a tall, handsome kid with Lydia's bone structure and what had to be his father's height. "Can't I stay?" he asked, poking his head in the window. "Hi, Marcia. They're just starting to get stuff on TV now. Mom, the Bay Bridge fell in!"

Marcia had already heard that on the radio. The helicopter traffic reporters were swooping around the bay, finding damage.

"The buses won't be running," Lydia said.

"I can walk. It's only twenty minutes."

"All right, honey." She kissed him. Marcia raised her index finger good-bye and pulled away from the curb. "I think he'll be safer up here," Lydia explained in a shaky voice. "If there's a big fire, he can go into the park. He could get away."

Marcia took her hand. "He's OK," she said. "All of us are all right." Ten minutes later she watched the first pictures come in of the collapsed Cypress structure. The reporters kept talking about cars falling off the top of the accordioned freeway. "They don't know there's a whole other deck underneath!" Marcia cried. "Lydia! Come here and see this!" Tears started rolling down her cheeks as Lydia came out of the kitchen and Marcia pointed wordlessly at the screen. Smoke billowed out from the sandwiched section. Marcia closed her eyes. When she opened them the helicopter had merely gone on another few hundred feet. Two miles of buckled roadway, the voice was saying. A truck was teetering from the upper deck.

"We should go down there," Marcia said. "We should go down and help. Those people are trapped in there."

Lydia had remained standing, mesmerized by the television. Now her eyes widened in panic, sudden as the shutter of a camera. "Marcia, no. Please. I—I don't want to leave. I'm scared to leave. Cory will come home. The fire downtown...what if it comes up here? What if something else catches on fire?" Her voice was rising. Marcia stood up. "Marcia—"

"No, no, I'm not going," Marcia hastened to reassure her. "I just got up to hold you. It's all right. We'll stay here. We'll make sure the fire doesn't come. I think they've nearly got it out anyway."

When Cory came home, Marcia and Lydia were sitting in front of the TV. Marcia fixed him a sandwich, and he ate it while they discussed whether there would be school in the morning. The television was noncommittal on the subject, as least as far as Berkeley was concerned. Lydia had already been called by her department chairman. Nothing at UC Berkeley was cancelled, but she wanted Marcia and Cory to hole up in the house while she was gone. In fact, she didn't want either of them to set foot out the door. "I'm going to have to leave really early," Marcia told her gently. She hadn't mentioned Fairview Street yet.

Lydia shook her head over and over, as if by sheer willpower she could make Marcia take back what she'd said. "Because of your house?"

Marcia squeezed Lydia's hand. "No. Because of work. This is catering hell. We had all these World Series parties. Now they're off. I've got to unschedule everything, and then the problem is not knowing when it'll start up again. Day after tomorrow? Next week? Next month? Maybe people will cancel entirely. I almost hope they do."

Finally they all went to bed. Marcia and Lydia lay awake side by side, not speaking, for what seemed like hours. One aftershock made Lydia bolt out of bed. She came back under the covers and lay there rigidly. After awhile she said, "Marcia, what are you thinking about?"

Marcia shook her head. "The house."

"Was it bad?"

"It was disastrous."

"I'm sorry."

Marcia chuckled. "My dad always said I should get into real estate." Marcia had grown up in the marijuana hothouse of Mill Valley, her years at Tamalpais High lost shepherding giggly, stoned friends around as she downed six-pack after six-pack. After she'd graduated, her parents had cashed in their equity and moved to Seattle, though she heard from them most frequently via postcards stamped Curacao or Sitka. "Buy houses," her father told her. "Then you can spend your golden years cruising."

"Cruising?" Lydia yelped with delight, relaxing for a moment from her earthquake-trauma.

"I can never tell if he gets it," Marcia said. "But the thing is, they let their real estate plum ripen while they were living their lives. I'm supposed to compress thirty years into six months—or three, according to Reba the tyrant."

"And then there are little difficulties."

"Like the house falling down."

"Marcia!"

"It was just the porch." She sighed, rubbing Lydia's shoulders and back, trying to get the muscles to loosen. Lydia pressed against her. "Put your arms around me," Lydia said. "I need to feel you."

Marcia pulled her close, kissing the spot on her backbone that Lydia most often wanted scratched. She had just begun to slip off when she heard Lydia say, "Sometime we really should talk."

Marcia knew she meant "about us."

"You're right," she said, but she closed her eyes and nuzzled her face into the smoothness of Lydia's skin. She lay wide awake until she heard Lydia's breathing change. Then she rose up, kissed Lydia's cheek and settled down again, curling herself against Lydia's back. I love you, she thought. She didn't say it. She was a thief in the night.


Marcia arrived at Fairview Street at six-thirty the next morning, after reassuring an anxious Lydia she would return at six that evening on the dot. She wandered from floor to floor, wondering if she should clean things up or do something more constructive. She decided to measure the window frames that had come out of plumb.

It took her two windows before she realized the frames weren't the problem, the house was. She put away her pad of paper, got a garbage bag from the kitchen, and climbed the steps to start picking up fallen plaster. A few minutes later she wandered back downstairs to stare at the front porch. What the hell were they going to do about it?

Reba came in the back entrance. "Hi."

"Hi." By an unspoken pact, they drifted off to different parts of the house. After awhile they swept back to the kitchen, as if caught in a tide, nodded at each other, and then swam out again beyond the breakers. Dale and Sarah arrived during their second tour back to the kitchen. They all greeted each other. They all went away. They all came back.

"I'm not getting very far," Dale said at eight-thirty. Polly had arrived with the thermoses from her Peet's run, giving them a reason to stop roaming around.

"It's shock," Polly opined.

"What do you mean?" Dale asked.

"I heard it on the radio. Unfocused, unable to order priorities, inability to get things accomplished. Every task seems to have equal weight. Nothing seems important. Shock."

"That's interesting," Sarah said.

No one else responded.

Marcia thought they were in too much shock to care. "We could have the meeting we didn't have last night," she suggested. "But we have to do it fast. I've gotta get to work."

"Meet now?" Polly goggled.

"Then we don't have to do it tonight," Marcia amplified. Last night's meeting had been delayed because Marcia had insisted she had to help the Giants, down two games to none, win the third game of the series in person. She hadn't mentioned the possibility that their rehab group might meet tonight to Lydia, fearing hysterics.

"Good idea," Carol said. "I have a topic. What to do. I have a solution. Do a Bronx."

Everyone sat there blinking stupidly. "A Bronx?" Reba finally queried.

Carol made a violent scything motion with her hand. Marcia, who was sitting closest, jumped back nervously. Carol looked at her with disdain while Marcia glanced at Dale for moral support. The few lines in Dale's face had deepened like the new fissures in the earth. Carol's nuts, her eyes told Marcia.

"Burn," Carol expanded. "How much is our fire insurance?"

"One-forty," Polly reported. "We were going to raise it as we went—"

"So we lose some labor. Most labor. Nearly all. But we get back our money and get free of this place. We're out."

They sat, stunned. It was amazingly quiet in the world around them. Most people were staying home from work, and some, no doubt, were afraid to leave their houses at all. The serenity of the day—engendered by the awesome force which had reordered their everyday life—made what Carol suggested obscene. Marcia imagined the sheer noise of the spectacle, the flames leaping into the sky, rafters falling two stories to crash through the street level floor, the whoosh as fire engulfed room after room, the confusion of the pigeons who still roosted on the ornaments, the fear of elderly Mrs. Jackson next door. She didn't think anyone—human, animal, or bird—could bear it. She was surprised, in fact, by her own reaction to the crippling of the Bay Bridge. What was the Bay Bridge to her? Yet its fallen platform was profoundly disturbing in a way she didn't understand, as if her own emotional underpinnings were somehow linked with these concrete and steel structures that she had, if anything, scorned in a hippie-dippy, back-to-the-earth way.

Far worse was the collapse of the Cypress freeway, which was so devastating she could hardly stand to think about it, yet it was hard to think of anything else.

We're already reeling from destruction, she thought; in fifteen seconds we've had enough to last us a lifetime. For us to purposely destroy this house for our own gain would be...would be—she couldn't imagine anything horrible enough. "No," she said.

Reba looked at her. "No? Just that? You were the one who was so against buying the house."

That seemed so irrelevant she didn't know how to respond to it. "Look, what gives us the right to burn down this house? When we first got it, I thought it was so pathetic, like it wanted to collapse. Well, it's still standing. It survived a seven point earthquake with half its interior walls torn out. Who are we to decide it needs a coup de grace because it happens to suit us?" She shook her head. "Not to mention, of course, the illegality and *conventional* immorality."

"Oh no," Carol said sarcastically. "Instead in *unconventional* but *typical* dyke fashion we'll talk about the house's spirit and how we should nurture it."

"But we won't bring up preservation," Sarah snapped. "Or accountability. Or how it would affect the neighborhood to lose one of its landmarks. God forbid that we should think ourselves responsible for something outside our own concerns."

"I want a vote," Dale interrupted, before everybody started yelling at each other. "Burn or no burn, yes or no."

"What about a debate?" Polly asked.

"I vote no," Marcia said.

"One no," Dale reported. "I don't want a debate. I don't want to talk about it at all."

"What if we tie?" Reba asked. "Let's see if we do," Dale said. "I vote no. Two no's."

Reba glared at her. "I vote yes."

Carol. "Yes."

"I vote no," Sarah said.

Everyone looked at Polly, who first peered up at the ceiling as if the answer were written in the sagging plaster, then stared right at Reba as she said, "I vote no." Reba began to puff up like an enraged cobra, and Polly's voice got wheedly fast. "I'm sorry, honey. I just don't think it's fair."

"Fair to who?" Reba exploded.

"The house. Us. We don't know what will happen. Maybe it won't be so bad, maybe it will. But we have to live with what we do, we can't do stuff we disagree with just because we think it'll help us in the future. Besides..."

she shivered. "We're all shaky. I just don't think I could take it emotionally."

"So that's that," Dale said. "Let's go to work."

Marcia had to leave to get to her job. Dale walked her out to the Ranchero. "Is Lydia all right?"

"She's pretty freaked. Even though she had to go to work, she wanted me and Cory to sit by the woodstove all day. I promised her I'd be back early."

Dale nodded, then turned around and looked at the house. "Guess we're stuck with it."

"Guess so," Marcia said. "Next time don't say it can't get worse."

Dale nodded slowly. "I did say that, didn't I? There ain't nothin' like a forty-year-old fool."

After all her anxiety during the night, there was little for Marcia to do at her job besides pick up the pieces. Party-givers were cancelling their events right and left. Marcia spent a couple hours contacting employees and food and drink suppliers. Then she drummed her fingers on her desk for a solid minute, dialed a number, and listened to the ringing. When Annie answered in her best raspy bottom-of-the-well, pickled-olive-in-the-martini voice, Marcia hung up gently and closed her eyes. You didn't stop caring about people. That was the problem. People stuck with you, kept on after you, like an amputated limb that still hurts...

How have I let myself become this vulnerable? And now fear was all around her, a solid sea that had risen up to engulf everyone. People moved like zombies but their eyes shone with a strange intensity, as if the real them was trapped inside a nonresponsive body and they were desperately trying to communicate their panic. Fear had leapt out of the box and become universal. Everyone else's anxiety seemed to amplify her own, until she only wanted to crawl into a cave and cover up her head.

But dark as they were, caves didn't erase caring. She hadn't even managed to expunge Annie from her life. Did she expect Lydia would withdraw gracefully? Lydia needed her. Marcia couldn't figure out how that'd happened, but she suspected that Lydia had understood more than

Marcia had all along. No matter how new it was, she did love Lydia, was already part of her. As much as Lydia needed her, she needed Lydia and the locus of warmth and family she felt with her. It just is, she told herself. Maybe you didn't mean it to be, but it already is.

When she got back a little after five, Lydia was making spaghetti sauce. She turned to Marcia, wooden spoon raised in the air. If everyone else's eyes were bright, Lydia's were searing. "I don't like the aftershocks," she confessed. "They scare me."

Marcia kissed her. "I know. It's really disconcerting."

"Do you think it will happen again?"

"Yes. But not for awhile." Marcia realized she hadn't eaten anything all day. She reached out for a piece of baguette. "They baked?"

"Yeah. In the East Bay. I heard on the radio that the restaurants in the City are really upset because they can't get their bread. Almost all the bakeries are over here now." She paused. "This is hard, Marcia."

"What, baby?" The baguette tasted like heaven.

"I feel like I can't let you out of my sight." She put the spoon down and stood in front of the stove, looking at Marcia with her burning eyes. "I know that's bad. I know I'm supposed to act aloof so you'll feel safe. I was trying to do that before, but I can't do it now. I'm surprised myself at how much I need you to be here."

Marcia got up from the table and crossed over to Lydia so she could hold her. "No games," she said as she massaged the steel hardness of Lydia's shoulders. "We don't have to do that. You don't think my being afraid is a game, do you?" She almost hadn't said it, so weary unto death was she of her own fear, but she wanted to know.

"No, I know it's not. I know you're telling me the truth. I just don't understand why." She hesitated as Marcia moved her fingers up to the back of her neck. "I never thought something could throw me like this. It makes me be exactly the way I hate, clingy and tearful. It's like the earth shifted and I don't know where I am unless I'm holding your hand."

"Well, the earth *did* shift. But you'll feel better soon, and then you'll wonder who this jerk is that's hanging around your house."

"Don't say that."

"I'm sorry," she said. "Look, honey, let's not sit in front of the tube tonight watching earthquake news, okay? I think that makes it worse."

But Lydia was unable to settle down, alternately pacing or being strangely passive and acquiescent. When a big truck rumbled down Euclid, she practically shot out of her chair. Their only animated discussion was about the earthquake kits Lydia was making for them to carry in their cars and keep in their houses.

Lydia wondered what Marcia would think about her buying Cory an old car. "To carry his earthquake kit in?" Marcia asked.

"Well, he can't take it on his bike."

"Lydia, you worry way too much about Cory. The kid's a survivor."

"You hardly know him," Lydia protested.

"I know enough for that. I can tell things about people."

Lydia looked at her and nodded. "You're right. So then how can you be frightened of me?"

Marcia couldn't answer that beyond the obvious: it wasn't really Lydia she was afraid of. And Lydia was too skittish to concentrate on a subject for more than a few minutes, so they didn't get much further. Marcia was relieved when Cory got home and they finally went to bed.

They copied the same nervous pattern the next night, though after that first evening, Marcia thought they might as well watch the endless reports on the news. When Marcia awoke during the long dark hours, she would find Lydia lying stiffly next to her. "Can't you sleep at all?"

"No."

"Can I do something? Make you something hot?"

Lydia shook her head. "No."

Finally, very early Friday morning, Marcia said, "Lydia, would you rather I go home? If you're trying to be still to let me sleep, maybe you can't relax enough to sleep yourself."

"No, please don't leave." Lydia clasped her hand. "I want you to stay."

"OK. Did you try counting sheep?"

"I wish the shaking would stop."

"I know." She squeezed Lydia's hand and then drifted off until a particularly big jolt jarred them both. Lydia leapt out of bed and went to the door. "Cory," she called, "are you all right?"

They both heard his sleepy voice. "Mom, it's just an aftershock. Go back to bed."

Lydia came under the covers and pressed hard against Marcia, burying her nose in Marcia's neck. Marcia held her, stroking her back, wondering how much uncertainty about their relationship was contributing to Lydia's anxiety. Fear begets fear begets chaos. Lydia slid further down, tentatively nuzzling the curve of Marcia's breast, and Marcia shifted her weight to offer her nipple to Lydia's searching mouth, then drew her close as she began to suck. Lydia fell asleep soon afterwards, but Marcia lay awake for more than an hour. Just as she started to go under, she thought, "Please let me not be afraid. I don't want to be afraid anymore."

Friday evening Marcia drove Dale home because Polly wanted to borrow Dale's truck. Marcia was halfway to Dale's when she spotted an open flower stand and pulled the Ranchero into a red zone. "Hang on," she said. Dale untwisted her long body from the depths of the Ranchero's sprung passenger seat and followed Marcia across the street to the white pushcart surrounded by buckets of flowers. "Let me have five of those blue iris," Marcia told the curly-haired saleswoman, "and three stems of the white chrysanthemum. No, not those. Over there. Great."

"Flowers for your sweetie?" Dale asked laconically.

"Yeah."

"You in love, buddy?"

"Seems so," Marcia admitted. She was fishing in her pocket for bills as the seller wrapped the flowers in butcher paper.

Dale fingered a rubberband-bound bouquet of yellow roses. "You tell her yet?"

"Naw."

"Why not?"

The saleswoman was watching them covertly, taking a long time to tie the bundle of flowers with string.

"I don't know," Marcia said. "It's a secret."

"Between who? You and you?"

"Women like to be told," the seller informed them unexpectedly, glancing at Marcia and then looking out into the street. An ironic grin tilted up the corners of Dale's mouth. "See?"

"I'm buying her flowers," Marcia said. Then she sighed. "Okay, I'll tell her. But I have to be ready first."

"Sure you do. How much?" Dale asked the woman.

"Seven dollars," the seller said. This time she smiled at them openly.

"Seven dollars!" Marcia rolled her eyes in agony. "For a few iris?"

"Cough it up, sport," Dale advised. "The sooner you get married, the sooner you can stop this expensive romancing and instead lie around like a dead sloth. But you gotta tell her first."

# CHAPTER 13

"Hey, Marcia!" Billy shouted. He clattered down his steps in bedroom slippers with fuzzy yarn duck heads on the toes and leaned in the window of Marcia's Ranchero. She had swooped by her house Saturday morning to pick up her mail on her way to Fairview Street. "Cute," Marcia said, pointing at his footwear.

He risked a smile. "Hey. Were you here?"

No one needed to ask "when." "Yeah, I was here. I checked for gas leaks at both our houses."

He nodded. "Figured. That's what I told Pop. You coulda left a note. He thought maybe you were squashed on the Cypress." Billy's eyes shone with glee. "He even sounded kinda sad about it."

Marcia shook her head as she laughed. She spent so much time worrying about trivia that she missed the important stuff, like that people might be concerned a-bout her. "God, I'm really sorry."

Billy shrugged. "Anyhow, he wants to know have you seen Lucas."

"No, why? Is Lucas missing?"

Billy guffawed. "You gotta ask? His brain cells went missing a long time back. I don' even know why Pop cares."

A shaft of fear hit her stomach. "Do you think *he* could be on the Cypress?"

He snorted. "Are you kidding? How'd that dude get a car?"

"That's not very nice," she chided.

"So who's nice?" He winked at her, and Marcia began to relax. Maybe he'd recovered from the weight of too much gratitude; Marcia had worried that he'd run from her forever. Kids bounce back fast, she reminded herself. "You better watch yourself up there on Fairview," he warned her now. "I didn't know what block it was before. There's two crack houses within a hundred yards of each other."

"What do you know about crack houses?"

"Oh, man!" He rolled his eyes comically and started to stroll away, his duck's heads bobbing. But then he veered back to add, "Anyhow, you just be careful, okay? We don' need no more family emergencies."

He tipped a nonexistent hat as she pulled away from the curb. What a sweetie, she thought. He called me family. She blinked back sudden tears as she angled past a double-parked truck to get across San Pablo. A vision of Billy in an officer's uniform swam into her head until she blanked it out angrily. I can't keep acting like his life's a tragedy, she told herself, or that I'm disappointed even though I am. He's got to know he has something ahead of him besides prison. I'm as down as if he left his own life back there on that porch. But at least he's talking to me again. At least now he can look me in the eye.

Lydia decided she wanted to spend Sunday afternoon at Marcia's house, particularly since Cory, unwilling to stay home an entire weekend to humor his mother, had gone to play baseball at the park. Lydia said she wanted to do nothing but sit in Marcia's garden, and Marcia managed to get her there by three, after a packed morning at Fairview Street.

One of the clematis, a fall-bloomer, was going nuts on the pergola, its giant purple flowers set off by the few tiny pink blooms of a climbing rose. A few feet away was the vegetable section, with its neat raised beds and overhead wires for twining crops. Marcia had planted cherry trees and rhododendrons everywhere, interspersed with various kinds of irises and species geraniums. The large wooden bench in the pergola was overhung with ferns and begonias in baskets, and it was here that Lydia lay, her hand over her eyes. After watering her yard, Marcia went inside to clean the kitchen, occasionally glancing out at Lydia, who was so quiet she was almost invisible in the riot of greenery.

When Lydia came back in the house, Marcia was lying in a filling tub, underneath a thick cover of suds from a pine-scented bath emulsion. Marcia saw with relief that Lydia's eyes were much calmer, and that she seemed to have recovered her humor. She leaned against the door frame, watching Marcia. "Very lovely," she said.

Marcia smiled. "Not so lovely as you."

"No?" Lydia came to the tub and knelt down, trailing her fingers through the water to brush the top of Marcia's thigh. "What's so lovely about me?"

"Well, your breasts for one thing. You've got gorgeous breasts. Firm—"

"Still."

Marcia waggled her head back and forth, acknowledging this point. "Still." She shrugged. "We're both getting older. Anyway, you have these beautiful firm alabaster breasts with round nipples that feel so hard against my hand.... Why don't you take your shirt off?"

Marcia reached out to caress Lydia's breasts through the cloth, but Lydia shook her head. "I didn't say you could touch." She did, however, unbutton the cotton shirt and drape it over the toilet seat.

"I could spend hours just staring at your breasts," Marcia continued, scrunching way down in the water so she could put her feet up at the end. Her bathtub was a clawfoot, half again bigger than a normal tub. "But then there's your ass." She raised her eyebrows. "Absolutely gorgeous. Firm—"

"Still."

Marcia sighed. "Still. Curved like silk."

"Silk doesn't have a shape."

"Shaped silk."

Lydia rolled her eyes and then unbuttoned her jeans and slipped them and her underwear down her legs. "You're such a bullshitter. Do you really like the way I look?"

"Are you kidding?" Marcia asked, honestly surprised. "I love the way you look!"

"Sure, sure." Lydia climbed into the bathtub, and Marcia turned off the tap. The water level rose precariously. "Put your hands on the rim and leave them there."

Marcia obeyed, relieved Lydia was feeling more herself. Maybe she would even be able to sleep again. Things might start getting back to normal soon, whatever that meant, wherever normal happened to coalesce in the clamor of their busy lives. One point was clear. As far as Marcia was concerned, pre-Lydia was no longer the status quo. Marcia couldn't give her up now.

Lydia was rubbing the bar of glycerine soap all over Marcia's breasts, pausing to pinch here, caress there. Then she slowly moved the soap down, her fingers busy all over, running between Marcia's lips, the cheeks of her ass. Marcia was already beginning to slip into a trance. "Left-handed compliments," Lydia said, calling her back. "I know I'm getting older. You don't have to remind me."

"Lydia!" Marcia said, shocked. "You were the one—"

"Shut up. I don't recall giving you permission to say anything."

"But—" Marcia was full of turmoil. Could Lydia seriously believe she didn't find her attractive? Suddenly there was nothing more important for Marcia to prove.

"Since you're so eager to open your mouth, why don't you do something constructive with it? And move around. I want you against the tap, not me."

They shifted positions, crawling past each other in the big tub as little wavelets sloshed on the floor. Marcia looked at Lydia, her eyes pleading. "May I touch you?" At Lydia's nod she soaped her hands and began rubbing them all over Lydia's body, between her toes, under her arms, along her sides until Lydia began making noises much like the doves that nested on the overhang of Marcia's back stairs. Marcia licked Lydia's nipples, rejoicing as they rose under her tongue, loving how Lydia thrust against her as Marcia nibbled at her, using a gentle suction to coax Lydia's nipples between her teeth. As she sucked and bit, she slipped one soap-slick finger into Lydia's ass, causing her to jump and then sigh. "Lydia," Marcia said.

"I don't want to talk now," Lydia told her. "You never want to talk when it's important, and you always want to when we're making love. It's perverse, Mars."

"Just my nature," Marcia mumbled. Besides, what would she say? Couldn't Lydia feel Marcia adoring her? Marcia knew how tuned in she was when she was topping—Lydia must be the same, must be able to use her prospector's pick to mine deep inside Marcia's veins and see that something had changed. She tried to find Lydia's presence inside her skin and failed, then stared into her agate eyes, but all the greens and golds and browns had run together, and it was like looking at pebbles under a fast current, hazy and hard to pick out one by one.

A smile was spreading across Lydia's face as she touched Marcia's cheek. "Come on, baby. I told you I wanted you to use your mouth. Do I have to hurt you before you'll do it?"

Marcia felt Lydia's warmth shift to her as if she'd stepped into a shaft of sunlight. She must know, Marcia told herself. "No...but—" It was so hard to think logically when she was bottoming, she skipped from sensation to glimmer to trance, none of it in order, none of it predictable. "How can I go down on you underwater?"

Lydia leaned over to kiss her fingers. "I'm sure you can find a way."

The way, of course, was to hook Lydia's legs over the rim of the tub, thus raising her cunt to surface level. Marcia began wishing very soon that she hadn't used the bath emulsion because suds were tickling her nose and imbibing pine-flavored water wasn't what she'd intended. And she felt cramped, half on her knees, her elbow crunched against the hard porcelain of the tub.

But as she lost herself in Lydia's folds and crannies, as her tongue alternately drummed and explored, trailed off and returned, the discomforts faded until she thought she could do this her whole life—that is, until Lydia began gyrating her hips and water sloshed against Marcia's nose. She lifted her head, a grin on her face. "Hey, lady, you better come soon before I drown."

Lydia's eyes twinkled. "Did I ask for your input?"

"No, but on the other hand, if I start floating, you might lose what input you do want from me." She ducked back down, using her hands to raise Lydia's buttocks another strategic inch. But a few moments later, she couldn't resist looking again, so pleased was she by Lydia's relaxed face and beatific smile. "You're gorgeous," she said.

"Don't lie."

"I'm not lying."

"Are you able to breathe down there?"

"On and off. Hopefully I'll survive. Otherwise you'll have sacrificed the whole deal for one last glorious swan song."

Lydia caught her under the chin. "And what whole deal is that, my too-talkative one?"

Marcia rushed ahead, not letting herself think about what she was saying because her head had been trampling on her heart too long already. "Me. Me fucking you to the end of time." Her wet hair fell across her eyes, and she shoved it back. "You fucking me to the end of time."

Lydia got quiet, and Marcia could hear the clock ticking from her bedroom. "I didn't know I had that option," Lydia said finally.

Marcia swallowed. "Well, you do."

"Don't say something you don't mean."

"I'm not. I haven't said anything I don't mean all day."

Lydia looked unconvinced. Her eyes had become slitted, her lips tight. Marcia swallowed painfully. She could feel the closeness between them slipping away, past her, out of the bathtub, through her bedroom, into the yard.

The tension in Lydia's face, which had lifted for the first time since the earthquake, was back full-force, her body stiff and graceless.

Through the waves of disappointment washing over her, Marcia realized she had no one to blame but herself. Had she expected a grateful Lydia to fall thankfully into her arms? Lydia would be cautious, expecting Marcia's ambivalence to resurface.

"Marcia," Lydia said, startling her. "I know nobody can promise a future. But you can state an intention. I want you to think, okay?"

"I've thought," Marcia said. "I've had weeks to think."

"No. This is more important to me than anything. You think again."

Monday morning Marcia found her rehab partners staring at a spray-painted message on the broken-down front porch: "What goes around comes around."

"It's spelled right," Carol said. "Which means it probably wasn't any of those teenage punks from down the block." She was referring to a whole household of kids who occasionally asked if they wanted their cars washed and then called them bitch or freak when they refused. Tormenting the rehab team was small-time, however, compared to infuriating Mr. Thomas of the anal-retentive lawn. Sometimes Marcia feared for Mr. Thomas' heart.

"That's a stupid thing to say," Sarah told Carol.

Carol shrugged.

"I think it's someone we know," Polly said.

"Like who?" Marcia asked.

Polly shook her head. "I remember something like this from high school." All of Polly's meaningful experiences seemed to have occurred before her eighteenth birthday. "I can't put my finger on it."

"It's a man's writing."

"Umm-umm. Woman's."

"Who cares?" Reba said. She could never stand an unsolved puzzle. Finish it or forget it. "Let's get to work." But only twenty minutes into the day, as Dale switched on the table saw in the kitchen and began marking up a series of boards with her flat pencil, Marcia heard someone knocking politely on the back door molding. "Hi ya," called a black man so tall he dwarfed the small white man standing behind him.

"Harrison!" Dale said from her saw. She sounded cheerful but guarded: somewhere a dragon was lurking. Rocketing to the front door, she strolled down the ramp, forcing the men to follow her. Dale never moved fast. Marcia wandered outside after them, her eyes narrowing.

Harrison was murmuring something to Dale. He didn't introduce his short friend, who either was negligible or didn't have a name. Marcia saw Reba's face appear in one of the upstairs windows. Her mouth made a wide "O" and then she vanished. Sarah and Polly poked their heads up a second later and then ducked. Jesus, Marcia thought, who the fuck are these guys?

"So, Dale," Harrison said in a louder voice, now that he'd exhausted topic one, which seemed to be about the demise of a certain termite inspection company, "you gals kinda seem to be doin' stuff outside of what you got permits for. There's also—well, some question about this two-unit stuff."

Jesus! Building inspectors! Marcia hurtled into the house and got two clean paper cups and poured in hefty doses of Peet's best French roast, along with cream. She came outside and handed it to the men with a smile. "Coffee? Pretty day, huh?"

"Yeah, it's great," the short guy said. He sipped at his coffee.

Harrison flashed his teeth at her. He knew exactly what she was doing, but he appreciated the coffee anyway.

Dale was in the middle of a lengthy explanation about how the earthquake had created new damage. She said they planned to apply for FEMA funding, and that's why they hadn't come to the city to, say, take out a permit to rebuild the front porch.

Harrison nodded. "Yeah, that FEMA stuff is stupid. My chimney went...can't even get those guys on the phone." He paused, whistling softly through his front teeth, tapping his clipboard against his thigh. "Got this call...kinda funny. Says there never were two units here."

"That's completely untrue," Marcia said, for once righteously indignant. Harrison gazed at her from under his arched eyebrows, a look of faint surprise on his face. He apparently considered Dale job boss and the rest of them peons.

"Don't know about that. Nothing in the city records."

Polly appeared in back of Marcia. "But there's even two electrical meters," she said.

Another peon heard from. Harrison was tapping his thigh faster now, and he'd stopped whistling. "You're kidding."

"No, look," Dale took up. "Right over here." All five trooped around the corner of the house and stared for a long minute at the two electrical meters. They were covered with dirt and cobwebs, and inside one was a strip of paper with a penciled date in 1954.

Harrison was now shaking his head to go with the thigh-tapping. "I told you that woman's nuts," he said to his colleague. "She's a fox but she's got a fried brain."

The short man shrugged. He had inhaled his Peet's French roast and seemed to be angling for more.

"Vernita Foster," Polly guessed. "Foster's daughter," she told Marcia though Marcia knew very well who Vernita Foster was. "And she spray-painted that sign on the front porch too. I knew it was a woman's writing!"

Harrison glanced at Polly sharply. "Hmmm," he muttered. "Too bad." They all paused for a moment to contemplate the waste of gorgeous Vernita's slipped mind. Then Harrison led the way to the back yard again and spoke to Dale. "Anyhow, we gotta do a run-through here, see where you are, what still needs to be done."

"We could do it now," the short guy said hopefully. He gestured with his paper cup. Marcia started up the ramp to get the thermos, but Harrison made a big show of looking at his watch. "Naw, we gotta go do some other stuff first. Earthquake's made a helluva mess. Maybe sometime next week, huh, Dale? We'll drop on by." He grinned at her. "See ya." They both waved and went off through the side gate. The three rehab partners listened to their car start. Everyone waved again as the men pulled away. Then they dashed into the house where the rest waited in the kitchen breathless.

"That bitch," Polly said.

"Jesus, we're fucked!" Dale moaned.

"But why?" Marcia said. She knew something disastrous had happened but she didn't understand what. They'd made their case about the electrical meters, hadn't they?

"For one thing, the kitchen."

"We tore out the kitchen upstairs," Reba said. "It was never registered as a two-unit."

"But the electrical meters," Marcia bleated.

"It doesn't matter about the meters," Dale told her crossly. "We can do anything we want with existing structures. If we'd left the kitchen upstairs intact, we'd have no problem. But they'd never in a million years let us put in another whole new kitchen downstairs."

Sarah sunk to the floor, her hands wrapped around her knees. "I told you," she said. "I told you we shouldn't have faked the blueprints."

Marcia's head was swimming. "You mean we can't do two units even with the electrical meters?"

"Forget the meters!" Reba barked. "What matters is he gave us some time. We have at least a week's reprieve to create what we claimed was here in the first place."

"Why?" Polly wondered. "That's the real question."

Dale answered that. "He probably thinks it's funny that a bunch of old dykes are remodeling a junker on Fairview. And he's a pretty good guy."

Carol had her hands on her hips. "What the fuck can we do in a week?"

Marcia was still faint. "You mean he was nice?"

"Sure," Reba said. "They could have come in that second. He gave us time to build as much 'existing structure' as we can. That means both the kitchens and the upstairs bath and the back entrance."

Carol was shaking her head. "There's no way."

"We have to hire people," Sarah muttered.

"Flunkies," Dale said.

"Slaves," Reba added.

"Hire people?" Marcia moaned. "With what?"

"Money. We all have to kick in. We'll get it back, for god's sakes. Are we going to sacrifice the profit on two units to save a couple thousand bucks?" Reba was in a militant mood, her chin out-thrust.

"Of course not," Marcia surrendered.

"I think we should hire men," Carol said.

"No, we have to hire dykes," Sarah told her from the floor. "I know these younger women who do construction. I can call and see if they're busy."

"Why? We can get a lot more work out of men."

"We're hiring women," Dale told Carol.

"This is an emergency," Carol insisted.

Marcia remembered when she'd constructed the pergola in her back yard. She'd overdone it, really, buying huge beams and cross-braces, and she'd cursed herself as she'd driven home with her load, thinking how long it was going to take her to haul the pieces into the back. Lucas and Billy, hanging out on the porch, did it in exactly three minutes. "Maybe we should go for men," she said doubtfully.

"We'll hire dykes," Reba sighed.


The next day, four women in their twenties showed up at the job site. Lauren Yamaguchi had a penchant for tight jeans and cowboy boots. Kimberley Brewer, with the lines shaved in her scalp, was more into torn T-shirts and leather. Marcia never did find out Jennifer or Janey's last names, but placid Janey had her sleeves rolled up over bulging biceps, and Jennifer's half-inch buzzcut crested up higher in front where she'd spot-bleached it. Sarah kept talking out of the corner of her mouth to flinty-eyed Lauren, who tilted her head forward to listen but never said a word. Marcia felt a twinge of hope—the quartet radiated confidence.

Reba, always the general, gathered everyone in the back unit's nonexistent kitchen while Polly served coffee. "The only way we could afford to rehab this house was to do it as two units," Reba explained. "We had to change the floor plan, and of course we couldn't go through the city in case they turned us down. Now they're on our backs." She nodded with conviction, as if everyone knew Berkeley city officials were always searching for lesbians to oppress. When she began listing the jobs that needed to be accomplished in one short week, Marcia felt her optimism plummeting, but their employees showed no dismay. They evinced little sign of anything, in fact, staring off into the distance with apparent boredom, except for Lauren, who was attentive (Marcia put this down to what she thought were vestiges of Asian politeness), though her eyes had finally started to glaze as Reba came to a stirring finish.

Both the glazed look and any mistaken assumption of courtesy were eliminated as Lauren followed with her own staccato lecture. "Look," she snapped, "as far as we're concerned, this is a job for which we're being paid too little. The only reason we're giving you the low end of our sliding scale is because we're all queer. You're not doing anything laudatory here."

She crossed her arms over her chest, a perfect match for Reba's MacArthur imitation, while Sarah blanched but then rallied to mumble, "Right on."

Reba sputtered out a mouthful of coffee. "Well," she said, and could go no further.

The favor of employment they'd been granting the younger set had been neatly turned on its head, and now they found themselves in the supplicant role. None of them were pleased by this reversal, Marcia thought, even Sarah, but it was probably closer to reality since construction jobs had mushroomed since the earthquake.

"Fine," Polly smoothly stepped into the breach. "Kimberley and Janey should build the interior walls we showed you earlier, and Lauren and Jennifer can do the staircase for the back unit. Above all, we need to establish that unit's existence. The six of us will be splitting up, one group putting in the second kitchen downstairs, one group putting in the master bathroom upstairs. Can you do it?"

"Sure," Kimberley said. "But we'll divide ourselves."

"Fine," Polly agreed. The six rehab partners glanced warily at each other as Kimberley partnered with Lauren, Janey with Jennifer, and all trudged off to separate areas of the house.

"What do you think?" Sarah asked quietly.

"Not a whole lot," Dale said.

"I don't get the idea they're very impressed with us," Reba said. She seemed perturbed.

Marcia stood up. "That shouldn't make any difference, should it? Come on, let's get going."

They all scattered, carrying circular saws, tool belts, wrenches. Reba went to the electrical supply store to get wire. Dale abandoned her saws to make sure the kids, as she called them, really did know what they were doing. Marcia began drawing out a plan for kitchen cabinets. She was in charge of the impossible: stepping up the two-week wait for decent cabinets to two or three days. She hadn't decided yet how she would do it. Sarah went down to the tile store to pick up kitchen and bathroom tiles. Luckily they had already had one color coordinating meeting, so they had a very minimal master plan. It would have to do.

By ten Marcia had her kitchen design, and by twelve she'd located a set of returned base cabinets at one kitchen supply store and a set of top cabinets at another. Truitt had the same pattern in a bathroom cabinet that could be altered to function as a small island. The stain might be different on the top cabinets, but Marcia decided she could sand and restain them if they were really much darker. She also purchased countertops for both kitchens and fancy new drawer pulls for the front unit.

When she got back to the house with her cabinets tied in various positions around the rusted bed of the Ranchero, everyone was sitting in the sawdust of the front unit's kitchen, eating a late lunch. Polly had gone up to Andronico's to buy salads, while Kimberley had dashed down to San Pablo to a fancy Italian deli. When Marcia walked in, her five partners were gazing with jealousy at piles of ham, cheese, smoked turkey, and baguettes littering a two-foot-square piece of butcher paper.

"Good eats," Carol commented. The four employees smiled and continued spreading hot mustard on torn-off chunks of baguette, then rolling up ham and turkey slices to balance on top.

"So," Lauren said, waving a piece of cheese, "you own this place, right?"

Reba shrugged. "Well—"

"You do or you don't."

"Yeah, we bought it. We're planning to sell in a month."

"Didja think about how you were gonna be speculators?" Kimberley asked.

"No," Reba told her. "We thought about how we were going to make a profit."

"Kimberley and Lauren's point is that—" Sarah began.

"What are you," Reba asked Sarah, "their interpreter?"

"I'm surprised you bought in this neighborhood," Lauren said.

"Why?" Reba asked blandly. "You guys could do it. Try one of the transition areas in East or West Oakland."

Lauren and Kimberley flashed each other glances, while Janey's handsome face passed from still to startled. Jennifer was the only one who responded. "We just have different ways of looking at it," she said, more to her friends than to the rehab partners.

"I think the whole concept of 'transition neighborhood' is not to anyone's liking," Sarah explained to Reba. Silence as everyone chewed literally and figuratively.

"Well, you gotta do something with your money," Reba declared. Marcia hopped to her feet and signaled to Polly and Sarah. "Help me move the cabinets, OK?" She was deluged by volunteers.


Two days later, Marcia returned with six more lo-cal boxes of salad from Andronico's, but this time she carried the bag upstairs to the very front of the house, where the other five waited, as far from their employees as they could get. They ripped into their salads with sublimated venom. "They didn't want to eat with us anyway," Marcia reported. "They preferred the back yard."

"Kimberley told me this morning that we were gay and they were queer," Polly said.

"What's that supposed to mean?" Carol asked.

"It means they're more PC than we are even though they oppose the whole idea of PC," Dale said. "Gay means wanting to pass."

"Pass?" Reba cried. "If we wanted to pass we'd be wearing panty hose and working in the fucking Financial District."

"Lauren said we're gentrifiers," Sarah said. "Of course she's right." She chewed on a carrot reflectively. "I think they're kind of cute."

"You would!" Reba snapped.

"I do too," Marcia admitted. "Jennifer's really funny. So is Kimberley once you get her to drop her hostile number."

"Kimberley said no friend of Mother Earth would have sixty-seven thousand bucks to spend on a rehab project," Sarah said glumly.

"Shit!" Reba shouted. "You didn't tell them how much money we put in, did you?"

"No, of course not! I'm just paraphrasing."

"Good, 'cause they'll think we're rich or something." Reba speared a cherry tomato with her plastic fork. "Anyway, I can't believe they have the gall to say a goddam word. What were they doing in 1970, sucking their mothers' tits?"

"They probably were, that's the amazing part," Dale said.

"But I don't see why we should be blamed because they don't have enough imagination to buy their own house and fix it up," Polly complained.

"I don't think it has to do with imagination," Marcia said. "I think money's the problem."

"I don't," Dale told her.

"Part of it's money," Sarah said. "Social class is now being determined by generation, which is part of the reason they're so up-front with their anger. It happened somewhat to us—our earning capacity is lower than our parents."

"We're dykes," Dale pointed out. "Our economic expectations are automatically diminished 'cause there's no prick involved."

"Straight people our age don't earn as much either," Sarah told her. "They're just more pissed about it than we are because there *is* a prick involved."

"How'd we get back to us?" Polly asked.

"What happened to us in a mild way has hit them like a sledgehammer," Sarah continued. "They can't hope to buy a house. They can hardly find jobs."

"So they have to buy in Outer Mongolia," Carol said.

"Ruth is going to inherit our house," Reba mused.

"Ruth is an only child," Dale pointed out. She began cutting up a green apple with her knife. "It's so weird how you can think you've been following this principled course and then look down to discover you've been walking on another map the entire time."

No one responded to this observation. Instead they scarfed down their salads, Marcia even eating the pickled vegetables she'd mistakenly shoveled into her plastic box. It was amazing how perplexity could pique an appetite.

"Can we fire them?" Carol asked.

"For what?" Sarah said. "For thinking they're more revolutionary than we are? They're doing good work."

Everyone was fair enough to agree to that. The four younger women had accomplished a great deal in only three and a half days. The interior walls were completed, and they would finish the staircase by the end of the afternoon. Carol now had Janey and Jennifer climbing around the outside of the house re-attaching the fallen decorative elements.

"They're just trying to make us feel bad," Polly said.

Sarah shook her head. "I think we're the ones making us feel bad."

This time they had no salad to hide in. "That's real deep, Sarah," Carol finally said.

"Too deep for you anyway," Dale retorted. "C'mon, let's get back to work."

"It's only been fifteen minutes," Polly complained, looking at her watch.

"It's been fifteen minutes too long," Carol told her. They all climbed to their feet with a chorus of groans, rubbing aching backs and joints.

"We sound like a bunch of old ladies," Sarah sighed. No one answered her.

# CHAPTER 14

"We shoulda hired men," Carol said in her usual truculent voice. She and Sarah and Marcia were painting the front bedrooms while everyone else finished the kitchens and baths. Their employees had been so efficient that the three older women were on "free time," a good description, Marcia thought sourly, since her paychecks from work had dwindled to almost nothing.

"Do you know if Polly got coffee this morning?" Marcia asked. She was sick of talking about their employees.

"It's all gone," Carol said. She poured more paint into her roller pan and ascended the ladder.

They painted in silence for awhile. Downstairs was alive with pounding and sawing. Marcia was edging trim with an angled brush, enjoying how the paint flowed on smoothly and evenly. "You married, Carol?"

"Yeah," Carol grated. "Why d'ya ask?"

Marcia shrugged. "I was just wondering. I don't know anything about you."

"Well, that's how I like it."

"Okay. Forget it."

Sarah caught Marcia's eye and grinned, while Marcia stifled a chuckle. Then Sarah started singing something under her breath that sounded like, "Two-by-fours bloomin' in the pit of my love, baby," but couldn't have been. No doubt it was too much for Carol because she spun around and said to Marcia, "So what about you?"

"Not now."

Carol had a smirk on her face. "I bet."

Silence. Then Marcia said, "What do you mean?"

Carol shrugged. "You know."

"No, I don't."

Sarah put down her paint brush. "What *do* you mean, Carol?"

Carol shrugged more elaborately. When she saw her two partners were still in the dark, she explained combatively, "Well, it's probably hard for you to find anybody to do that sick shit you like in bed."

Marcia's heart stopped beating for a second and then engaged with a sickening lurch. She fired a quick look at Sarah, who had flushed red to the roots of her cloud of hair. Furious at her own reaction, she nevertheless felt the open parts of her flee to somewhere walled-off and safe. "Finding someone's never been a problem," she said in a cold, neutral voice that sounded far away.

Carol was pleased at the consternation she'd caused. She dipped the roller into the pan and began rolling the wall Sarah had just cut-in.

"Let her alone," Sarah demanded in a shaky voice. If it could be said that Dale wanted to avoid the ticklish subject of S/M, Sarah preferred to bury it under a ton of concrete. Marcia hadn't expected her to speak up.

"It's all right," Marcia said. "We can talk about it." Not that anyone would. Dykes would rather have root canals than talk in a real way about S/M.

After a minute or two of silence, Marcia shrugged and began painting again. But then Carol said slyly, "C'mon, Sarah, you can't tell me you don't think it's sick to beat each other with whips."

Marcia swung around to face Sarah, who was still flushed, her hands clenched into fists at her side. Sarah threw Marcia a beseeching look, which Marcia interpreted as "Must I defend you?" Yet when Marcia started to speak, Sarah interrupted her.

"I don't like it," Sarah admitted, her eyes on Marcia. "But if both people want to, I don't see anything wrong. Lots of people like being tied up, for instance."

"That's different," Carol asserted.

"At what point does it turn different?" Marcia wanted to know.

"Don't act dumb," Carol said to her.

Marcia shook her head.

"I'm gonna go get some beer," Carol announced. "Want some?"

"Not me," Marcia said.

"Oh, right. Sarah?"

"It's kind of early. But—okay."

Carol slammed out the door. They could hear her pounding down the steps. "She does everything like an elephant," Sarah said. Her voice was still quivery.

"Sarah, look—"

"It's just hard for me, Marcia. I was thinking about it last week. Nobody asks me what I'm doing anymore 'cause they don't want to talk about Flame. I realized it's like that for you too, with this thing everybody avoids mentioning." She heaved a big sigh, trying to get her breath. "When no one talked to me, first I thought, fuck you guys, I don't give a shit what you think about me. But I do!" She tried to breathe again and started crying instead.

"Sarah!" Marcia tossed her brush on a pile of newspapers and caught Sarah's elbows in her hands, pulling her close. "Sarah, honey, I'm sorry. You're right. I should have thought how that would make you feel." She was, after all, one of the guilty parties in the conspiracy of silence surrounding Flame and Crewcut and anyone else Sarah met at the clubs. Marcia and the rest had made Sarah responsible for bringing up something they all found unsavory, so naturally enough, Sarah had kept her mouth shut.

Marcia held onto her hard. "We'll talk, all right? You tell me everything that's happening with you." Christ, she thought, if we can't do this for each other, who can we do it for?

Carol burst in carrying two cans of beer in each hand and skidded to a halt. "Jesus. Kimberley's kissing the jock in the hall and you guys are feeling each other up. Fuckin' dykes."

"It's so wonderful working with you, Carol," Sarah said, scrubbing her hand across her eyes. "You're such a peach."

"Let me do the sarcasm," Carol told her. "I'm a lot better at it."

Harrison and his short friend returned on Thursday morning, 9 a.m. The rehab crew had been hoping for Friday or even the following week. Harrison halfway apologized. "Lotsa stuff happenin' with the quake," he explained. "Hard to keep a schedule." He and Nameless walked around the house. The back staircase was built, though not glassed-in. Since everyone was arguing about how to finish it off, it had been left for later. The upstairs kitchen and back bedroom had been turned into a master bath/bedroom suite. All the plumbing was in, the walls tiled. A slight film of plaster dust and dirt lay on everything. Reba had achieved that by coating the floors and walls with KY and then reversing the direction of her vacuum cleaner, thus spraying the contents of the bag over everything in sight. It lent it a very lived-in look, as if the master bath with its skylight had been there forever in the middle of a Victorian on Fairview. Harrison could hardly restrain a grin.

Downstairs was even better. They had bought used pipe at a salvage yard and used it to establish the double connections in the back-to-back kitchens. Marcia had mounted her cabinets so that one could no longer see where the washer and dryer had stood in the former laundry room. "We replaced the cabinets, of course," Polly said. She was playing tour guide, leading the two men around. Harrison reached out to fondle one of the new old pipes. "Great," he said. "'Course you might have to replace some of this old plumbing." This time he couldn't prevent himself from chuckling. When Marcia looked at the pipe later, it was still labeled with an orange price sticker from the salvage yard.

"So, two units, three existing baths, two kitchens..." Harrison was writing notes on a pad of paper. "What was the former access to the upstairs of the other unit?" he asked innocently.

"A walled-in staircase," Reba answered quickly. "But we tore it out. It was just terrible." Luckily the foundation from the utility shed remained to support such a claim.

"Uhmm-hmm." Harrison walked down the ramp and around the house. "Now this bay?"

"Well, the bay was here, obviously. Putting in the french doors is a remodel."

"Uhmm-hmm, other access..." A car pulled up at the side of the house, and a squat woman in her early fifties wearing a tape measure clipped to her belt got out. She had curly short hair, a bulldog face, and a swing to her walk that said she wasn't going to take shit from other lesbians. She strode up to the little group, which had now grown into a crowd as Harrison was coming to the end of his visit. He was observed, helped, or hindered by all six from the rehab crew as well as the four employees. "Julie!" he exclaimed. He sounded like Dale had when she'd greeted Harrison: aware of the dragon underneath.

Unlike Harrison, however, Julie's dragon was off its leash and surging to the surface. She gave a courtly but ironic nod to Sarah, whose face had paled, and then she regarded the women in front of her as if they were students on a disciplinary hour. "Did you run these changes through the architectural integrity department?"

Dale chose to answer. "Well, on their way through planning they go through your department."

"Yes, but you informed us at the time that you weren't altering the exterior."

"Well, we haven't changed the footprint or the roof structure."

"What about that staircase? It wasn't there before."

"It was; you just couldn't see it. It was walled-in," Marcia said. She had almost begun to believe this story.

"What about that?"

"That" was the twelve-foot mystery wall. "We certainly didn't put that there," Marcia said. "And we're planning to get rid of it."

"The french doors in the bay? Did you apply for an integrity review on that?"

"Well, no, but—"

"You didn't apply for a review on any of these changes, did you?"

"We didn't need to," Dale maintained. "Besides, all these changes are for the better. Surely you wouldn't like us to leave all these nice packing crates piled on top of one another?"

The woman took a step closer, her thumb hooked in her belt. Harrison and his partner took about five steps back, observing the confrontation of Julie and Dale with nervous amusement.

"You're missing the point. It's not your decision. Every substantive exterior change goes through our department, and I would certainly call what you're doing here substantive."

"And how long might this routing through architectural integrity take?"

"Six to eight weeks."

"That's unfortunate," Dale said, "for people who have to go through architectural integrity. Luckily we have nothing that qualifies under your definition."

The woman gave her an icy smile. "That's for us to determine, not you. And it might take us six to eight weeks to even *make* that determination."

"Too bad they can't just whip 'em out and see whose's longer," Polly whispered to Reba, but loud enough for at least Marcia and Harrison to hear. Harrison bit his lip in glee, but Marcia couldn't fully enjoy the moment because Reba was hissing at her, "Get Dale the fuck out of here, Marcia. Now."

"Really," Dale was saying. "And does your department make it a policy to obstruct people who are remodeling residences in low-income—"

"Jesus, Dale!" Marcia cried, grabbing her by the elbow and spinning her around to face her. "We've gotta get going! We forgot about that appointment with the FEMA people." Dale's jaw was beginning to set stubbornly, but Reba took up the cry: "Oh, no, we can't lose that loan! Go on, you two, we'll finish up here."

Marcia hustled Dale into the Ranchero, which luckily was only thirty feet away, and sped off before Dale had a chance to throw a real fit. They'd gone three blocks when Dale said, "I blew it, huh?"

"That was completely, totally, ridiculously—ah, who gives a fuck. That woman's gonna do what she's gonna do."

"But it was dumb."

"It was dumb; it wasn't fatal."

"Fuck her," Dale said.

"Agreed. Maybe Harrison can handle her. He seems on our side."

Dale moved the seat back and stretched her long legs. "See, what's happened here is that Harrison thinks we're cute and funny whereas she, being a dyke herself, doesn't see anything cute about us. And that's what's going to cause the trouble in River City."


The trouble was big enough to shut them down. The workers were paid for the rest of the day (over Polly's objections, who wanted to pay to the hour) and let go. But perhaps Harrison had influence, or by the time Amazon Julie got back to the office she'd vented her spleen. For whatever reason, architectural integrity made its determination that it had nothing to review by Friday afternoon. "Should we call back the troops?" Sarah asked.

"Why?" Reba questioned.

"Aside from their being so damned self-righteous, it was nice to have the help."

"They aren't free," Polly pointed out.

"Let's call them in a little later," Reba decided, "after their other project is over—it's a two-weeker, Jennifer said. How 'bout that? They could build the front porch while we do the exterior painting."

"And put up the side fence," Marcia pointed out, "after we get rid of all those packing crates."

"Agreed," Dale said. "Now let's move it. Even I'm starting to worry. The radio was talking about interest rates rising again. We need to get on the market."

"To market, to market," Polly misquoted, "to snare a fat pig."

"Indeed," Reba said.

# CHAPTER 15

Marcia spent a frustrating Wednesday attempting to dig postholes on the far side of the driveway for her three-foot-high planter boxes. The boxes would raise the trees and plants to a level where they could be seen when cars were in the driveway, so that the end of the property wouldn't seem to peter out in a gravel wasteland. Unfortunately someone had buried tons of castoff concrete and wood only inches below the hard-packed earth.

As she dragged the posthole digger, her pickaxe, and a trenching shovel from one impossible area to the next, she thought about Lydia. Since their tryst in the bathtub, Lydia had remained guarded and cool. Clearly she needed proof that Marcia meant what she said, but what kind of proof? One thing Marcia knew for sure—the balance of power had shifted into Lydia's court, and Marcia didn't like it. But was steering the horse more important than letting it drink? Didn't Lydia *want* Marcia to love her?

"I guess we do need to talk," Marcia said that evening as Lydia put a bowl of soup in front of her.

Lydia made an amused noise. "We could walk across burning coals instead."

Marcia didn't answer. She ate a steaming noodle delicately, trying to keep the hot bits off her tongue. Lydia

183

had no call to be sarcastic, she thought. She was about to repeat her suggestion when Lydia said, "I just keep wondering what you find so enticing about fear."

"Enticing?"

"Sure. You wouldn't hold onto it so fiercely if it didn't do something for you."

"Jesus," Marcia said. She finished her soup, hot as it was, and took her bowl to the sink, then hovered over Lydia and snatched away the bowl as Lydia scooped up the last spoonful. "C'mon, let's go lie down, okay? I've decided I don't want to talk."

"You never want to talk, except to tell me a million stories of your past."

"You've got a million stories of your own," Marcia retorted as they walked into the living room. "That's why we have to change lovers occasionally, so we can tell all our old stories again."

"You're so romantic, Mars."

"But I am," Marcia said, certain of this fact. "You're pragmatic, I'm romantic."

"I see," Lydia said. She had halted in the living room, as if undecided about where they should settle, but now she continued into the bedroom. Marcia followed her and flopped on the bed. Lydia leaned on her elbow, watching Marcia with one eyebrow cocked, almost as good as Dale. "Sometimes you're such a mystery to me," she said, taking Marcia's hand and weaving their fingers together into a strong warm knot. Marcia was amazed at how their bodies craved each other even when their minds couldn't connect. She moved closer until they were pressed against each other, their legs in a looser jumble than their fingers, wishing she'd figured out this stuff about their bodies earlier. How come all the signs had been there but she hadn't been able to read them? Too preoccupied. Too scared. "Do you think," she asked hesitantly, embarking on her usual journey of indirection and disguise, "that we keep ourselves busy to avoid intimacy? I've been thinking about that lately. Like maybe the underpinning of middle age is avoidance."

She glanced at Lydia out of the corner of her eye. Lydia's face was scrunched up, as if she were giving

Marcia's question deep consideration. But then she shrugged. "Since I'm not frantically busy like you are, I don't think I'm the best person to ask."

Marcia sighed and pulled Lydia close, so Lydia's chin jutted into her neck. She was afraid to suggest that two were needed to make it work; that it wasn't just herself holding them back, that Lydia wasn't there to take them where she claimed she wanted them to go. And Marcia heaping all the blame on her own head was a dynamic too disturbingly familiar from her years with Annie.

They lay still for a while, Marcia with her eyes closed, liking the taut warmth of Lydia's body and the strength of her fingers laced in her own. "So tell me one of your stories," she said finally.

Lydia chuckled. "All right. You're always curious a-bout why I got into plants when it seems I have no interest in them, right?"

"It's pretty strange," Marcia said.

"Well, I did have an interest in one plant—sensimilla."

"Oh no! Lydia, please, not some hippie nightmare—"

Lydia poked Marcia and then flipped on her back and caught Marcia's hand again. "Once upon a time, Jeff and I wanted to move to the country."

"Who didn't?" Marcia interposed. She had spent her twenties mapping out complicated plot rotation plans for cross-fenced ten-acre parcels. The closest she'd actually come to leaving Oakland, however, was purchasing three rabbits. Three grew to twenty and Marcia still hadn't managed to convince herself that bunnycide was the object. A friend came over and reduced the herd to nine-teen, but Marcia couldn't eat a bite.

The rabbits went, along with Marcia's country dreams.

"Cory was three at the time," Lydia continued, "and Jeff was doing graphics for Macy's. We figured we could make a fortune growing dope. So I signed up for a bunch of classes in plant science at Cal Extension, and I just got fascinated. Of course we never made it to the country, and Jeff became a computer nerd. But I guess I should be happy. He paid for my doctorate, and I even wound up with the kid." She laughed. "He actually *is* kind of a nerd.

I see him now and wonder how I could have lived with him all those years."

Marcia looked over at her, watching Lydia's long lashes brush her cheeks as she rested, her face relaxed. "But I guess," Lydia said thoughtfully, "how it finishes isn't a reason not to start." Her eyes opened suddenly, and Marcia found herself scrutinized by a piercing agate gaze.

"Wondering if you'll feel the same way about me?" she joked.

Lydia wrinkled her forehead. "Maybe."

"Was Jeff into S/M?"

"Yeah, sure. In fact, when I realized I liked women, that part really upset me. I figured dykes weren't into this stuff. I thought I'd have to sacrifice one part of my sexuality for the other."

Marcia smiled. "Little knowing—"

"Little knowing I'd happen upon a gorgeous hunk who loves being beaten. When it suits her." She watched Marcia for a long minute. "I just keep thinking we could be going deeper here."

Marcia bit her lip. "This going deeper," she said finally. "It's not just me."

Lydia stared at her salmon ceiling. "I guess that's true." Then she twisted around to rub Marcia's belly with her fingers. "Tell you what, Marcia, you be a little more obedient and maybe I'll let you top sometimes."

Lydia switched from Marcia's belly to her nipples, and Marcia could feel herself responding fast, though she worried that their going deeper discussion had gotten derailed. But it was so much easier to show what they meant to each other by making love. Lydia's face had eased and her fingers had become supple and wise. Marcia didn't want to send them back to the hard stuff, where they stammered and gritted their teeth and couldn't think of what to say. "You'll *let* me?" she asked, playing to Lydia's lead.

Lydia grinned at her. "You got it, babes. Don't forget who's boss around here."

"Yes, ma'am."

"Mistress."

Marcia was surprised. "Really?"

"You're such a punk. You're never going to top at this rate. But then, that's just fine with me." Her fingers moved under Marcia's T-shirt, teasing and pinching until Marcia was whimpering with pleasure. "C'mere, pull down your pants. You still got those bruises from last week?" Marcia wrestled with the buttons on her jeans and then squirmed as she felt the delicate tracery of Lydia's fingers on her behind. "Ah, they've almost faded," Lydia said softly. "That's a shame. You want more, baby?"

Embarrassed, Marcia mumbled, "Yes."

"Can't hear you. What'd you say?"

"I said yes."

"What?"

She fairly shouted, "Yes, ma'am, I'd like some more bruises on my butt."

Lydia smiled at her. "Good. Happy to oblige. Take off your clothes and go get that cat you hate so much."

Marcia went into Lydia's closet, moved two boxes, and dug out the heavy many-tailed whip. She handed it to Lydia, who kissed her hard before she unfastened the cuffs from the bed, strapped them onto Marcia's wrists and then attached them with carabiners to rings mounted on opposite sides of the closet door frame. Her arms outstretched, hands about a foot above her head, Marcia stood facing a solid line of Lydia's clothes—good sound-proofing, Lydia told her as she came up behind her and stroked her back and buttocks.

"But you can yell as loud as you want anyway, hon, because Tina next door is out of town and nobody else is around."

"I don't know about that," Marcia said, aware of just how loud she could yell.

"I do," Lydia said. She ducked under Marcia's arm to stand in front of her and stroke her cheeks. "Remember when you were crying?"

"Sure."

"I want you to cry again, but this time for me." Lydia's face was half in darkness, but Marcia could feel her excitement.

Marcia swallowed, not wanting to disappoint her. "I'm not sure I can cry on command."

Lydia grinned at her and slid back under her arm. "Oh, I can make you cry."

Marcia turned half-around, her eyes concerned. "But what if I can't—"

Lydia smiled at her and stroked her cheek. "Don't be so worried," she said, and began the steady flogging that would raise bruises. Marcia was yelling within minutes. Lydia varied her strokes from soft brushes to two-handed slams, across Marcia's shoulders, her butt, and her thighs. She stopped every few minutes to check the circulation in Marcia's hands and to rub against her as Marcia leaned back, straining to imprint every inch of herself on Lydia's belly and breasts. Occasionally Marcia wiped the corners of her eyes on her upper arms. "I'm not crying," she told Lydia, though she did seem to be wet everywhere—juices were streaming down her leg, and Lydia's roaming fingers spread that slickness all over, from Marcia's nipples to her back to her stomach. Lydia even stepped again in front of Marcia to paint it on her lips as Marcia dangled panting from the cuffs. "The only lipstick I can get my boy to wear," Lydia said, the light from the bedside table reflecting the gleam of delight in her eyes. And she licked the tiny wet trails down Marcia's cheeks and agreed, "Oh, no, a few tears of pain don't count."

But finally, a sob caught in Marcia's throat at the tail end of a yell, and Lydia sucked in her breath and then slammed Marcia hard twice across the buttocks. Marcia's head fell forward and she began weeping. Lydia tossed the whip on the bed and unsnapped her from the rings, then helped her to the bed. "I told you I could make you cry," she said.

Marcia dug her nose into Lydia's shoulder and licked her breast, nuzzling the heavy sway of it. Then she raised her head, her eyes shimmering with tears and want. "Fuck me."

"With pleasure," Lydia told her.

Very early the next morning, they stood on the front porch, watching Cory on the sidewalk below them performing the graceful movements of T'ai chi. Lydia had her back scrunched up against Marcia's front, and Marcia was rubbing Lydia's crossed arms as Lydia murmured in contentment. Suddenly Cory bounded up the steps, almost bowling them over. "The garbage truck's coming! I forgot to put it out!" He dashed into the house and then scrambled past them again to pelt down the stairs, carrying the key to the garage.

Lydia's eyebrows knit in annoyance.

"C'mon, Lydia, at least he's doing it, right? So what if he does it one second before they arrive."

"I suppose," Lydia said. Cory came back up the stairs and went into the house. Lydia turned around to face Marcia. "You're pretty cute, hon. You'd make some woman a good husband."

Marcia grinned, tickling Lydia in the midriff. "Oh, yeah? But who, that's the question." Then she leaned forward and kissed her hard. "See ya, sweetie."

She'd been at the Fairview house for about an hour, at work on her driveway section, when she heard the familiar whine of Cory's scooter. She wandered out from the back yard, carrying her pickaxe.

"Hi, Marcia."

"Hi, Cory."

He stood tall as a crane and just as gangly. Lydia's husband must have been a monster, Marcia thought. Otherwise where'd that height come from? "Wanta come see what I'm doing?"

Cory inspected the paths she'd made, the deck off the french windows, the raised beds, the proposed pond area. She showed him where she would put the planter boxes and how much trouble she was having digging the postholes. There was even a huge log, she said, that she'd found right before she'd given up yesterday in disgust. "Gee, this looks kind of fun," Cory said, digging at the ground with the toe of his cowboy boot which had no doubt cost Lydia a fortune. "Where's the log?"

"It's over here." He took the pickaxe from her. "But, Cory, you're dressed for school—"

He threw off his sweater and started pickaxing with a steady rhythm, moving around the log, then prying it up at various angles with the pick. Marcia watched him, amazed how far he could dig in the pick on a single swing.

Within three minutes he'd pried out the log. Then he grabbed the posthole digger and began, at her direction, making neat holes in the hard earth. Ten minutes later he'd done more than she could do in an hour, and he seemed to be enjoying it too. Finally, however, she could no longer stand the suspense. "Cory, I'm sure you didn't wake up this morning and say I think I'll go help Marcia dig out logs, although this exhibition has convinced me that male muscle is a truly wonderful thing. Now what's the deal?"

He blushed, then answered with a question. "When—uh—when did you know you were gay?"

She'd expected almost anything but that. Does he think he's gay? He had a girlfriend down in San Jose whom he saw when he went to visit his father, though that didn't mean anything, especially not at seventeen...but no, something else was behind this. "When I was really little," she answered. "By the time I was six, I'd figured out that girls weren't supposed to marry girls, so I hid my intentions from then on. I didn't come back out of the closet for thirteen years."

"Couldn't you talk to anyone?"

"There wasn't anybody to talk to. There weren't rap groups or social services or gay parades. Nobody was out. I didn't know any real lesbians. I didn't know if there *were* any others." She paused, watching him. "Your mom told me you were mad when she came out."

He levered aside a piece of cement that had gotten in the way of his digging and hoisted it onto the driveway. "Naw, I didn't care. I mean, I yelled at her and stuff. I figured I shouldn't be too easy on her. I thought it was my responsibility to point out what a big mistake she was making."

"But if you didn't care, why'd you think it was a mistake?"

"'Cause it's really hard. I mean, look at you guys. She really likes you, and you get along OK." He dribbled to a finish, as if he'd meant to say something else entirely. Then he brightened. "I like how you play it cool." He looked at his watch. "Guess I oughta get going."

"Cory, did something happen this morning?"

He swung the pickaxe and hit something hard a few inches down. She could see the shock of it run up his arms and snap his neck back. "Shit!" he yelped.

"You should stop doing this," she told him, then winced as he stubbornly swung the pick close to the same spot, but this time it dug in deep. "Stupid concrete," he muttered. "Well, ya know, you probably don't even remember 'cause it's so dumb, but, uh, ya know I was around when you and Mom were talking on the steps?"

"Yeah," Marcia prompted. "The garbage."

"Right. Well, ah, Mom said you'd make a good husband—" he smiled at her weakly while Marcia raised her eyebrows, wondering what he'd made of that remark—"and you said for who and I knew you were kidding—"

"Whom," Marcia corrected automatically and then added, "yeah, I was teasing."

"But see, she went right inside after you left and cried for a long time. I mean, I could tell you were kidding, I don't know why she couldn't. She's just so sensitive now, 'cause of the earthquake I guess."

Marcia's stomach sank. "Oh, no. Listen, Cory, I'm sorry I hurt your mother."

"It's not your fault," he told her with a shrug. "She's just gotten real erratic." He hung the pick on the side fence. "I really oughta go now."

"Thanks for telling me," Marcia said. "It was a nice thing to do, for all of us, OK?"

He flushed again. "I gotta go."

Marcia smiled at him. "When I need some more muscle—"

"Sure," he called, already half-out the gate. "Anytime."

Marcia pulled the pickaxe off the fence and sat down on the driveway's packed dirt. Something truly was wrong if Lydia couldn't take being teased after last night, when sex between them had reached the ecstatic level. Of course, that's probably exactly why she *was* so sensitive. You're not too swift in the thinking department today, Marcia told herself. She walked into the house and dialed Lydia's office number. "Lab," Lydia answered.

"Ah, hi."

"Hi." Lydia's voice was cool.

"How're you doing?"

"All right. Why?"

"Well—listen, Lydia, we really do have to talk."

It was so quiet the line hummed. "Why are you calling me at work to tell me this?" Lydia finally asked.

"Because—because I thought you might have misinterpreted something I said earlier today when really of course I'm not interested in anyone but you." Now why had she said that, she wondered. It sounded defensive. It sounded as if she were standing in the middle of a harem of dancing girls, for god's sakes.

The line was humming again. Reba turned on the chop saw, and Sarah responded by switching on a tape of what sounded like a woman moaning over a background of Gregorian chants. Maybe, Marcia thought anxiously, Lydia is saying something significant and I can't even hear her. "Lydia?"

"Yes?"

"I thought you might have said something."

"No, but can't we discuss this tomorrow? I have that meeting tonight and now I'm right in the middle of a procedure."

"The yams are restless? Okay, fine." Marcia hung on the line while Lydia disconnected. She sat there with the receiver on her lap until the phone started beeping at her and then she returned it to its cradle. "Bad news?" Sarah asked.

"No...uh, not really." Marcia wandered into the front hall where Dale was reframing for the carved front door, one of the early costly purchases they now regretted making. "Hi."

"Hi."

"I just did something stupid."

Dale stuck her pencil behind her ear and knelt down to measure the door jamb. "Number nine-thousand four-hundred fifty-one."

"With Lydia. Actually," she clarified, "first I did the stupid thing and then I made it worse. I called her up and I was defensive and dumb."

Dale tilted her head to the side. "Nine-thousand four-hundred fifty-two."

"Thanks for putting it in perspective," Marcia snapped.

Dale held up her hand and Marcia hauled her to her feet. "Gee," Dale said, "that's getting harder and harder to do." She pursed her lips, staring at Marcia. "Lydia really likes you a lot, you know."

"You think?" Marcia was as eager as a pup.

"And you like her too if you'd only let yourself feel it. Just the way you answered me now proves it."

Marcia sighed. "I do like—love her. But the whole thing scares me. I thought I was in love with Annie too."

"You were!" Dale exploded. "You *were* in love with Annie. After seven years you'd grown apart. It happens. It's not a crime. And it sure as shit doesn't mean a thing about anyone else. Annie is not Lydia. You can learn from experience but if all you learn is fear and avoidance, what you've taught yourself is to be dead."

"Jesus, Dale."

"It's true."

"But how could I have been so mistaken about someone I lived with for years? That's what I don't get."

Dale sighed with frustration. "You really meant it when you asked who was crazy, didn't you? Well, I meant it when I said it didn't matter. Those last two years you hardly saw each other. What pissed you off was you felt burned that you'd taken care of her for years and then it turned out she was fine by herself."

"Well, wouldn't that piss you off?"

"No! It was your choice. Anyway, she *did* need you, she just didn't need you anymore, and you didn't need her either. If you use what happened with Annie as an excuse to not see Lydia, you're being a coward."

"For crissake—" But then she stopped because when Dale bent down to pick up her hammer, a spasm of pain crossed her face. "You're really having trouble, aren't you?" Marcia said. "Come on, let's go sit out on our broken-down front porch for a few minutes."

They involuntarily glanced towards the top of the staircase and then stepped outside on the splintered boards of the porch, shoving the door over the opening to the house to give themselves some privacy. There was one fairly level area they could nestle in. "Tell me what's going on," Marcia said.

They knew each other too well for Dale to ask how Marcia had known anything was going on. "I feel like I'm falling apart," Dale confessed. "I thought—I don't know why, this seems so stupid now—I thought I could handle doing this—work on weekends or in the evening, tile someone's bathroom or stuff. I never realized we were going to take on such an enormous project. Even then it looked good at first. I figured I could work for myself, invest my five thousand at good appreciation, plus get paid for my labor, and all I needed to do was bridge the gap of not getting paid until after we'd sold." She took a deep breath. "I didn't think about how my back would be so fucked I can hardly work here much less anywhere else, and how my money's long ago run out, and how I can't fucking probably even go to Berlin—" She took another deep breath, trying not to cry. "I mean, you see what's happening over there."

Marcia was perplexed. "Yeah, I'd think you'd be wild with joy. They're dancing in the streets."

"Oh sure, the Wall coming down is great, but it's all unsettled now, which means who knows what could happen? It's weird how it's so close to the earthquake. Everything's gone nuts."

"Dale, let's stick to you."

Reba's head appeared in the open window above them. "Girls, I'm sure this is a fascinating discussion, but I fear I'm going to have to administer discipline soon." The window slammed shut as Marcia and Dale rolled their eyes.

"The thing is, if it gets horrible over there and Renate comes now, she can't work here. There's a ten-thousand dollar fine if people get caught hiring a foreigner. How the hell am I going to support us when I can't even bend over!"

Marcia was about to propose her usual, that Renate marry an American gay guy so she could work legally, but instead she was suddenly furious with both Dale and herself. Annie was becoming like a duck in a carnival game, popping up alive and well no matter how many times Marcia shot her. And Dale continued to agonize over

Renate, as if a solution didn't exist. We're either sisters in self-destruction or stupidity, she thought. She hugged Dale's shoulders, wishing more than anything they could solve each other's problems.

Dale had been watching cars pull up at the drug garage across the barricade. "Guess I shouldn't worry," she said glumly. "I don't know why she'd even want to come to this mess we've created for ourselves."

"She'll come because she loves you," Marcia told her.

Dale nodded. "You're right. I don't know why but she does. Guess she's got her head screwed on a little crooked."

# CHAPTER 16

Marcia was balancing a double cappuccino, a toasted dry bagel, a single latte, and the local gay rag's latest edition while she tried to open the recalcitrant door of her Ranchero. She was hurrying because she wanted to show Dale the marriage column, and she was late to Fairview Street—her morning check-in at the catering company had taken longer than usual today—but even more pressing, a shiftless mob of teenage boys was roaming down the block looking for trouble, and she would prefer to be in her car when they came upon her than standing out here in the oil stains.

She'd just slipped onto her cracked sprung seat with a sigh of relief when she realized one of the boys was Billy. He saw her at the same time, and they did a quick double-take, then an even faster assessment, both deciding to acknowledge the other: Billy apparently figuring his reputation could stand the strain of knowing a middle-aged white dyke, Marcia allowing herself another couple minutes before she got to Fairview Street. Besides, she wanted to find out what had happened to Lucas.

"What'cha doin' up here?" Billy greeted her, giving his puzzled friends a little wave which meant they should put themselves on hold.

"I work here," Marcia said, pointing at the catering company behind her, with its confusing logo of a waiter wearing a chef's hat, carrying a tray of hors d'oeuvres. Company lore said the original owners wanted to put a martini shaker in his third hand, but the artist objected. Billy nodded with comprehension, and both were embarrassed, faced with this blatant evidence of how little they really knew about each other; Marcia, for instance, had no idea what Billy was taking in school.

After they'd absorbed that blow, Billy wanted to know how Fairview Street was going. Marcia shook her head. "It's all right, I guess. Mostly exhausting. Has Lucas surfaced?" For some reason, Billy didn't like the change of subject. His face clouded over, and his brows dropped. Then he shrugged, as if he could care less what happened to Lucas. "Well, has he?" Marcia pressed.

"I guess."

"He either has or he hasn't."

"He's in detox," Billy finally admitted with a grimace.

"Huh." That knocked her back a step. It was about the last thing she'd expected. "Did he go in on his own?"

A faint tendril of hope began to grow in her. "Why are you so upset about it?" she challenged. "It's *good*. If he can sober up—"

"Oh, you know that's bullshit."

"Why?"

"'Cause he's such a fuck-up." Billy stated this with the assurance of a science teacher telling a class of first graders that the earth is round. "I don' know why you and Pop pay him any mind at all. I don't. I mean, I just don't expect anything out of him except crazy shit, y'know?"

He gave another elaborate shrug. "I cut him loose a long time ago."

"You did not," Marcia protested. "What are you talking about? The three of us are always hanging out together."

"Were," he corrected. "But I don't mean that. I mean I cut him loose up here." He tapped the side of his skull. "The dude's gone for me. I wouldn't spend a second looking for him. Only reason I asked you that day was 'cause Pop wanted me to."

Marcia was shocked speechless. When he saw she was not going to continue arguing with him, he raised his hand. "Look, I gotta get goin'. You be careful, Marcia, OK? See ya."

She nodded, though she wanted to dive out of her car and scream at him that his entire rap about Lucas had nothing whatsoever to do with Lucas and only with his own anger and self-hate, but she could hardly do that in front of his friends.

"I'll talk to you later," she told him. She watched him rejoin his pals and swagger down the sidewalk. People moved away fast, practically did backwards flips to get out of their path. Don't step aside for them, Marcia thought. They're just kids. Part of them wants to know they scare everybody but most of them just hopes to belong. All you guys that jump back are scaring them more than they're scaring you.

She pulled next to the curb at Fairview Street and slid out of the car, once more balancing her cups and bag. Dale was out back cutting lumber with her Skilsaw. "Jeez," she complained, "if I'd known it was going to take so damned long for you to get here with a simple latte—"

"Don't hassle me. It's been an ugly day so far, and it just looks as if it's going to get worse." Then she remembered, and her face brightened. "However, there is one ray of sun."

Dale looked pathetically interested in any optimistic news. Marcia tore the lid off her cappuccino, now cool, its foam all but gone, and opened the newspaper to the classifieds. "Look, I finally found the perfect one. This guy wants to live in Europe, so he needs a European wife. He's forty-five so it won't look funny. See, German, Belgian, or Dutch, he says." Dale, drawing a thick pencil line across another two-by-four, made no comment. "This way Renate can work here," Marcia explained, rolling her hands, expecting applause once the amazement at finding the appropriate groom had worn off.

Dale tilted down her safety glasses, positioned her saw, and made the cut. Then she shoved the glasses back up with her forearm. "You just don't get it, do you?"

"Get what?"

"Why the fuck should Renate have to marry a man so she can marry me?"

"Ah, come on, Dale—"

"No, I won't come on! I am sick of this shit! I am not going to be 'practical' or 'accommodating.' I've done all the fucking accommodating I'm ever going to do for het society. I want to marry her, period, and I'm not going to do something sleazy or undercover so she can live over here. She's applied for her visa, and when it's approved, she'll come."

"But—"

"Look, Marcia, I think why you're not getting this is on some level you still feel apologetic. Maybe it's because you're into S/M and three-quarters of the lesbian community and even me has made you feel like shit." Dale shook her head and the thick plastic glasses bobbed around in her short hair. "I am not in the least apologetic. I'm more enraged than anything else. As far as I'm concerned, it's the fire next time. That's why there's no fucking way Renate is marrying a guy."

Marcia sat down on the wall she'd just constructed behind the lavender plants. She ran her hand over the plump tassels, as swollen as big bees.

"Hey, I didn't mean to make you feel bad," Dale said after a moment.

"No, what you said is right. I can't believe it, but you're right." She stood up and walked out of the yard, leaving her cappuccino and the newspaper on the stone wall. Behind her, she heard Reba calling: "Hey, where's she going? Marcia!" and an unintelligible reply from Dale, which at least shut Reba up.

Marcia walked down one block, then another, her thoughts incoherent. Finally they coalesced into a single incident at work the day before, when she had been talking to Judy Inman, who had come in to pick up her paycheck. "Oh, there's a spider on you," Marcia had said as she reached up and brushed the spider off Judy's breast.

"Oooo, I'm so scared of them!" Judy cried. She was a big, bluff woman in her forties with three teenagers and a husband who drank. The two had continued talking for another couple minutes before it occurred to Marcia that perhaps Judy had been offended that Marcia had touched her breast, or that Judy might have even thought Marcia had invented the spider in order to touch her breast. Of course not, Marcia had told herself at the time; no to either scenario. Judy had thought nothing beyond that she had a spider on her dress, and she was no doubt glad that Marcia had gotten rid of it for her. But still Marcia had been relieved when Judy had finally left, and then she had sunk down at her desk to berate herself.

Who had she really been angry at, she asked herself now as she whipped around a corner. Surely not at Judy. Even if Judy had been offended, that was her problem, not Marcia's. No, Marcia was mad at this homophobic demon who lived in her head, who leapt up at odd moments to spout pure drivel, or who clouded her vision so she couldn't see the simplest things but would instead throw the sheets over her head and hope no one would notice the lump that was her if she stayed quiet enough.

The most infuriating part, she thought, is that none of this is me. Oh, yes, what I do in bed is part of me, but that's all it should be. I don't want to think about it, to focus on it. It assumes an importance it shouldn't have, and then people say, "Hey, why are you making this into such a big deal? My sexuality isn't the end-all of my life." Honey, it ain't mine either, but you make it be by your hate. That was the cruelest cut of all, to blame the oppressed for their oppression. Like telling black people they have a bad attitude when from day one they're defined by nothing more than the color of their skin. Like those people diving out of the way as Billy walks down the street. How much energy is spent on pure psychic survival, on fighting those inside and outside demons? Who has anything left to be who she really is?

And thinking about being who she was, she started to notice *where* she was, which was in the middle of a block walking towards a group of teenagers that did not include Billy, who were arguing about something and getting louder and more physical by the second. In spite of her thoughts a moment earlier about acting scared, Marcia made an abrupt about-face and started back up the street, heading for a group of older guys who were doing a landmine crack business. In the time it took her to walk down the remainder of the block, four cars came and went in quick five-second transactions.

When one of the men noticed her approaching, he said something, and a circle of faces turned towards her. She considered crossing the street. No, she thought, it's noon, it's a public sidewalk, and goddammit, it's even more suspicious to cross the damned road.

As she drew close to them, the hairs on the back of her neck rising, one man separated off from the rest. He walked beside her for a block, neither of them speaking, as if he were the sheriff escorting her to the edge of town. When he turned back without a word, she nearly collapsed in relief, but all the way back to the house she kept reviewing her options for defense or escape step-by-step—grab that baseball bat carelessly left on the lawn, run over to that house where women sat out on the porch. And all the way she castigated herself. Who am I to be so damned self-righteous and say people shouldn't be frightened? Yet how strange that I marched down these same streets minutes earlier, so completely caught up in my own rage that I saw no threat. Perhaps there really was no threat—though that seemed Pollyanna-ish. Still, Marcia thought, her fear was vastly exaggerated, way out of proportion to reality. And why so terrified today? Because she was feeling estranged from Billy and Dale, not to mention Lydia?

Something in me is changing, she thought, no matter how hard I try to resist. She was like the fault lines that defined the earth plates that made up California, moving in her center while her edges stayed stuck. A moment would occur when her edges had to finally catch up with the inexorably moving mass, and the resultant explosion was going to shake her for months.

She turned into the driveway gate of the house, crunched across the gravel, came back to the same wall, sat down, and sipped at her cold cappuccino. She stared into its mud-brown depths and saw nothing.

Dale sat down next to her and put an arm around her shoulders. "You don't live in a vacuum," Dale said to her.

"All this stuff matters, even if just in all the energy we have to spend pushing it away. We make jokes about how mean we are to each other, but we forget that hurt hurts."

Marcia smiled. "Now you're apologizing for me."

Dale grinned at her. "Hey, somebody's gotta. Tell everybody to fuck off. Live as if the world told you you could do it. It's people who are messed up, not the world."

"Sometimes I think I need to rehab me," Marcia said.

"Amen."


Lydia still had not called a day later, so Marcia phoned her. "Lydia, remember when I called you at the lab the other day and said I thought we should talk?"

"Ummm," Lydia said.

"Are you humming or what? Anyway, the thing is—"

"Listen, Marcia," Lydia interrupted, "I've decided that more than talking we need to do something fun with each other."

"But you always want to talk."

"And you don't. So why this sudden need?"

"Well-"

"There's something reactive here, something hidden under the surface."

"Cory heard you crying."

"I knew it. So you decide we should talk."

"Well, shouldn't we?"

"Because you pity me?"

"Lydia, I don't pity you, I *love* you!" This discussion was definitely not going the way Marcia had intended.

"You choose the nicest ways to tell me. Has it ever occurred to you that you never commit yourself to anything unless someone absolutely forces you, flushes you out, and then you just go to ground somewhere else?"

"Maybe we shouldn't talk," Marcia said heavily. She couldn't believe Lydia was saying this, especially over the phone.

"It doesn't mean I don't want to be with you, babe," Lydia went on. "I want you to come out and be with me. But you can't be with me unless you're with you, and you think being with you means being on your own."

Marcia closed her eyes. Lydia wanted her to trust, that's what this was all about.

"Mars."

"What?"

"Look, I was crying that morning because I was crying, okay? I didn't mean to start off on you. And I meant it about us doing something fun."

Marcia couldn't imagine what could be fun after this conversation. "Like what?"

"Well, I was thinking of a luxurious weekend at a B&B. I know one near Nevada City that has four-poster beds and a wonderful hot tub. But I knew you'd refuse because you can't afford it, so I'm willing to go backpacking."

Marcia's eyes widened. She hated backpacking even more than she hated talking. "Well—"

"Obviously not your favorite activity," Lydia surmised.

"It's November."

"Best time. Uncrowded, beautiful. Let's go tomorrow. No doubt you haven't noticed but it is Friday night."

Marcia thought fast. Reba had scheduled them for ten-hour days both Saturday and Sunday. The kids, as Polly called them, were returning on Monday to construct the front porch and the side fence. Marcia had finally finished building the boxes along the driveway, though she had the pond and the entire front yard to go. She rolled her eyes. Reba kept insisting they had to get on the market before the holiday slump. But if Lydia wanted her to come out and be with her, that's what she was going to do. "Fine," Marcia said. "But let's take my car, okay? And I'll bring everything we need."

"How come you have the equipment if you hate backpacking so much?" Lydia asked suspiciously.

"It's a recent antipathy."

"Come by early," Lydia told her.

"I will," Marcia promised. "I'm sorry I made you cry, OK?"

"Just come," Lydia said.

# CHAPTER 17

Marcia turned up on Lydia's doorstep at seven a.m. Lydia appeared in her robe, her eyes misty, shaking her tousled hair. "I told you to get here early," she admitted. Ten minutes later, her backpack by her side, she stood staring into the empty bed of the Ranchero. "Where's the stuff?"

"Trust me," Marcia said. "I said I would provide, and I will."

"We're staying in a tent cabin?" Lydia guessed. "I didn't know there were any still open. But it's okay, I guess. It is pretty cold."

The moment Marcia was on the highway, she began to feel better. She realized how exhausted she was.

She'd been working close to thirteen hours a day, five at work, eight at the house. She couldn't garden in the dark, so at night she'd helped glass-in the back staircase, which they'd done with the aid of rented flood lamps. Maybe, she thought, she could get Cory to help her dig out the pond. The listing agents, Marcia told Lydia, were coming the following Thursday, by which time the exterior of the enormous house had to be prepped and painted.

"It seems impossible that you've done all this work in so short a time."

"It *is* impossible. All I want to do is sleep."

"Well, you'll have plenty of time for that," Lydia said, "as long as you didn't pick a place too far away. We can rest from the phone, from the sound of radios and televisions, just us and the trees and the birds."

Marcia slipped a tape into the Ranchero's stereo system. Reggae music started pounding out of the speakers. Lydia smiled at Marcia and curled up against the door, making notes on a yellow legal pad affixed to a clipboard. She had to give another speech, and she'd told Marcia she hadn't done a thing about it since the earthquake.

Marcia zoomed by buses bound for the casinos as she tapped out the rhythm on the steering wheel. When some guys pulled near them and waved, she lowered her aviator sunglasses, looked them over, and then sped on. Lydia tried to say something above the pounding of the heavy bass.

"What?" Marcia shouted.

"TURN IT DOWN!"

Marcia did, quickly. "Sorry," she said.

"I'm glad I didn't know you when you were drinking."

"Why? Everyone says we're so dull and glum. Reba calls Dale and me 'the Republicans,' you know."

Lydia shook her head. "Yeah, well, this boring bit you affect is only a thin veneer over otherwise unmitigated craziness. Kind of like a semi-transparent stain that hides nothing."

Marcia laughed. "That's what Lucas says."

As Marcia had come down her front steps with her overnight bag that morning, Billy had sauntered out to tell her that Lucas was still on the straight and narrow. But Billy predicted that with a screw-up like his uncle it wouldn't last long.

"Did you like him better when he was drinking?" Marcia had snapped, irritated with Billy's attitude.

"Sure," Billy had retorted. "Now he looks like he's dead."

"Who cares what he looks like? He's stronger now than he's been in years. It takes guts to ask for help."

Billy had made a dismissive noise and slouched off, unimpressed with Marcia's logic, which, she admitted, she hardly believed herself or at least never followed. She still hadn't talked with him about why he was so upset with Lucas or with her, partially because she was always on the run.

I have to make time for him, she promised, yet here she'd wrested a weekend free from Fairview Street and instead of talking to him, she was going away. I'm on too many tracks, she thought. No wonder she kept heaping on the coal. If I could only finish this run, then I could switch rails. "How're the yams?" Marcia asked Lydia.

"They've been uncooperative lately," Lydia said. She made another note on her legal pad. "At least I enjoy it." She glanced over the top of her reading glasses at Marcia.

"The perfect job," Marcia said. "Socially redeeming, fascinating, contemplative..." Kind of like landscaping, she thought, if one weren't doing it at a dead heat. Maybe she *should* consider a career change—

"It's not socially redeeming," Lydia said. "In fact, one might even call it the opposite."

"Oh, Lydia, what's unredeeming about feeding the world?"

"Because the kind of basic research I do is generally used by companies to make expensive products that Joe and Molly Farmer can't afford to buy. Apart from that, those expensive products and technical advances have unexpected consequences."

Marcia glanced over at her. Lydia was tapping the legal pad on her knee. "Here's an example: for fifty years a Third World village has been gathering seaweed which provides thickeners for ice cream and yogurt. I come along with my fancy equipment which will select and seed an area with a variety of seaweed that contains far more thickener than the mix the villagers have been collecting. The villagers can't afford my expertise, but agribusiness decides it's now worth their while to set up a factory. So I've increased both the quality and quantity of thickener, but I've put an entire village out of work."

She looked over at Marcia. "And it's really much worse than that. We've pillaged germplasm from Third

World nations for decades and sold it back to them as products. Because of our emphasis on capital accumulation, we've discouraged research that would help farmers be self-sufficient. Agribusiness wants commodities, and that's what they pay us to develop, even in our little ivory towers."

Marcia shot past the Nevada City exit and Lydia's fancy B&B, which would have been paid for by the innocent yams, a variety Lydia told her had been gathered in Indonesia. "Nothing's simple, is it? Even what should be."

"Often what seems simplest turns out to be the worst," Lydia said. "But making those kinds of choices is far more than I can sort out. Just to feed the world's population for the next forty years will take the total amount of food produced in the last ten centuries, and we're trying to do it with a third of the earth's croplands decimated."

"You're kidding. You're not. That's a lot of thickener. Wouldn't it be easier to kill everyone off?" At Lydia's laugh, Marcia said, "I'm halfway serious. We have to stop people from breeding like rats. You know what Dale thinks?"

"I hate to guess."

"That we've created a disaster of such magnitude we *must* deny it, which in turn allows us to continue destroying everything."

Lydia sighed. "That presupposes we even care, which I think is debatable." They were silent for about twenty miles as they climbed higher and higher in the Sierra Nevadas.

Finally Lydia said, "I want you to come with me to my brother's wedding."

"Oh. Where is it?"

"In Roanoke, Virginia."

Marcia grimaced. "I don't know. There's about six places in the world I feel comfortable, and I bet Roanoke isn't one of them."

"Come on, Marcia, what could happen?"

"Death. Disablement. Despair. Disaster. The parade of deadly D's."

"I'll pay for your ticket."

"Hell, no." Marcia glanced over at Lydia. "All right, I'll go. And I can pay with the wonder of plastic. What do I have to wear?"

"The horrible dilemma of every butch. Whatever you like."

"You sure you want to introduce me to your family?"

"Of course. You think you're so reprehensible?"

"Noooo, just checking."

"You sound insecure. Maybe you need some confidence-building."

"No doubt."

By this time they were approaching Donner Pass. Lydia remained silent until they'd shot over the top and begun descending into the Nevada desert. "Marcia, where exactly are we camping tonight?"

"Umm, well, in a lovely room at Fitzgerald's with a queen-sized bed. Fourteen bucks a night for two."

"Fitzgerald's is in Reno," Lydia said.

"That's true."

"And I suppose we'll go hiking in the game room at Harold's Club."

"Backpacking through the Sands," Marcia added. "We can have a campfire at the Eldorado buffet, all the roast beef you can eat."

She glanced over to see how Lydia was taking it. If Lydia threw a fit, there was always Option Two, which was stopping in Truckee and charging the equipment they would need on her credit card. But a slow smile was spreading across Lydia's face. "Marcia, you're in a barrel of trouble."

"Oh, good," Marcia said. She floored the accelerator.


They were sitting in a booth at Tony Roma's, under a hanging plant bigger than both of them. Lydia had just polished off a full slab of baby back ribs while Marcia watched her in amazement. "How can you eat like that and stay so slender?"

Lydia shrugged, uninterested. She was watching the numbers light up on the Keno board at the front of the restaurant. "Didn't you have nineteen and seven?"

Marcia checked the hashmarks on her card. "Hey, good deal. I got three out of three. Forty bucks."

She tipped the Keno runner a five, then relaxed back against the plush green upholstery. We should have done this ages ago, she thought. Then she noticed Lydia gazing at her. "What's wrong?"

"Nothing," Lydia said. She stirred some sugar in her coffee. "Did you and Annie switch all the time?"

She glanced up with what Marcia had come to think of as the asking-about-Annie look, half-resigned and half on pins and needles. Apparently Lydia either feared being unable to compete with Annie or that Annie had somehow scared Marcia so much she was unsalvageable.

"We didn't do S/M."

"You're kidding."

"No, I'm not kidding. I'm sure you haven't done S/M with every single one of your lovers either."

Lydia acknowledged the truth of this statement. "You were together a long time. I'm surprised, that's all."

Marcia shrugged. "We did the whole non-consensual emotional turmoil thing that people do. You know, you always imagine it'd be healthier to convert some of that energy into S/M, but it doesn't work that way. I don't think it comes from the same place. In any case, she was—unwilling, let's say. She just never got it."

"What do you mean?"

"She thought it was wimpy to have safewords or fantasize fearful or dangerous situations when you were actually safe. She thought if you did S/M you should do it"—Marcia indicated quote marks by wiggling two fingers on each hand—"'for real.' No safeword, no caring, just beat someone up."

"But that's not S/M, that's abuse! How could anyone find that sexually exciting?"

"Exactly. Which is why we never did anything." Marcia sighed and sipped at her own coffee.

"At first I thought she was purposely being obtuse, to be annoying or because she really didn't want to do it so to fob me off she came up with an alternative she knew I'd never go for. But then I began to wonder. Maybe she really didn't see the difference."

"That's impossible," Lydia asserted.

Marcia shrugged. She'd spent enough energy puzzling over Annie when they were together; she saw no reason to waste time on it now. "Wanna split?" she asked.

But Lydia shook her head. She was still thinking. "Maybe there was no sexual turn-on in it for her, so she figured S/M's appeal must be that push-pull psychodrama you sometimes see in abusive relationships. Maybe she even thought that's what you wanted. You can be much more dramatic without a safety net."

"Very perceptive," Marcia said tightly. "But if she thought that's what I wanted she wasn't listening."

Lydia tented her hands. "Why are you so bitter, babe? I mean, I had a horrible relationship with Jeff, but I've moved beyond it."

"Good for you," Marcia said. "Come on, let's leave."

She actually felt like laying her head on the table and going to sleep. It seemed like a good way to escape when you couldn't drink your way out of a discussion.

Lydia watched her for a long moment, tapping her fingers on the table. "*Did* she abuse you?"

Marcia said nothing. She stared into the dregs of her coffee, wondering how to answer. The waitress came and filled up their cups.

After another minute or two ticked by, Lydia said, "I assume your silence means yes."

"I don't want to talk about this." In fact, she wanted to disappear under the table.

"You have to," Lydia told her.

Marcia closed her eyes. "She never really hit me," she said slowly. "It was more—like an underlying current of violence. She would scream and push me or throw things or say she was going to kill herself. I tried not to set her off, I tiptoed around her anger, terrified she'd turn it on me if I did something wrong. Of course I almost always did do something wrong even if I did nothing. I hated it, it made me sick. I kept thinking how stupid it was because I was bigger, stronger. But I knew I could never defend myself because I wouldn't hit her back. I loved her, how could I hit her? I kept wondering, if I couldn't do it to her, how could she do it to me?"

Lydia reached across the table and took Marcia's hands in hers. "So you lived with her for seven years and you never felt safe."

"No," Marcia said, and her relief at finally telling someone was so palpable a waterfall was cascading off her shoulders. "I never felt safe."

"Why the hell didn't you leave?"

"I thought she'd die without me. Turned out that when we finally split up, she began to live. Isn't that a joke?"

Tears welled in Marcia's eyes. Lydia stroked Marcia's palms, then lifted her right hand and kissed her fingers. "So could you, honey. You could start living too."

"How're you doin'?" Lydia leaned over Marcia's shoulder as Marcia scattered powder blue chips in various patterns around the roulette layout.

"Embarrassingly well," Marcia said, indicating the big pile of chips in front of her. She pulled some striped chips marked five dollars out of her pocket and handed them to Lydia. "Here, take these so I won't spend them."

"She's doin' great, lady," the man next to Marcia said. He had a Clark Gable-style moustache and a cowboy shirt.

"He's seen *The Misfits* too often," Marcia told Lydia.

The little ball rattled about in the wheel. Marcia had a half-chip on the winner. The dealer raked in the rest of Marcia's chips and then counted out and pushed across a tall stack of blues.

"I feel guilty," Marcia said to Lydia. "I just keep winning and winning. This has never happened to me before. I mean, I often win at roulette, but not like this." While Marcia was talking, she was throwing her blue chips all over the layout, some across four numbers, most over two, a couple on single numbers. Lydia's eyes widened. "Marcia, how much are each of those worth?"

"A quarter."

"Well, you've just spent about five bucks."

"That's OK."

The ball spun into a slot. Marcia slapped the table. "Hot damn!" It was one of her two single numbers. The cowboy groaned as his chips were raked away. He turned in a twenty dollar bill for more chips. Marcia tipped the dealer four chips, then handed a striped fiver to Lydia.

"Marcia," Lydia said.

"Hey, don' bother her, lady, she's winning!"

"Don't tell her what to do," Marcia said to him. "What?"

"Do you want to leave soon?"

"OK." Marcia was tossing her chips around again. This time she came out slightly behind, only bagging a quarter-chip's worth.

"Don' listen to her. Never quit when you're winning."

"Better to quit when you're winning than losing."

"Marcia."

"What?" The ball was spinning again. Marcia was scattering her chips, less this time.

"I'm sort of—uhmm—"

The ball spilled into one of Marcia's doubles, and also one of the cowboy's. "Thank god," he said. "Don't listen to her," he told Marcia. "You leave in the middle of a winning streak it's bad luck forever."

"I'll chance it," Marcia said. She shoved her chips across the table. "I'm cashing in." A moment later she moved with Lydia past the craps tables. "What's wrong?"

"I was just thinking. Uh, what if there's an earthquake and we can't get back?"

Marcia nodded. "Yeah, I thought of that on the way up. It's frightening, isn't it? It's scary to be home and it's scary to be away." She took Lydia's elbow and guided her out of the casino until they stood on the narrow street flooded with crawling cars. Cruising was the big Saturday night activity for Reno's teenagers. "Do you want to phone Cory?"

"It's midnight," Lydia said.

"Do you want to go back? We can if you like. I'm awake enough to drive."

Lydia kissed her on the cheek. "No, let's go up to our room. I just mostly wanted to tell you. And I guess I wanted to see if you'd leave."

"An alcoholic I am, a gambling addict I'm not. I'm too cheap, you know that. Besides, I can't stand to win and I can't stand to lose."

Lydia laughed. "OK, tiger. Let's hit the sack."

Marcia awoke to the lonely whistle of a train. She lay next to Lydia, listening to the chuffing on the tracks below, the quiet hum of heat in the big hotel, and the reassuring sigh of Lydia's breathing, steady as a heartbeat. She could touch the smooth warmth of Lydia's thigh and sense the muscle and blood and sleek throbbing strength underneath, as if she had X-ray vision in her fingers. Funny how she could be so perceptive in some ways and oblivious in others. Dale had been telling her for months that memory makes us human but it can also drown out what we need to survive. Lydia could caper on the edges because, unlike Annie, her edges weren't razor-sharp. Of course Annie hadn't been able to do S/M—she couldn't trust herself not to commit mayhem. Yet mayhem had permeated their relationship anyway, and it was still reverberating through Marcia's being.

I'm safe now, Marcia thought. I've been safe all along, I've only doubted my own judgment. Lydia and Annie are nothing alike. She lay in the dark, feeling as if she were cascading down a mountain to sink into a warm sea, while all around her was the glow of twinkling lights.

But then she vaulted from the sea, once again stunned by her own blindness. In all the time she'd tried to explain S/M to Annie, it had never once occurred to her that she wouldn't have felt safe enough to do it with her. Why *had* she stayed with Annie for seven years? For security? How secure could it have been when she was too terrorized to make love as she wished? Only by breaking through with Lydia had she been able to understand she'd almost consigned herself to a truncated life out on her porch for no reason but fear. Lydia was right: instead of accepting that she'd made a mistake, she'd blamed life, relationships, love, anything else.

Lydia moaned in her sleep. Marcia moved close and Lydia nestled against her, pushing her butt tight against Marcia's stomach. Marcia wrapped her arm around Lydia, cupping Lydia's breast in her hand, and listened to her breathe.

# CHAPTER 18

Marcia turned up for the final push at Fairview Street at six a.m. Monday morning, to find Polly and Reba already edging countertops, with Reba striding about like Rommel in the desert and Polly sleepy-eyed and yawning. Marcia went upstairs to eat the strawberry muffin she'd bought the night before. The street was quiet, the drug garage closed for business. Mr. Thomas had mowed his lawn again that weekend, keeping it to a neat half-inch.

When it got light enough to work outside, Marcia began tearing down the packing crates, breaking them up, and loading the junk into the Ranchero. Sarah drove in around eight, followed by Dale. At eight-thirty the Fearless Foursome arrived, Kimberley in a growly mood and the others tired, they said, from their last job. Kimberley and Jennifer began sinking postholes along the section Marcia had already cleared, while Lauren and Janey went to work on the front porch.

Dale came out to supervise the posthole digging and instead began an argument with Kimberley which Marcia couldn't follow since she had to keep dragging broken packing crates to Dale's truck, now that the bed of her Ranchero was packed full. But she turned the corner just in time to hear Dale say in the voice of sarcasm she had perfected over the years: "Are you telling me you're a better lesbian than I am because you sleep with men?"

A pregnant pause. Jennifer bit her lower lip while Marcia strolled over, intending to mediate. "Can you believe it?" Dale said to Marcia. She lifted her hands beseechingly to the heavens. "Oh, Go-o-od! I think we need a reality check down here."

"This is such bullshit!" Kimberley snapped.

Marcia snagged one of Dale's lifted arms. "Stop harassing them and let them work," she told her.

Jennifer decided to talk. "Kimmy, let's not start—"

Kimberley rounded on her. "I'm not afraid to defend my right to sleep with men and identify as queer."

"We aren't here to debate," Marcia interrupted calmly, thinking she sounded like Reba. "We're here to work. And that's what we're all going to do, right now." She made a motion with her head to Dale, and both of them went off. Behind them Marcia could hear Kimberley muttering something about fascists and Jennifer remonstrating with her.

"Hey," Dale said, tapping her fingers on her breastbone insistently as they climbed up the steps to the side deck. "Fascists, huh? Where were they when we were marching against the war? Who's got FBI files two inches thick? Who's been beaten up and spat at and—"

"What do you care who they sleep with?" Marcia asked her. "They could sleep with *insects*, who gives a shit?"

Dale bit her lower lip, thinking. "Insects," she said. She went into the house, chuckling. Marcia turned on her heel and went back to the packing crates. She was ignored by Kimberley and treated to sympathetic rolled eyes from Jennifer. Out front Lauren, perhaps sensing discord, added to the fire by putting on a tape that sounded like a bunch of synthesizers had fallen into a drum kit. Kimberley made a special journey to the porch to tell her to turn it up so she could hear it in the back yard. Sarah, emissary to the young, dressed in her baggy overalls with her tool belt dragging off her hips, came outside to tell Lauren to turn it down. Marcia had just brought another load to Dale's truck when Reba joined the fray at the front porch.

"It's our right to listen to music at the job site," Lauren told Sarah.

"Is that in the Constitution?" Reba asked.

"Tell them to turn off that junk!" Polly shouted from the large unit's bedroom window.

Sarah threw her a look and then turned back to the others. "Let's just try to find something we all like."

But Kimberley was unwilling to be mollified. "You've treated us with disrespect ever since we came here. I've never had to put up with shit like this on a job. It's homophobia, pure and simple."

"Homophobia?" Reba sputtered. "Hey, honey, take a look."

"Just because you're gay doesn't mean you're not homophobic. In fact—"

"Let's not get off on that again," Jennifer told her as Polly appeared at the front door, her cheeks splashed with angry crimson blotches and her hands clenched into fists.

"Homophobia coupled with power," Lauren added. "You're paying us, so you think you've bought our submission. You guys have been so coopted you make the CIA look good." With a flick of her finger she turned up the volume. "Now let's all go back to work."

"Don't forget they sleep with men," Dale called from the sidewalk where she was repairing the picket fence. "And insects!"

Reba formed a pistol with her right hand, shot Dale through the heart, and blew delicately on her index finger. Then she swiveled back towards them, a brilliant smile on her face. Reba the charmer, Marcia thought. That role usually belonged to Polly, but her perpetual good cheer had lately been replaced by forced smiles and nervous chatter, as if she knew a wolf was in their midst, a gaunt stalker that only needed someone to notice him before he ripped them apart.

"We can work this out very easily—" Reba began, but fury had apparently washed away Polly's caution.

"You're absolutely right, Lauren," she said, her whole body quivering. "We're paying you, so we get to decide about the music. If that's oppressive, tough shit. Maybe in a couple hours, we can decide again. Maybe you can have it on softly. Right now I've had it and I'm not going to take it one more second." She plowed over to Lauren's tape player and punched it off.

There was a moment of intense silence. It was Jennifer who finally found her voice. "You can't touch her tape player."

"Why?" Dale shouted from the walk. "I thought owning property was fascist."

"Shut up!" Reba yelled back at Dale. "Look, Polly's sorry she touched your player." Lauren had begun to breathe again, which Marcia considered a good sign, Kimberley's eyes refocused, and Janey stopped gnawing on her lip. But Polly was still trembling with leftover adrenaline, and she kept swallowing and clearing her throat with a hacking sound that was hard to listen to. "However, as you can see," Reba continued, "she's very upset by this. Now I think we should all work for a couple hours and you can turn it on at lunch, okay? Maybe we'll split so you can eat in peace."

"With their boyfriends," Dale called. She raised a broken picket in triumph.

Kimberley seemed about ready to sprint down the walk after her, but the rest, recovered from the shock of Polly's overt action, had cooler heads. Everyone went back to work except for Marcia who rambled across the front lawn to tell Dale to cool it. "They don't have it so easy, you know," she said. "When do we go out? Hardly ever. They get hassled constantly. Gay-bashing is up everywhere. We were beaten up and tear-gassed in crowds of thousands. They're being set on by thugs in twos or threes. They're on the front line all the time. So what if some of them sleep with men occasionally? That doesn't invalidate their experience of being gay. If people could do what they really wanted without fear, most everyone would be bisexual."

"Not me," Dale said.

"All right, not you," Marcia said, giving up. "I'll be around back."

"This is crazy," Dale said when Marcia returned from a brief trip to Top Hat at four. "Wouldn't you call this panic self-driven?"

"Reba-driven," Marcia groused.

Dale perched on Marcia's wall and ran her fingers across the lavender buds. "Polly's kinda losing it."

"I've never seen her so mad," Marcia agreed. "I didn't know she had it in her. Of course, living with Reba would drive anyone bonkers."

"Polly knew what to expect when she married Reba," Dale said. "But she never could have predicted the stuff we've run into with this house."

Marcia shielded her eyes from the glare of the sun. "Is it that different? The four of you have done these jobs together for years."

"With other people's money," Dale said, "and for someone else. We didn't have our own bucks in it. Remember Polly made such a big deal of putting in her separate savings? We all did, me, Sarah, you... I think Reba feels responsible for everyone and her money."

"That's the trouble with being an egotist," Marcia said. "You think everything's your fault."

Dale grinned. "Call this project 'Reba Should Have Shrugged.'"

"Exactly. But think how Polly must feel propping up Atlas *plus* the weight of the world."

Reba threw open the rear unit's bathroom window. "News flash!" she called to them. "Sixty-eight and three-quarters hours 'til D-Day!"

"Come on, Dale," Marcia said. "I think we just had our weekly ten-second break."

Tuesday Marcia had a load of top soil delivered; by Wednesday she'd planted the driveway boxes with a mix of semidwarf fruit trees, climbing roses, and perennials, set bougainvillea and bamboo in the containers on the side deck off the french windows, and edged the lip of the pond's polyvinyl sheet with rocks she'd gathered at the tail-end of the Reno trip. Pond-filling and planting came Thursday morning; by one Marcia was misting the new transplants, shaking her head at all they'd accomplished.

Three sides of the house were painted, the front porch was sturdy again, and the packing crates had been replaced with a six-foot-tall redwood fence. The yard would be new-looking, but its design structure was strong and attractive.

Reba acted as tour guide for the two agents while the rest of the rehab crew and the employees worked on the fourth side and finished off details: mounting light fixtures, towel bars, bathroom mirrors, and closet shelves. When the agents left, Reba gathered the rehab crew in the upstairs front bedroom, leaving the employees to continue painting. "One twenty-five for the rear unit, one-sixty for the front."

"That's great!" Sarah said. "That gives us a hundred-ten thou profit!" She lowered her voice as Carol jerked her head to indicate listening ears out the window, although it was probably impossible for the younger set to eavesdrop over the tape player that Polly had allowed to be set at a reasonable volume.

"There's the real estate fee," Reba cautioned.

"There's our labor costs," Marcia added. She was rapidly calculating in her head. Even with everything tacked on, they had doubled their money.

"Still—" Polly said. They were all starting to smile.

"Still it's good," Reba agreed. "Now, they had some comments. They thought the floor plan was terrific." Marcia poked Dale. "And they loved the bathrooms, especially the small unit's."

"Good going, Sarah," Polly said.

"They loved the deck off the bay window." Marcia preened. That had been her idea. "And they really loved the back yard. They said it added twenty thou to the price of the house."

"Hey!" Dale clapped Marcia on the back.

"But—"

"Why did I know there'd be a but?" Marcia wondered.

"They said the house has no curb appeal."

"Curb appeal?" Dale questioned.

"Marcia, you didn't do a fucking thing with the front yard! It looks like the Mojave desert out there! And it's really typical of you. You just didn't think."

"What's that supposed to mean?"

"I mean, you like to be in a garden. I've been in your back yard. So you figured no one would want to be out front. Well, being *in* one isn't the purpose of a garden," Reba shouted. "The point of a garden is to fucking impress people as they drive by!"

"Gee, pardon me for being so crass that I didn't fully appreciate that, Reba."

Sarah stepped lightly on her toe, so Marcia clammed up. Sarah was right; there was no point in picking a fight. But it turned out a fight was in the offing anyway. After Reba had explained that they needed to put flowers in every room and have bread and cookies baking in the ovens, filling the house with wonderful smells for Open House Sunday, Polly announced that she and Reba were taking a long-deserved rest.

"What kind of rest?" Dale asked with an edge of fear in her voice.

"She means we're not going to do this anymore," Reba said. "We decided last night."

Dale ran her fingers through her short hair. "Gee, this is great to hear right before I go off to Germany. I'm glad to know I won't have a job when I get back."

Polly's eyes brimmed over with tears. "I'm sorry, Dale, but I hated every minute of it. I think we were all really shitty to each other. It wrecked it for me. I just don't want to do it anymore."

"I didn't realize how hard it would be," Reba took up. "I didn't think about how everybody would have money in it and we wouldn't be getting paid and what that would mean.... I know all you guys think I'm a hard-ass, but I was just trying to keep us going and get Dale to Germany and make our money back..." Marcia had been lying on the floor; now she raised herself on her elbows so she could see Reba. Was what we valued most about ourselves always the very thing that drove everyone else nuts?

"I can get to Germany on my own, thanks," Dale was telling Reba, her fingers twitching. Dale in a rage could be volcanic; Marcia began to edge across the floor towards her.

"Hey?" she said softly.

Dale shook her off. "If we're going to be so honest, what's this shit Polly was telling me this morning about the Neighborhood Watch?"

"Fuck that," Reba exploded. "Mr. Thomas came over here and wanted us to write down the license numbers of cars coming to the dope garage. He said we had the best vantage point from these windows. We'd get the goddamned house burned down."

"Pretty ironic given that you wanted to burn it down yourself a month ago," Dale told her.

"So that's why Mr. Thomas hasn't waved at me the last couple days," Marcia mused.

"How come you didn't ask the rest of us?" Sarah said. "Maybe we would have wanted to help."

"Our street did that last year," Marcia said. "Our whole neighborhood did it." And had driven out the druggie renters across the street, opening up the house to the art students. Of course, they'd had just-retired Robert to spearhead the operation, sitting on his porch with a notebook and a pen day and night.

Carol had been slouched in a corner smoking a cigarette. Now she dropped the butt in the dregs left in her beer can.

"So go write down the numbers," she challenged, jerking her head towards the windows. "And make a big fucking point of it too so everyone can see who's such a righteous asshole."

No one moved and none of them looked at each other either. After a long minute, Carol snorted and stood up, throwing her jacket over her shoulder. "Mail me my check," she said as she walked out the door.

Polly rose too, sniffling. "Come on, Reba."

"I'm sorry," Reba told them. She waited until Polly had started down the steps to add, "She's really mad at me, too. I'll talk to you guys later."

Sarah and Dale and Marcia were left sitting in the stillness, the smoke from Carol's cigarette settling in hazy layers around them. Dale leaned over to raise the front window. They could hear the heavy bass from Lauren's tape player and Jennifer shouting something to Kimberley about where to eat dinner that night. They still hadn't looked at each other. "Maybe I should move to Berlin," Dale said.

"No," Marcia told her.

"Can you believe this?" Sarah asked.

"We saved the bats," Dale offered. "We got bat karma from here to New York."


Marcia went to her own house that night. There were twenty minutes of messages on her machine, some six days old. She listened to them in a fog. Then she phoned Lydia's machine, telling the tape she was too exhausted to come over and that she would see her Friday evening. She took her clothes off and lay in bed in the dark. A few hours later, she heard someone knock tentatively on her door but she didn't get up to answer.

Friday she spent her entire day at Top Hat, surprising Ted, who looked miffed that he didn't have her desk to mess up but relieved after two servers suddenly became ill and one woman's car broke down. When Marcia got home from work, Lucas was sitting on the top stair of her front porch, rocking back and forth, his arms wrapped around himself, his face gray and gaunt. She had never seen him look so bad. "Lucas!"

"Hey, Marcia. Old devil whupped my ass, huh? Sent me on home here to look at the bay."

Marcia unlocked the door behind him and came back out with two Cokes. They sat facing the Golden Gate, watching the light fade from the sky.

"What'cha doin' here?" he asked after awhile.

"I live here."

"You do and you don't."

She tilted her head to the side, acknowledging this point. "You want something to eat?"

He shivered. "I'm not much on eating yet."

She nodded and faded off for a time, enjoying the night air and Lucas' silent presence. Finally she had to come back to earth. "Hey, Lucas. Is Billy—acting kind of weird with you?"

"You mean, is he mad at me? Sure he is. He's mad at you too."

She was affronted. "Why?"

"'Cause you're never home for him to talk to."

"He doesn't want to talk to me. He runs in the other direction everytime he sees me." Except the past couple weeks, she admitted to herself.

Lucas chuckled. "Guess he just wants you around to run from." He lit a cigarette and sipped at his Coke. "'Course, he's got plenty to be mad about."

"Yeah, but why us? We're the ones helping him."

Lucas nodded. "Sure. We're gonna help by standin' around wavin' good-bye when he gets on that bus to the CYA."

He sipped at his Coke while Marcia took a deep breath, her head pounding. When you're seventeen, she reminded herself, you still think the adults in your life can work miracles, can change almost anything. She remembered her dog Mattie, how he would turn and look at her reproachfully with his big brown eyes whenever it was raining outside. I don't want to go out in this! Make it stop! That's all Billy asked. He just wanted them to make it stop.

The phone rang. Marcia hesitated, then rose groaning under the force of Lucas' wordless chivvying.

"Marcia," Lydia said, "I thought you were coming over tonight."

"Oh. Well, I'm just sitting out here with Lucas."

"What happened with the agents?" Lydia asked.

Marcia gave her an abbreviated report. "That sounds good," Lydia said. "But you don't. What's wrong?"

"I'm a little depressed."

"End of project blues?"

"I guess. I'll tell you about it later."

"Don't forget the wedding."

"How could I? It's not every day I go to Roanoke." Marcia hung up the phone and went back out on her porch.

"Headin' up there?" Lucas asked her.

"I don't think so," Marcia said.

"Go on," he pressured her. "Woman calls you, wonderin' where you are, wants to see you, you get in that shitkicker car of yours and bring her flowers too if you know what's good for you."

Marcia laughed at him. "You got it all figured out, don't you? Well, solve this. She thinks I don't trust her."

Lucas nodded, rubbing the corner of his mouth with a long index finger. "Trust is a sometime thing. Has more to do with you than her anyway."

Marcia sighed. "That's what she's afraid of." She flipped up her palms in surrender. "OK, OK, I'm going." She squeezed Lucas' shoulder. "Hang in there."

"Sure," he said, his eyes haunted behind the swollen lids, "sure I will."

# CHAPTER 19

Marcia unlocked the dull green door to their motel room, stepped aside for Lydia to enter, and then came in behind her, carrying her small duffel by its shoulder strap as well as a paper sack stuffed full of presents Lydia had brought for her family.

"Dale and Sarah are out of a job," Marcia was saying, "but we've already gotten two full-price offers on the small unit."

"You're kidding!" Lydia said, tossing a garment bag across the bed one second before Marcia pitched herself next to it. "You didn't tell me that."

Marcia nodded. "Yup. They have to be sold together, of course. Tenants-in-common. One couple is so anxious they're actively recruiting a family with kids to buy the big one. 'Where else,' they asked us, 'can you find a three-bedroom house for one-sixty?'"

"With french windows leading onto a gorgeous deck."

"With a hand-carved front door."

"With a back yard with a pond and dozens of roses."

"With bullets flying everywhere you look." Marcia turned on her back and lay her arm over her eyes. She could sense, however, that Lydia was regarding her with exasperation.

"Marcia, how can you stand being so determinedly miserable?"

"You gotta admit it didn't turn out so hot, Lydia."

"Oh, I don't know. Doubling your money isn't bad."

"I don't mean that. I mean Reba and Polly pulling out and the earthquake and the kids thinking we're so bad and even Mr. Thomas' Neighborhood Watch business."

"Well, what'd you expect, tiger? Did you really believe you were going to write down the numbers of those cars and risk having the whole thing blow up in your faces?"

Marcia flipped up her palms. "Yeah, I guess I did. I mean, I did it before."

"In a different situation. And I don't know why you're depressed about Reba. It's not like you wouldn't continue being friends, is it?"

Marcia smiled. "No. Reba's already making noises about taking on a limited role. Sarah's started calling her 'low-profile Reba.' Polly—well, I think she's wanted out for a long time. We're all older and it gets physically harder every year. Their pulling back is probably a good thing. It just felt bad coming at the end like that, and it leaves Dale and Sarah in the lurch."

Lydia took off her shoes and socks and began massaging her toes. "Getting older is a good reason for you to make the switch to landscaping while you still can. Get together with Dale and Sarah and quit your job at the catering company."

"I've been thinking about that. But where could we buy? It'd have to be a quote-unquote transition neighborhood again, so we'd be pricing people out..."

"It's not quite so monolithic as you make it appear, Mars. Take Mr. Thomas. Your rehabbing that wreck across the street from him and selling it at those prices jumped the value of his place about thirty thousand. Whenever a street is mostly owner-occupied, you're helping, not hurting. Besides, you could convert empty warehouses to live-work artists' spaces if you wanted."

Marcia grinned. "Lot of landscaping opportunities with a warehouse."

Lydia poked her. "My kitten always looks on the bright side."

"First I'm your tiger, now I'm your kitten. What does that mean?"

"It means I want to bite your neck."

Lydia pounced on the bed next to Marcia, on top of the garment bag, but Marcia fought her off. "Honey, I really am kinda down." She pulled Lydia close and said, "It's hard for me to make love when I feel this shitty. It's too intimate and too affirming. I know that sounds contradictory—"

"No, it doesn't," Lydia said. "You feel like a rat."

"Yeah."

"Okay, let's talk about that for a minute. I've been thinking about this rat business."

"And you've rationalized a bunch of stupid excuses."

"Do you mind if I tell you what I've done? Or do you just want to have this conversation with yourself?"

Marcia bounded up off the bed and began to pace around the room. Lydia watched her patiently for a few moments until Marcia ran down a little. Then she said, "You know, I figure my being willing to wear a dress will allow me to make about—oh, maybe four hundred thou more than you will in the course of our lifetimes." She tilted her head to the side as Marcia stopped pacing and blinked at her.

"What do you mean?"

"Exactly what I said. I play the game at those conventions I go to. I wear a very nice skirt and a silk blouse and a scarf and I have my hair done and I wear lipstick. People flock around me because I look good and I'm good at what I do. I know how to act with people. You could give a shit how to act with people though you're good at what you do too, at everything you do, at managing and landscaping and living in general. But because of who you are, you won't get paid for doing those things, no matter how well you do them. So you don't have a pension plan or health insurance or anything else, even sick leave. Yet still over the course of fifteen years you manage to amass fifteen thousand bucks. You know as well as anyone else that fifteen thousand bucks is worth shit in this society. You can't retire on fifteen thousand bucks." Lydia shook her head. "Doing that house is your way of taking care of yourself. I have to admit that at first I had my reservations. But then I saw how unbelievably hard you've worked on it and what it meant to you and what your choices were. And I started thinking about how everything can be looked at in a lot of different ways."

"Yeah, but—"

"Let me finish. You tell me we have an individual responsibility to act morally, and you're right. What you're ignoring is that we don't have individual freedom of action. We're interconnected with everyone, and those connections are unbelievably complicated. To pretend otherwise is just naive. Sometimes we're forced to make choices we don't like."

Marcia rubbed her hands through her short hair. "That's not an answer, Lydia."

Lydia tipped her head to the side. "Maybe there is no answer."

"You better hope there is," Marcia told her, "or we're in even worse trouble than I thought." She stopped stalking around the room and came back to lie on the bed, moving close to Lydia. "You're a scientist. How can you say there's no answer?"

Lydia grinned at her. "There's two kinds of questions, the ones you can solve and the ones you can't. I concentrate on the former and leave the others to philosophers and theologians."

"Or politicians," Marcia countered. "Or to no one, which is what I'm really afraid of."

She and Lydia stared up at the ceiling, but their hands, as if disconnected from their bodies, crept across the covers until they found each other and hung on tight. "When I was younger," Marcia said, "I thought we'd wipe out poverty and prejudice in one generation, that we were so different from the ones who'd brought us concentration camps or nuclear bombs. I guess I still think we can be noble, but I never expected to be so disgusted with us at the same time." She flipped on her side so she could look at Lydia. "And you're right. I'm no worse, but I'm no better either. I expected more of myself." She shook her head. "Here I've spent all these years worrying about being despised for what I do in bed when I should have been concerned that I have the integrity of a snake. Disappointing myself is a lot worse than disappointing the moral fucking majority. Now I understand why people turn to religion—so they can stay open to *something*."

Lydia reached out to touch her cheek. "So what're you going to do, tiger, start chanting?"

Marcia wrinkled her nose. "That's not really my style. But I do want to keep feeling. Guess I'm just a pain junkie at heart."

Lydia laughed. "I'm telling you, you're never going to top at this rate."

A smile flitted across Marcia's mouth that finally settled to stay. She rose to her knees, caught Lydia by the elbows and pulled her from the bed to give her a kiss. "It's so nice to see you smile," Lydia told her when they broke for air. "Your whole face lights up like the sun just rose behind your eyes."

"How can I feel so blessed after what I just said?" Marcia wondered. "That's the trouble with being alive. It really grows on you after awhile."


Lydia's parents were small and round like dumplings, and her brother Randall was only a couple inches taller than Marcia. Sister Edie was the tomboy in the family—Marcia decided she and her husband were the het equivalents of Castro Street clones. They dressed alike, moved alike: it was hard to imagine they hadn't grown up together, twins. Randall's bride was funny, no-nonsense, and impatient with all the brouhaha surrounding her wedding day. All of them descended on Lydia and Marcia the moment they got out of their rental car.

Marcia stayed in the background where she was most comfortable anyway, enjoying everyone's delight in seeing Lydia, and savoring Lydia's excitement at introducing her to Randall and Edie. Lydia's parents, however, had telegraphed their displeasure, her father distant, her mother remarking that perhaps Lydia had asked Marcia to accompany her only as a polite gesture. Marcia decided to stay out of their way to prevent Lydia from getting annoyed at them.

Everyone was upset Cory had not come. "He could-n't," Lydia lied gracefully. "He was behind in school and he said he just couldn't do it."

He wouldn't was more to the point. He had announced that a church wedding when one was not religious was hypocritical. Marcia thought he had latched onto this objection as an excuse not to go—he would spend the time at his father's in San Jose, near his girlfriend—but she had endured three evenings' worth of discussions before Lydia had given in. Now she sat in the pew thinking not about Cory but Billy, who would graduate from high school on a Friday in June and go directly (that Monday, he had told her) to California Youth Authority for one long year—or even eighteen months, he had added, but that was unlikely. But all this was old news. She hadn't spoken to him in a couple weeks though she had no doubt that it had been Billy knocking on her door the evening she hadn't answered.

"How you doing, babe?" Lydia whispered to her. She reached out and took Marcia's hand, pulling it into her lap.

"Okay."

"You were better, but now you're sad again."

"I feel bad about something else."

A smile flickered briefly across Lydia's face. "I wonder if that's an improvement." Then, a moment later, "Do you think he'll ever shut up?"

The minister was droning on about the responsibili-ties of being married. Marcia had once assumed she'd have a lifelong relationship, which was part of why break-ing up had not been an option with Annie. But no matter what had happened with Annie, she still felt the same as she had when she was a kid: she would be most happy married. And now she'd even found the right person, but Lydia kept insisting she knew Marcia better than Marcia knew herself. Of course, Lydia's perception was probably accurate—Marcia knew she puzzled out her feelings with the same misplaced optimism that she attempted *Atlantic Monthly*'s acrostic.

Finally the wedding was over—Lydia's mother had glared when she'd looked up to see Marcia and Lydia holding hands—and they sped off to the reception in the rental car, passing dozens of shopping centers which all seemed to be either closed down or under construction. "Why don't they just open up an old one?" Marcia asked, but Lydia was too busy grousing about her mother to pay attention to malls. When they arrived at the private club, Lydia went off to get champagne, then reappeared with a cheese spread on a cracker for Marcia. "They don't seem to have anything nonalcoholic," she apologized. "I'll bring you some water when everything calms down a bit."

"Fine," Marcia said.

"I meant to tell you how wonderful you look," Lydia said, touching her cheek. "Very sharp."

"Thanks," Marcia said. After trying on everything in her closet, she had finally chosen black slacks and an open-collared silk shirt that matched her eyes. "Hey, you can walk around, you know. You don't have to sit here with me."

"I will. I just want to decompress for a minute or two. It's discombobulating being here, you know? It's a very different reality."

Marcia nodded. "Remember the six places I feel comfortable? Luckily almost all of Europe is one of them."

Lydia tapped her hand. "Next time France." She sailed across the floor at intervals, fetching crackers and once a glass of water. A band set up and began playing old standards. Lydia drank more champagne. It didn't seem to have much of an effect on her until she turned to Marcia and said, "Let's dance."

Marcia glanced involuntarily at Lydia's mother, who met her quick look with a mystified expression. "Oh, honey, I don't think that's a very good idea."

"Why not?"

"Why not," Marcia echoed rhetorically, gazing out at the dance floor filled with couples of all shapes, ages, and sizes. It could not be denied, however, that each couple was a male-female pairing. They swooped and dipped along to "Strangers in the Night." Lydia's sister Edie waved over her husband's shoulder. Marcia waved back. "Let me count the ways. First there's your mother watching us every two seconds to make sure we don't do anything horrible. There's the rest of your relatives. It's your brother's wedding. We're in Virginia. Everyone would freak out. It would cause a horrible fuss, which is not fair to your brother."

Lydia was tapping her fingers on the shiny tabletop, watching Marcia. "You didn't learn much from your young'uns at the house, did you? The discomfort straight people feel is their problem, not mine. Furthermore, my brother would prefer that I caused a horrible fuss, if such a thing were to happen, than to not dance with my girlfriend at his wedding."

Marcia sighed. "I have a perhaps more sober view than you do. You've really been slugging down the champagne."

They were quiet for a moment. The band segued into "Goin' Out of my Head." "I want to dance," Lydia said. "If they want to freak, they can. They all know I'm gay, they just haven't watched it be manifested. I see no reason why we have to sit here like wallflowers while they dance."

A waiter interrupted them with a trayful of champagne. Lydia plucked one from the slick surface. Marcia was about to refuse when the waiter handed her a glass from the back. "Perrier," he told her. He winked. "I noticed earlier you weren't drinking," he said.

"Thanks." She watched him serve Lydia's sister and husband, just coming off the dance floor. "Good waiter," Marcia said thoughtfully. "I oughta bring him home with me." She realized with a start that she was feeling better. How strange to begin to come back to life here, at this reception in Roanoke.

As she raised her glass, Lydia reached across the table and tapped her wrist. "I could *order* you to dance with me."

Marcia smiled at her. "Nice try, hon, but that doesn't work out of bed."

"Or in bed, either, very often."

"Is this a complaint? Shall I call the complaint department?" She pretended to be speaking to someone over her left shoulder. "Hey, Harry, the lady's got a love beef. Call the supervisor, OK?"

Lydia's sister appeared at their table. "Aren't you two going to dance?"

Lydia made a face. "Marcia's afraid of Mom. Or that God's going to strike her with a thunderbolt, I'm not sure which."

Marcia burst out laughing. "Lydia!"

"You are, it's true."

"Well, I don't know about God," Edie said, "but I'd forget about Mom. She'll survive." She strode off to the bar.

"See, all these straight people you don't want to offend are offended that you think they're so shallow that you would offend them." Lydia giggled. "Did I say that right?" The band swung into "Moon River." Luckily there was no singer. Lydia mouthed a silent "Please." Marcia stood up and held out her hand. "How can I resist such a heartfelt wish?" They sauntered to the dance floor, Lydia stepped inside Marcia's open arms, and they began moving together easily. The band didn't grind to a halt nor were there gasps all around. No one threw boulders. In fact, the worst that happened was that every one of Lydia's female relatives, with the exception of her mother, wanted to dance with Marcia. By the end of the evening, Marcia was begging for a dance with Lydia's brother. Randall, resplendent in his tuxedo, appeared at her side. "You want to lead?" he asked her, grinning.

"Hell no, that's why I dragged you over here. Sweep me away." She hadn't followed for years, not since she and a gay guy friend of hers had entered dance contests, but apparently it was like riding a bicycle—she hadn't forgotten.

"Listen," he said past her shoulder, "you like my sister?"

"I like your sister a lot." She thought about it as he whirled her around the floor. "Correction. I love your sister."

"Good. 'Cause I know she's crazy about you. She was so unhappy when she was married to Jeff. She kept on trying long past the point she should've quit, I guess 'cause of Cory, but also because I think she didn't know what else to do. Then her relationships with women haven't really been good. I think she'd sort of given up until she met you."

When Marcia came back to the table, Lydia was half-plowed from the champagne. "It's so nice to have a permanent designated driver."

"Let's go," Marcia said. "I think things here are winding down."

"OK." Lydia rested her head against the seat back on the way to the motel. When she got into their room, she tore off most of her clothes and flopped on the bed. Marcia undressed more carefully. "Lydia," she said, "you might want to get under the covers."

"All right." But Lydia didn't move. Marcia gave her 'til the count of ten, and then crawled under the covers herself. She switched off her bedside lamp and lay in the darkness. After a few moments, Lydia said, "I'm not as drunk as you think."

"No?"

"Do you like my family?"

"Yes. I found your brother particularly edifying."

"Randall? Why?"

"He said something that started me thinking. I realized that my self-involvement has reached unprecedented heights, that not only am I often blind, I'm even blind to those I care about the most."

"What are you talking about?"

"I'm talking about how whenever I tell you I want to be with you and you say I should go home and think about it some more?" Marcia upturned her statement at the end, but Lydia didn't answer. Instead she reached out her hand and Marcia grasped it and pulled it to the base of her throat, where she could feel her own pulse throbbing. "Well, I realized that at some point you have to believe me. Because we can go on forever pretending I'm too scared when for a long time it's been you who's too frightened to accept that I'm telling you the truth, that I love you."

Silence. A car started up, drove out of the parking lot. "I was wondering when you'd figure that out," Lydia said. "Now that you have, there's nothing more to say." There was a long pause. "You're right. I am frightened. But I don't need to go home to think about anything. I know I love you. I have from that first day at the Botanical Gardens."

Marcia smiled. "When I threw myself at you?"

"Naw, you were being very cool. At least until we got to my house and I changed into my vest."

"You already knew I was a pervert."

"Your reputation preceded you."

They lay close together. Little bubbles of happiness kept breaking inside Marcia's chest; she moved Lydia's hand from her throat to between her legs. They fell asleep like that, Lydia clasping her cunt, her lips moving silently against Marcia's breast.

# CHAPTER 20

Marcia awoke to quiet groans which finally coalesced into a single sentence: "Ohhh, god." She raised herself up on her hands and peered at Lydia, who was lying with the pillow over her head. "Problems?"

From somewhere beneath the pillow emerged garbled words.

"Do you remember what we talked about last night?" Marcia asked. Wouldn't that be a kicker, she thought. But Lydia allowed that she knew exactly what had gone on.

"Given your state of inebriation," Marcia said, "you might want to reconsider. I'm not the nicest person in the world. In fact, I'm moody and egotistical and ill-tempered."

"All of which you take total delight in," Lydia said tartly, ripping the pillow off her head. "These unpleasant behavior patterns are under your control, you know. They're not engraved in the sky so you can act out on them whenever you want to fly off the handle. However, as I already said, you'll do. Now let's switch subjects. You have some experience with this bit."

"The hungover bit?"

"What should I do? I feel absolutely horrible."

"Does the idea of drinking a beer make you sick?"

"Jesus!" Lydia exploded. "Ask an alcoholic a question, get an alcoholic answer."

Marcia shrugged. "It'd make you feel better." Lydia dragged the pillow back over her face. "All right, all right, I'll go get you something." She pulled on her jeans and a shirt. Then she opened the door, felt the wind on her face, and added a sweater, two pairs of socks, and her leather jacket to her wearing apparel. "It's freezing out here," she reported to Lydia. Lydia grunted something. "OK," Marcia said, "I'm off to the Alaskan wilderness. If I'm not back in a couple months, send out the dogs."

It had, in fact, snowed that night. Marcia closed the door behind her and stood still for a moment, glorying in the clearness of the air, the sight of the mountains in the distance, marveling at how snow could make even a parking lot beautiful. She began cautiously picking her way across patches of slick ice, then clambered over a snow pile into another parking lot, that of a fast-food joint. She was so exhilarated about the hairs in her nostrils stiffening with cold that she hardly noticed the lines of people stretching to the doors. By the time her nose hairs had thawed out, however, she was wondering why a place that didn't even serve espresso was so popular. It had, as far as she could see, nothing to offer to anyone but the absolutely desperate. This is like visiting the United States, she mused. She had no idea what it was like to live in the States, though she had lived there all her life. The Bay Area and environs, with strong ties to Europe and Asia, were an anomaly within the greater anomaly of California. She was glad when she finally reached the counter so she could talk American and stop feeling so damned alienated. "I want two decafs and two orange juices," she told the teenager behind the register. "Hang on. Is that brewed decaf?"

The teenager boggled at her, but then she spotted the orange-handled coffee pot. "Never mind," she said. "Give me a couple English muffins, too. And do you sell aspirin?" Oddly enough, they did, in little foil packages of two. She shoveled out some money and carried everything back to the motel room. Lydia was still lying huddled under the covers. "You're mostly dehydrated," Marcia told her.

"Drink some of each, and try to eat at least part of the muffin."

Lydia sipped at the coffee. "It's decaf," Marcia told her. "Sleep is the best medicine. We have hours until the plane."

"I don't think I can sleep."

"You can if I make love to you. That's part two of your treatment. You come, you crash, when you wake up you're much better."

"OK, doc. Whatever you say." Lydia chugged some orange juice.

"Not too fast," Marcia counseled. "You're thirsty, but it'll sit in your stomach like a lead weight."

"A shower," Lydia said abruptly, leaning back against the pillows. "That's what I need. Come take a shower with me." Neither had taken a shower without a reduction control on it for years. "It's like a waterfall!" Marcia shouted. They spent nearly fifteen minutes underneath it, playing with each other's breasts, feeling deliciously sinful wasting all that water. "God, I can't stand anymore," Marcia said finally, shutting it off. "It's making me weak."

"Water, water, water," Lydia exulted. "Turn it back on."

"No, it's like heroin. You'll get hooked on it and want to do it at home." Marcia hauled her out of the shower and bundled her in a towel. "Go back in and lie down."

But when she came out of the bathroom a moment later, Lydia was rooting around in her suitcase, muttering to herself. "Can't remember what I brought.... Thought you'd still be languishing in the sloughs of angst." Meanwhile she was tossing items on the bedspread: a dildo packed with condoms in a sealed Jiffy bag, the handcuffs, the belt. "But—" Lydia looked up suddenly at Marcia, who was standing next to the bathroom door, arms folded across her chest, "actually, I didn't check with you first. Are you still too distraught over the course of human affairs to make love?"

"Not everything's a big joke, Lydia."

Lydia was unfazed. "How true that is. Your feelings are not a joke. We can continue talking later. But I thought we might do something else now if you want to. It could even make you feel better about yourself even though you think you have to have your life under complete control before you move an inch. It might get you back in your body. So—you wanna do it or not?"

"Yeah, I wanna do it."

"Good. Then shut up and get over here. You know what I keep forgetting every time I go to the leather store?" Lydia asked, pulling her down on the mattress. "The absolutely essential item for dealing with you, at least for dealing with you in bed, which is, I might add, the *only* time I have this problem with you. You know what I'm talking about, don't you?"

"No," Marcia said stubbornly. "I can't imagine."

"You're such a liar, Mars. Turn on your stomach." Lydia fell half on top of her, making Marcia grunt, then jerked her arm up hard, which made her squeal.

"Tell me what it is." Lydia reached underneath her with her other hand and began pinching her nipples. "Tell me."

Already Marcia couldn't remember the question. She was fast flying away, unable to think of anything but the sensations assaulting her everywhere, of her cunt throbbing.

"I can't remember," she said finally, at least recalling the second part, that a response had been demanded of her.

Lydia sat up on top of her, pulling her arm higher. "You really are a liar! I can't believe it. You just don't want to admit it."

"Tell me what you're talking about," Marcia begged pathetically. "I don't know anymore."

Lydia leaned close. "Marcia, answer me."

She felt engulfed by confusion. The more Lydia tormented her, the less able she was to concentrate on what Lydia wanted. To unravel the mystery of Lydia's question, to trace back the threads of conversation, she would have to think linearly. "Lydia," she mumbled with despair, "I can't do it."

Lydia laughed, dropped her wrist, and threw her arms around her, nuzzling her cheek against Marcia's. "Honey, you're just not paying attention."

Marcia smiled, relieved that Lydia had stopped trying to make her think. "I'll pay better attention next time," she promised, kissing the pulse at the base of Lydia's neck.

"And now we know there'll be a next time," Lydia said.

She rubbed the back of Marcia's head and Marcia arched towards her, turning to and fro under the pressure of Lydia's fingers, sighing with pleasure. "You ready to be mine now, baby?" Lydia asked her.

Marcia pulled herself away so she could look up at Lydia, who had a ghost of a smile on her face and worried eyes. Her hair cascaded over her shoulders to lie like the spread feathers of a bird's wing across her breasts. "You mean like out of bed?" Marcia asked.

Lydia watched her. "Sometimes."

Marcia thought about this for less than a minute. "Okay," she said, giving in with a whoosh. "You got me."

Then she seemed to go away, as if opening herself so much was too frightening to stick around for, but when she came back, Lydia was right there, staring into her eyes as she traced a line down her jaw.

"Baby," Lydia said quietly. It seemed to Marcia as if she were looking at Lydia through a layer of gauze, she seemed so soft and muzzy, the winter light glowing from her skin as if she were surrounded by candles.

"Lydia? I need you with me." She was surprised at how she sounded, as if she'd been running for miles. Lydia curled around her and held her while Marcia murmured against her throat. Then Lydia began sliding along Marcia's body, rubbing her thighs across Marcia's hips, her arms along her breasts, her face on Marcia's neck, until Marcia felt enveloped everywhere.

Before you can surrender you need to feel safe, Marcia thought. It doesn't matter whether or not it's S/M; it's just sex, just life.

Then something struck her. "Have you been frightened of me?" she asked.

Lydia didn't find this question unlikely. "Not anymore," she said, stroking Marcia's cheek. "You're here."

They lay quietly together until Lydia, almost as if by accident, put her hand on Marcia's breast. Marcia turned to her and they smiled at each other. "Go ahead," Marcia said. She raised her arms above her head, clasping her hands together and shoving them under the pillow.

"Close your eyes," Lydia told her, and then she licked Marcia's eyelids to make sure. She moved down to her nose and her lips, kissing her so deeply that Marcia began squirming, sucking on Lydia's tongue, listening to Lydia's breath catch and quicken. And meanwhile Lydia's hand was busy at her nipple, squeezing and tugging until the least touch made Marcia jerk in response, then cry out.

"You can't do that," Lydia cautioned.

"What?" Marcia gasped.

"Make noise," Lydia whispered. "You can't make noise above this." She blew a stream of air across Marcia's face. "Not above the wind."

Marcia was sure she was already making more noise than that; her heart was drumming in a conga-rhythm and she was huffing like a mountaineer at the summit. "OK," she said.

"OK?" Lydia questioned.

"Yes, Ma'am."

"Better. You're such a bad boy, it's going to be a real trial to get you to behave." Lydia was pulling at her nipple again while she sucked on the other one, biting like a terrier, and the combination of tweaks of pain with bolts of ecstasy made Marcia's heart pound harder, especially when Lydia began pumping hard against Marcia's thigh. Then Lydia stopped. "I don't want to come like that," she told Marcia.

"No," Marcia said. "I want to fuck you."

"What makes you think you've earned the right to do that?"

Marcia didn't know, so she remained silent as Lydia watched her for a moment, a slight smile on her face. In a flash she ran her hand up Marcia's neck into her short hair and yanked Marcia's head back, biting her throat until Marcia began moaning, then squeezed her nipple with her other hand until Marcia cried out. "What are you doing?" Lydia asked sweetly as she bent Marcia's thumb back.

"Making noise," Marcia said. "I can't help it."

"Don't tell me you can't help it. Who's in charge here?"

"You are."

"Then you control yourself. That's what it means to be obedient. Maybe you don't really want to be mine."

Was she serious? "I do!"

"Maybe you just can't take it then. Is that the problem?"

"No, I—"

"We're not playing a game here. You're mine or you're not. And when you're mine, you do what *I* want, not you. Understand?" By now Lydia had bent her thumb nearly to her hand, so Marcia could hardly talk. "Yes."

"Yes?" The pressure increased while Marcia searched frantically and then came up with the prize.

"Yes, Ma'am."

"Better." Lydia let go and then slid her fingers along Marcia's jaw to edge into her mouth, so Marcia could suck on them. And then they kissed again, with Lydia's fingers still in Marcia's mouth, her other hand running between the lips of Marcia's labia, so wet, Marcia marveled, that she was flooding these motel sheets. Marcia risked bringing her own hand down to Lydia's cunt, exulting when Lydia cried out at her touch. "Please," Marcia begged Lydia's chin, her cheek, her jaw. "Please let me make love to you."

Lydia was gasping. "In a minute, in a minute," for she was still busy at Marcia's nipples, pulling and tugging, and Marcia finally had to bite the pillow to be silent and then grab her T-shirt and ram it into her mouth. "You're being very good," Lydia told her. "I didn't think you'd be able to be so quiet."

Marcia smiled at her dreamily. "You told me to be."

"I love you, Mars. You have such a beautiful body, and you feel so good."

"I love you too."

Lydia smiled at Marcia's spaced-out face. "Can you even see me?"

Marcia finally managed to control her breathing. "I probably see you better this way." As her eyes cleared, she suddenly yelped, "A gag! That's what you were trying to get me to say earlier."

"You don't need a gag, babe. You need one of those speaking trumpets."

"For what? To shout to the heavens I love you? C'mere." She got to her knees, caught Lydia around the waist, and rolled her over on her back. "Now it's your turn to shut up," she said, and kissed her deeply, dropping her hand between her legs until Lydia was whimpering a-gainst her cheek, her hands scrabbling across Marcia's back like agitated crabs, one leg hooked around Marcia's thigh, straining to open further and further, so that Marcia might fall in.

Marcia unlocked her front door. Her house seemed silent, as if no one had lived there for weeks. She stood in the miniscule living room, the only part of her house that annoyed her, for more than a minute, thinking how much she loved even it. Then she walked to her bedroom and called her landlord. When she hung up the phone she sat down in the kitchen and cried. How come everything is so hard? she asked herself.

Someone knocked on her door. Billy stood there in the early morning gloom of her forty-watt light bulb. She let him in. "Milk and cookies?" she asked.

He looked at her as if she were nuts.

"It's what I used to give you when you came over," she explained to him.

"I know that," he told her. But he had obviously forgotten. He looked around at the unchanged rooms, at her jacket thrown across the seat of her favorite oak and rattan chair. "What's going on?"

The house had told him. Something had told him. "I'm moving in with Lydia."

He stuffed his hands in his Philippine jacket with a violent motion that almost tore the silk. "Hunh. When'd you decide that?"

"When I was in Virginia."

"When were you in Virginia?" he asked suspiciously.

"Until yesterday."

"You been here seventeen years."

She nodded.

"We're moving too."

"You are?"

"Pop's selling the house." He swallowed. "The lawyer. I mean, he doesn't have to sell it, but he wants to. To pay him, see. He said there's a lot of—"

"Equity," Marcia supplied.

"Yeah. Equity. Real estate agents are coming tomorrow. We're moving to Hayward."

"Hayward?"

He shrugged. "Doesn't matter. *I'm* moving to CYA. What do I care? Melinda's having trouble. People tell her her brother's a murderer. At school, see. In Hayward they won't know nothing. Nothing. And I'll be gone." He kept shoving his hands in the jacket so hard she was certain he would rip out the pockets. Marcia bit her lower lip. She wondered how to make him stop and then thought she shouldn't make him stop. He turned to her and his eyes were red. "You left, Marcia. I needed you and you left."

"Oh, Billy." Her face fell apart; tears started pouring down her cheeks. She had to sit, she was suddenly tottering on her feet. She sagged onto the couch and watched as Billy pounded at his own tears with the heels of his hands, as if he could force them back inside his eyes. "Stop doing that!" she told him, leaping back up and grabbing at his hands. "Billy, I'm sorry. I can't tell you how sorry I am."

"It doesn't help," he said. He kept trying to get a breath. "It doesn't help. Nothing helps. Now you're moving. To the hills. With your college professor."

"You like her."

He shook his head. "I like her." He started crying again and sat down on her sofa. "I don't want to go, Marcia."

"I know." It was so painful watching him cry that she wanted to gnaw on her knuckles for relief. She had to force herself to stay in the room. Here's when we need safewords, she thought. When it's real. When it's life. Billy could say a safeword and the kid he killed could come back to life and they could be in the front yard again, and instead of Billy shooting the kid they could back away from each other like she'd done that time she'd walked into a bear at Yosemite, she and the bear staring at each other as each of them took one step back, another step back, until they were fifteen feet apart and then they had both turned around and bolted in opposite directions.

Yes, Billy could do that with the kid. He could have done that with the kid. She drew a ragged breath.

"Hey," he said, smiling, "it's nice you're moving in with Lydia. She's real nice." Don't ask, Marcia thought. But he did. "She got any kids?"

"A boy," Marcia said. "Your age."

Billy nodded. Marcia would say no more about Cory. Nor would she tell Billy that Lydia had been saving a down payment, that when the house on Fairview sold they were going to combine their money and buy a place. She didn't know why she wasn't telling him. She thought he wouldn't want to know. They were already distant from each other, as if he had left and she had left and she had run into him on some street corner in downtown Berkeley after he was released from CYA, a year or two from now, and he was back working at his eighteen-dollar-an-hour job, and he and Miguel had jobbed together a car for him, some spiffy sports machine, and he was even bigger and stronger, having lifted weights obsessively the entire time he was at the Youth Authority, and he would be telling her that she'd be surprised how fine he was. I am surprised, she thought. Surprised that anyone gets out of this at all.

"We'll see each other, OK?" He stood up, somehow formal. They hugged. "You're so tall," she said to him. He towered over her.

"Yeah. Getting fat, too." He grinned. "Ya know, I'm working out."

"Billy," she said suddenly, "don't try to be tough. Just be yourself. The other kids will respect you more for that than anything else." And you're big enough to get away with it, she added to herself.

"Sure," he said. "You take care." He darted out her door, his eyes still red. She watched him go, and then she walked into her kitchen and sat in her favorite chair, staring out the window at her garden, which was disheveled and showing strain from dryness, even in December. Lydia had a small yard in the back. "Bring any plants you want with you," she had said.

"I want to bring everything," Marcia said out loud. What the hell am I doing? she asked herself. I'm moving in with someone I love, she answered. I'm taking a risk. It felt good. It felt horrible. How could it have happened that in order to do the thing she wanted most she had to do the thing she wanted least? She couldn't imagine leaving this place where she'd sobered up, where she'd lived with Annie, where the dog of her twenties lay buried.

Oh, she'd considered having Cory and Lydia come here—Cory, as a senior, could continue at Berkeley High. But she herself had nixed the idea—the desecration of her formerly laidback, almost rural black neighborhood ate at her until it was harder to stay than to go. If it weren't so hypocritical, she'd scream "Gentrifying fucks!" at her neighbors daily.

And if it was a mistake to leave—well, hadn't she been wrong plenty of times already? She couldn't continue living so cautiously, as if being wrong was the worst possible thing in the world.

She stared across her kitchen, remembering just a month earlier, when she'd been swooping by at intervals to pick up her mail or listen to her messages. So much of what keeps us busy, she thought, that demands our total attention, like rehabbing the house on Fairview Street, can vanish in an instant, as if it never happened. What's left is what was always there: friends and family.

"If I could only take you with me," Marcia said to her house and yard. If only she could create a small rend in the earth's fabric, a little unfilled space in Lydia's neighborhood, a void exactly sixty feet by one hundred into which she could neatly drop her lot. And thinking of rends made her remember fault lines and the terrible friction that built up along those lines as the bulk of the land mass pushed inexorably north or south. This was a case, she decided, where her middle had gone romping off without waiting for her edges to catch up. But where does the part of me that's me fit in with all this talk of edges and middles? Am I stubbornly sitting on my edge, resisting change to the end, or am I cowering in the middle, covering my eyes in fear? Hey, if I'm going to hang out in the middle, I might as well ride it for all it's worth.

She stood up, anchored her palms on the open door frame, and pressed so hard against the wood the muscles in her upper arms bulged out, staring at her garden until

the sun moved high enough in the sky to shine on her face,
until she couldn't see anymore through the light.

Photo by Debbie Bender

Linnea Due has never managed to make it out of Berkeley where she grew up. She divides her time between working as an editor at an alternative weekly and writing fiction and articles.

# OTHER TITLES AVAILABLE FROM
# SPINSTERS BOOK COMPANY

*All The Muscle You Need*, Diana McRae . . . . . . . . . . . . . . $8.95

*Being Someone*, Ann MacLeod . . . . . . . . . . . . . . . . . . $9.95

*Cancer in Two Voices*, Butler & Rosenblum . . . . . . . . . . . $12.95

*Child of Her People*, Anne Cameron . . . . . . . . . . . . . . . $8.95

*Considering Parenthood*, Cheri Pies . . . . . . . . . . . . . . . $9.50

*Desert Years*, Cynthia Rich . . . . . . . . . . . . . . . . . . . $7.95

*Elise*, Claire Kensington . . . . . . . . . . . . . . . . . . . . $7.95

*Final Session*, Mary Morell . . . . . . . . . . . . . . . . . . . $9.95

*High and Outside*, Linnea A. Due . . . . . . . . . . . . . . . . $8.95

*The Journey*, Anne Cameron . . . . . . . . . . . . . . . . . . . $9.95

*The Lesbian Erotic Dance*, JoAnn Loulan . . . . . . . . . . . . $12.95

*Lesbian Passion*, JoAnn Loulan . . . . . . . . . . . . . . . . . $12.95

*Lesbian Sex*, JoAnn Loulan . . . . . . . . . . . . . . . . . . . $12.95

*Lesbians at Midlife*, ed. by Sang, Warshow & Smith . . . . . . . $12.95

*Life Savings*, Linnea Due . . . . . . . . . . . . . . . . . . . . $10.95

*Look Me in the Eye*, 2nd Ed., Macdonald & Rich . . . . . . . . . $8.95

*Love and Memory*, Amy Oleson . . . . . . . . . . . . . . . . . . $9.95

*Modern Daughters and the Outlaw West*, Melissa Kwasny . . . . . $9.95

*Thirteen Steps*, Bonita L. Swan . . . . . . . . . . . . . . . . . $8.95

*Vital Ties*, Karen Kringle . . . . . . . . . . . . . . . . . . . . $9.95

*Why Can't Karen Kowalski Come Home?*
      Thompson & Andrzejewski . . . . . . . . . . . . . . . . . $10.95

Spinsters titles are available at your local booksellers, or by mail order through Spinsters Book Company (415) 558-9586. A free catalogue is available upon request.

Please include $1.50 for the first title ordered, and $ .50 for every title thereafter. California residents, please add 8.25% sales tax. Visa and Mastercard accepted.

Spinsters Book Company was founded in 1978 to produce vital books for diverse women's communities. In 1986 we merged with Aunt Lute Books to become Spinsters/Aunt Lute. In 1990, the Aunt Lute Foundation became an independant non-profit publishing program.

Spinsters is committed to publishing works outside the scope of mainstream commercial publishers: books that not only name crucial issues in women's lives, but more importantly encourage change and growth; books that help make the best in our lives more possible. We sponsor an annual Lesbian Fiction Contest for the best lesbian novel each year. And we are particularly interested in creative works by lesbians.

spinsters book company, p.o. box 410687, san francisco, ca 94141